F
BOW

Bowen, Peter.

Nails.

$23.95

DATE			

Nails

Also by Peter Bowen

Stewball
The Tumbler
Badlands
Ash Child
Cruzatte and Maria
The Stick Game
Long Son
Thunder Horse
Notches
Wolf, No Wolf
Specimen Song
Coyote Wind

Kelly and the Three-Toed Horse
Imperial Kelly
Kelly Blue
Yellowstone Kelly

Nails

PETER BOWEN

ST. MARTIN'S MINOTAUR
NEW YORK

www.minotaurbooks.com

Library of Congress Cataloging-in-Publication Data

Bowen, Peter, 1945–
    Nails / Peter Bowen.— 1st ed.
      p. cm.
    ISBN 0-312-31207-5
    EAN 978-0-312-31207-7
    1. Du Pré, Gabriel (Fictitious character)—Fiction. 2. Sheriffs—Fiction.
  3. Missing children—Fiction. 4. Montana—Fiction. I. Title.

PS3552.O866N35 2006
813'.54—dc22

2005054194

First Edition: February 2006

10 9 8 7 6 5 4 3 2 1

For Louis and Ella

Gabriel Du Pré's Toussaint

GABRIEL DU PRÉ — Métis fiddler, retired brand inspector, solver of puzzles

MADELAINE PLACQUEMINES — Gabriel's woman; children Robert, Thierry, Lourdes, and Chappie

JACQUELINE FORTIER — m. Raymond Fortier, twelve children, Du Pré's daughter

MARIA DU PRÉ — Du Pré's daughter, studying overseas

BART FASCELLI — very rich neighbor, alcoholic, runs earthmoving business, money out of Chicago

CHARLES FOOTE — lawyer, troubleshooter for Bart, manages Fascelli empire

BENETSEE — ancient medicine person, mysterious, always been around

BENNY KLEIN — sheriff

SUSAN KLEIN — former schoolteacher, now owns and runs Toussaint Saloon

HARVEY WALLACE — Blackfoot Indian and FBI agent, lives in Washington, D.C.

RIPPER — Charles Van Dusen, young agent, mad duck

PALLAS FORTIER — daughter of Jacqueline and Raymond, genius, determined to marry Ripper, if necessary marry his dead body

SAMANTHA PIDGEON — incredibly beautiful and brainy serial killer expert works for FBI, Redbone girl from California

FATHER VAN DEN HEUVEL — Belgian Jesuit, pastor of little Catholic church in Toussaint, physically very inept

JACQUELINE'S CHILDREN — Alcide, Pallas, Lourdes, Marisa and Berne (twins), Hervé, Nepthele, Marie and Barbara (twins), Armand, Gabriel, Colette

PELON — apprentice to Benetsee, often far away on some mysterious business

Nails

CHAPTER 1

Du Pré looked east. The sky was a patchwork of small fluffy clouds and the air was still. The clouds hung like balloons. A big jet roared down the runway and lifted off, the thunder of its engines faded. Soon it was just a silver speck far to the west.

The little white jet sailed in, almost silently, and the pilot reversed the engines and slowed it, then turned toward the private hangar.

"I bet she is six inches taller," said Madelaine.

Du Pré shook his head.

"Three," he said. "Bad air stunt her."

The door opened down and became a stair. A duffel bag was tossed out on the asphalt, then a backpack, and finally Pallas came down the steps carrying two suitcases.

Du Pré walked to her, Madelaine hooting behind him.

"It is too six!" she said.

Du Pré looked at his granddaughter.

"You are taller," he said.

"Yes," said Pallas. "I am taller than Jacqueline, she will not like that."

Du Pré picked up the dufflebag and the backpack and he and Pallas walked to Madelaine, and Pallas put the suitcases down and she kissed Madelaine and then she kissed Du Pré.

"We got one errand," said Madelaine, "then we go home."

"Good," said Pallas. "I miss them. Few days I will not miss them and be glad to go back, but for now I miss them."

They walked to the big SUV, a dark green one, and put Pallas's luggage in the second seat.

Then they got in and Du Pré drove to the box store. They bought a thousand dollars' worth of groceries, household supplies, tools, and odds and ends.

The store was busy. After Du Pré paid, they wheeled the three grocery carts and the big flat cart out to the SUV.

"Never get it all in," said Pallas.

"Then you take the bus," said Du Pré.

"Maybe we strap things on the roof," said Pallas.

Du Pré looked at her.

"No, Grandpa," said Pallas. "Not me."

They stacked and tucked and shoved and Pallas cursed fluently.

"You," said Madelaine, "watch your mouth, you ride on the roof, Pallas."

"I learn the best words from you," said Pallas.

Du Pré turned away to laugh.

They got in and Du Pré got on the highway east. They were soon out of Billings, and they passed the highway that went south to the Crow Reservation and on to Denver.

"I have never been to Little Big Horn," said Pallas.

"Not much to see," said Madelaine. "Looks like Montana, Wyoming, hills, grass, but it don't feel sad like the Marias or other places. . . ."

Other massacres, Du Pré thought, only then it was the Indians being slaughtered.

Me, I go to the Little Big Horn twice and I can't hear them there like I can other places.

Voices behind the wind.

"What you hear when you are there, Du Pré?" said Madelaine.

Du Pré shook his head.

"Horses maybe," he said. "I don't know."

Madelaine turned to look at Pallas crouched under a rampart of stuff that was piled on the seat and on top of the backrests.

"You are getting crap you are an Indian?" said Madelaine. "You are some Indian but French and Scot, too."

"Everybody likes Indians," said Pallas. "No, I just get dumb questions."

"Oh," said Madelaine. "Them."

"How is Chappie doing?" said Pallas.

"He is OK," said Madelaine. "Leg works pretty good. He has lots of colds."

"He will be around now?" said Pallas. "Your other kids don't come back here."

"They will come back," said Madelaine. "Just the lives they pick are far away."

Du Pré grunted.

Madelaine have four kids, two in the military, one in Africa, working for an oil company, one in Chicago, studying art.

Chappie is in Iraq. Bomb take off his leg and put out his left eye.

So he is retired from military.

Coughs a lot.

"So," said Pallas, "I have a month now. They tell me I have to wait until August to come, but I say no, I have to go now, have ceremonies to perform. Then they are able to find out I don't have to stay until August."

Du Pré and Madelaine laughed.

"Maybe we send you back with a warpole," said Madelaine. "Hang a bunch of scalps on it."

"Yeah," said Pallas, "that would be what they all call *awesome*. They use *awesome* when they mean *good* and *impacts* when they mean *effects*."

Du Pré laughed.

Pallas she can talk like some East Coast educated person, Du Pré thought. I just heard it.

"So it is all right?" said Madelaine.

Pallas nodded.

"Maria come for a week," she said. "From England, and I am so very homesick. They don't got mountains there and they got all these people. Pile in one place they would be a ver' big mountain, and after she is there a while I cry some and she says, well, get all you can and you can go back but not until you are done."

"She is your aunt," said Madelaine. "You listen to her."

"Sure," said Pallas. "She goes through a long argument, wins it because I am not talking back, and then she says she will break my nose if I quit."

3

"She will break your nose," said Du Pré. "That Maria keeps promises."

Du Pré fished the silver flask out of the console and he popped the top open and he drank.

He offered it to Madelaine.

She shook her head.

"What about me?" said Pallas.

"You are too young, drink whiskey," said Du Pré.

"Good," said Pallas. "I will take drugs then."

"Oh, crap," said Madelaine, fishing a bottle of pink wine out of the cooler at her feet. "Have some of my pink wine and leave your grandfather's whiskey alone."

"Now it is illegal to have booze in a car," said Pallas.

"Yah," said Du Pré.

"Montana, they are going to stop people driving with a drink," said Pallas. "How do they think they will do that without lots of people getting shot?"

"Federal government," said Du Pré.

"Oh," said Pallas. "Them."

"They say they don't give Montana highway money if Montana don't stop people who drink, go down the road," said Du Pré.

"So," said Pallas, "this government, one in Helena, passes laws they like in that Washington and then they forget them like the speed limit."

"Yah," said Du Pré.

"Remember when Jacqueline throws Raymond's piss, hits the Highway Patrol car?" said Pallas.

"Yah," said Du Pré.

"You think they would learn," said Pallas.

"No," said Du Pré, "they don't learn."

They drove on, silent, while Madelaine and Pallas drank pink fizzy wine and Du Pré smoked.

"Pret' soon you can't smoke in car, either," said Pallas.

"Yah," said Du Pré.

"Tobacco got lots of taxes now," said Pallas.

"Not where I get it," said Du Pré.

"Oh," said Pallas. "That is interesting."

"Crow come through often," said Du Pré. "They buy in North Carolina and they drive it back here. They say that anyway."

"Ah," said Pallas.

4

"You are going to give your grandfather crap about smoking?" said Madelaine.

"Sure," said Pallas. "He don't give me one I will."

"You are too young," said Madelaine.

Pallas pulled out a cigarette from her purse and she lit it.

Du Pré laughed.

"Don't they arrest you, Maryland, you smoke you are fifteen?" said Madelaine.

"Do if they catch you," said Madelaine. "I live in this house, other kids my age, all of us smart. We don't have a lot of trouble."

Du Pré snorted.

"Pissants," he said. "Biggest political party."

"Hey," said Pallas, "there is a coyote . . . ," and she stared out the window.

Du Pré glanced to his right.

The coyote was trotting along, sliding through the sagebrush.

A large bird flew up and the coyote leaped up and caught it.

"Sage grouse," said Pallas.

"They are pret' dumb," said Du Pré.

They came to the road north. Du Pré took the exit and then they crossed over the Interstate. He accelerated to about a hundred.

"Ah," said Pallas, "I am home."

The road was an empty gray ribbon winding north over the rolling yellow hills.

"They got pilots now watching for people like you," said Madelaine.

"Yah," said Du Pré, "they don't bother me."

The big SUV shot down the road.

Du Pré slowed when he came up to a hilltop. You never knew when a rancher hauling a piece of equipment at ten miles an hour might be just out of sight.

The puff clouds hung motionless.

"Those are Lucky Strikes?" said Madelaine to Pallas.

"Sure," said Pallas. "You want me to smoke something else?"

"Give me one," said Madelaine.

"I have not seen Chappie for maybe ten years?" said Pallas.

"Yah," said Du Pré.

"It is too bad," said Pallas. "I think all that Iraq business won't work out well at all."

CHAPTER
2

"That Ripper he is dead yet?" said Madelaine. "You are sleeping with him maybe?"

"He is alive, and no, I am not," said Pallas. "I think I don't like it he is in jail, child molestation, and it is me. Trouble is, no one minds their own business anymore. Noses in everything."

"Yah," said Du Pré.

Ripper was thirty-two, an FBI agent, and Pallas had decided he was hers some years back. Ripper's opinion was neither sought nor counted.

"So what is Chappie doing, he is now home?" said Pallas.

"Walks a lot," said Madelaine. "Gets used to his new leg. His wife divorced him three years ago, they did not have children."

They crested a hill and looked at a long stretch of road straight as a string north to the horizon. There were a couple of vehicles, a green van and an orange rental truck parked by the road.

Du Pré got back up to speed. The SUV was a very steady vehicle, heavy and well powered.

The van and truck were three or so miles distant.

Du Pré slowed when he was a third of a mile or so from them.

He stopped and pulled off behind the van.

A fat man in a soiled brown T-shirt was glaring into the engine compartment. He looked at Du Pré and then back at the engine.

Du Pré heard children's voices responding to a woman's voice. They were praying.

"You need help?" said Du Pré.

"It just quit running," said the man.

Du Pré looked at the license plate on the van.

Texas.

"You got a rag and some cold water?" said Du Pré.

The man looked at him.

"Your carburetor is maybe vapor-locked," said Du Pré.

"LuAnne!" the man barked. "Get a rag and some cold water."

"Praise Jesus," chorused the children.

A fat woman in a print pantsuit opened the side door of the van, got in, and came back out with a cloth dripping water.

Du Pré wrapped the cloth around the carburetor.

He whistled.

The fat man kept on glaring at the engine.

"Go and try it now," said Du Pré.

The man looked at Du Pré with stupid brown eyes.

"Go and try to start it now," said Du Pré.

The man jerked, as though he had been asleep, and then he went to the cab and opened the door and he got in. The engine ground, caught, ran.

Du Pré shut the hood.

He went to the window and he tapped on it.

The man rolled it partway down.

"If it starts to choke," said Du Pré, "put more water on the rag."

The man nodded, put the truck in gear, and drove off, and Du Pré had to step back to avoid having his feet crushed by the rear tire.

The fat woman herded the children into the van and she went off after the orange truck.

Du Pré walked back to the SUV.

"If they are stopped again," he said, "I am going around them. He was very stupid."

Du Pré put the SUV in DRIVE and he pulled back out onto the road.

The orange truck and the van were not that far ahead and Du Pré caught up to them, slowed until he could see round them, and he shot past.

7

He pushed the big SUV up to about one hundred miles per hour and the land fell away in moments.

Du Pré saw flashing blue lights ahead. He slowed down and a Montana Highway Patrol car shot past.

He got the SUV back up to speed.

In a couple of hours they were slowing down to enter tiny Toussaint, Montana, and Du Pré pulled up in front of the Toussaint Saloon.

They got out and went in.

"Pallas," said Susan Klein, the owner. "You have grown so!" She came round the bar and she hugged Pallas, who hugged her back.

She is like a colt now, all legs, Du Pré thought. She is a tall girl.

There were a few other people in the bar all of whom clucked and chuckled and welcomed Pallas back.

Du Pré and Madelaine sat at the bar. Susan brought a ditch for Du Pré and a glass of pink fizzy wine for Madelaine.

Pallas came and she sat next to Madelaine.

"Dry martini," said Pallas, "twist, shaken, not stirred."

"How 'bout a Coke?" said Susan Klein. "Or shall I have Benny, who you may remember is the sheriff here, arrest you for trying to buy alcohol?"

"Trying is a crime?" said Pallas. "They throw you in jail for trying?"

Susan filled a glass with ice and cola.

"Trying," she said, "is talking to a little blister like you."

"I'm sorry," said Pallas, not sounding at all sorry.

"Cheeseburgers?" said Susan, looking from Du Pré to Madelaine to Pallas.

Ten people came in then, all laughing.

"I cook them," said Madelaine. "You got enough to do." She went back to the kitchen.

Pallas eased over onto the stool that Madelaine had been sitting on.

"So," said Du Pré, "you are liking it there all right?"

"*Non*," said Pallas, "the work is interesting and I am glad for an education and I am going to get a good one. But it is dirty and stinks and it is crowded and there is no place you can go that does not have a lot of people in it. Not like here."

"No," said Du Pré, "not like here."

"No horses to ride," said Pallas. "There are stables, but they all have those funny little saddles and girls with irrigation boots only made of leather and little hard black hats."

Du Pré laughed.

"They can't ride for sour owlshit anyway," said Pallas. "I went to this one stable and found a good horse, talked with him, got on him we went off. I was on bareback and they shit rusty pickles. Called an ambulance. Me, I am riding the horse who likes me, and not in trouble."

The door opened and a man came in, dark, with a scarred face. A black patch covered his left eye, and he walked with a cane, a strange gait that seemed one step and a shift of body and then a rolling swing of an artificial leg.

"It is Chappie!" said Pallas. She got down from her stool and she ran to him and she hugged him.

He looked at her with his one eye.

"Pallas," said Pallas. "I was smaller the last time you saw me."

"Pallas," said Chappie. "Of course. You were driving my mother insane the last time I was here."

"She is all right I think," said Pallas.

The two of them walked over to the bar together and Chappie slid up on a stool.

Susan came down the bar.

"A big one," said Chappie.

Susan made a very strong ditch and she pushed it over to him.

"Thank you," said Chappie, "very much." He pulled a bill out of his shirt pocket and he put it on the counter. He had only two fingers on his right hand, and part of his thumb was missing.

Pallas moved to the far side of him.

Madelaine came out of the kitchen with three platters, cheeseburgers and fries and coleslaw. She slid the platters across the bar.

"You want some food?" said Madelaine.

"No," said Chappie. "Not now."

He drank a good half of his ditch, fumbled for a cigarette, lit it with a plastic lighter.

Du Pré and Madelaine and Pallas ate hungrily. It had been a long drive from Billings.

They finished.

Madelaine took the platters back to the kitchen. Water ran.

The door opened again and Lourdes and Hervé and several

other children of Jacqueline and Raymond rushed in. Hervé tackled Pallas, and she punched him in the neck.

"Owww!" yelled Hervé.

Pallas and her brothers and sisters ran out before Madelaine could make it back from the kitchen to throw them out.

"I was always hoping they kill each other off," said Madelaine. "Now they can carry her home, Jacqueline and Raymond."

"Raymond is working the towers," said Du Pré. Raymond was an electrical lineman now. He had gotten certified last year.

"Jacqueline probably got a horse, went up into the Wolfs," said Madelaine.

She came and sat between Du Pré and Chappie.

Chappie held up his glass and Susan made him another, made change from the bills on the bartop.

The telephone rang and Susan answered it. She listened.

"Oh," she said, "sure we can."

She put the telephone up.

A few minutes later, as Du Pré was finishing his ditch, a deliveryman came in. He looked tired.

Susan pointed to Du Pré.

"I have some boxes for Doctor Paul Van Den Heuvel," said the deliveryman.

"OK," said Du Pré.

"It says to deliver it to 10 Main Street," said the deliveryman, "but there are no numbers here."

"Catholic church," said Du Pré, "the white one down the road."

"Oh," said the deliveryman.

"But he is gone," said Du Pré.

The deliveryman nodded.

"I put them in the church," said Du Pré.

The deliveryman brightened.

"If you ever have any more," said Du Pré, "the church is never locked."

"This stuff is insured," said the deliveryman.

"OK," said Du Pré. He went out with the deliveryman, loaded the cartons into the SUV, and he signed the clipboard with the weird electronic pencil.

CHAPTER 3

Du Pré sat squished between Madelaine on his left and Lourdes on his right. The dining table was big, but Jacqueline's brood was bigger yet.

"Papa," said Jacqueline, carrying in a giant platter with a sizzling beef roast on it and mounds of new potatoes, "would you carve maybe."

Du Pré stood up and he pushed his chair back, pulled the knife he carried out of his boot, and he started slicing the beef. The rare beef fell away in leaves.

The children ate like wolves, said *maybescusenow,* and ran off to raise hell someplace or other.

Pallas and Lourdes went off together to ride.

"Don't say nothing to that Bart about Pallas and horses," said Jacqueline. "He will buy her one and the place to keep it in."

Du Pré and Madelaine laughed.

"Pallas is maybe going to rob banks she has a horse there," said Jacqueline.

Du Pré looked at his oldest daughter. Jacqueline had had twelve children, or thirteen, Du Pré could never quite remember, and she looked about twenty. She was still slim and her face was unlined, even though she had worked for years, day and night, to care for all of them.

"She don't need to rob banks," said Madelaine.

"She just do it to piss people off," said Jacqueline.

"Yes," said Madelaine, "that is maybe right."

Du Pré and Madelaine helped with the dishes.

"Raymond will be back tomorrow night," said Jacqueline. "It was too far to travel, clear over there, Plentywood."

They finished cleaning up.

The children had all scattered. It was late May and warm and the light kept late.

Du Pré and Madelaine walked to the big SUV. They drove on to Madelaine's place and unloaded all the purchases they had made in Billings. Du Pré hauled in the whole huge cooler the frozen foods and perishables had been in.

Madelaine tucked things away in the fridge or freezer.

"I got to find Father Van Den Heuvel," said Du Pré. "He is a doctor, too."

"Doctor?" said Madelaine. "We have had a doctor here all along?"

"Lots of different kinds of doctors," said Du Pré.

"I want to know what the hell kind of doctor he is," said Madelaine. "I have to take him for stitches, him shut his head in the car door two times."

"Three," said Du Pré.

The big priest was the most physically clumsy man in the county.

"I am going to take a long hot bath," said Madelaine. "Use those bath salts you gave me."

"Violets," said Du Pré.

"Lavender," said Madelaine.

They kissed and Du Pré went out to the big SUV. He drove back to the saloon, hauled the seven cartons out to the SUV, and then he drove over to the church. He went in the back where Father Van Den Heuvel's tiny apartment was.

There was a note on the desk.

"Arrastra Creek," it said.

Du Pré drove toward the Wolf Mountains and turned east when he got to the bench road that ran along the wheatlands. The soil on the benches was very rich and deep.

The winter wheat was nearly all headed out and would soon turn golden and cure in the hot June sun.

Du Pré drove, sipping from a bottle of whiskey. He put some fiddle music in the strange player that took the little plastic doughnut doohickeys.

Bandon Robideaux and his band blared out. Bandon was from Manitoba and he played fine fiddle but much differently than Du Pré did.

Du Pré turned off on the spur road that ran up to Arrastra Creek. There was a trailhead there, some pole corrals and a small parking lot, an outhouse and a green steel pump.

Du Pré pulled in beside Father Van Den Heuvel's battered old Plymouth. It was tan where it still had paint, but since Father Van Den Heuvel was no better a driver than he was a handyman or a runner the car lacked lights in some places and the doors and fenders were dented from his many errors in navigation.

Du Pré got out of the SUV.

He smelled smoke and he went toward it and he found the big priest burning a hot dog on the end of a coat hanger. He had built a big hot fire in the stone ring.

"Ow," said Father Van Den Heuvel, tossing the coat hanger from hand to hand.

"Use a glove," said Du Pré.

Father Van Den Heuvel gave a start. He was not much aware of what was around him.

He fished a glove out of his pocket and put it on.

He picked up the coat hanger with the weenie on it and he tried to shake off the ashes.

The weenie slid off and fell into the fire, which was too big to cook on.

"Shit," said the big priest.

"I got a bunch of cartons for you," said Du Pré, "to Doctor Van Den Heuvel."

"Cartons?" said Van Den Heuvel. He looked forlornly at his weenie curling black now in the hot flames.

Du Pré looked at the priest.

"Come on," he said. "You are starving. We go to the bar, feed you, take care of these cartons."

"Yes," said Father Van Den Heuvel, walking toward his old Plymouth.

"*Non!*" said Du Pré. "I will bring you back maybe tomorrow. You are not driving."

The big priest blinked at him.

Du Pré pointed at the passenger door of the SUV.

Van Den Heuvel got in.

Du Pré drove back to Toussaint while Van Den Heuvel dug around in one of the cartons.

"Oh boy oh boy oh boy," said the priest.

He held up a couple of books and some odd tools.

"Madelaine wants to know you are a doctor," said Du Pré.

Father Van Den Heuvel nodded. "Doctor of geology," he said.

"What is a priest doing being a doctor geology?" said Du Pré.

Father Van Den Heuvel turned back from his diggings.

"The Catholic Church," he said, "favors education as the only way to fight off good ideas. They have gotten good at it, having been fighting off good ideas for the last millennium and a half, and they don't learn. I was in secondary school and I applied for a novice's position and with that came the formidable power of the Jesuits. Get good grades and they keep paying tuition."

"Where you from?" said Du Pré.

"Belgium," said Father Van Den Heuvel. "And if you don't know much about Belgium, it has no rocks. I like rocks, and so I wanted to leave for some place that had rocks. Man, does Montana have rocks."

"Belgium," said Du Pré. "I got drunk there once."

"Good beer," said Father Van Den Heuvel. "Americans make lousy beer."

Du Pré laughed.

"So what is all that stuff?" said Du Pré.

"I got a grant," said Father Van Den Heuvel, "and I bought a lot of books and some gadgets. I think there is a layered gabbro formation under the Wolf Mountains. I don't know how a mountain range managed to get on top of one of those, but it did."

"Oh," said Du Pré.

Father Van Den Heuvel looked at him.

"I'm sorry," he said. "What happens with those is usually this: A huge meteor blasts a hole in the earth's crust and gabbro is the rock that wells up from the mantle. They have metals in them. Gold, platinum, palladium . . ."

"Shit," said Du Pré. "I don't want no damn mine here."

"It wouldn't happen for a long time," said Father Van Den Heuvel, "and things like that aren't secrets. There will be other people who will find it."

They rode along for a few minutes.

"How you make it from Belgium to here?" said Du Pré.

Father Van Den Heuvel laughed.

"I was an orphan," he said. "My parents died in a plane crash returning from Africa. I had been left at home while they went to settle affairs. They never came back. A bad uncle stole the money my parents had had, and I ended up in a Catholic orphanage. I had only myself to count upon. So I used the road that I had. But in time I could not lie any more, and I never did believe much that the Church teaches. It was less trouble to exile me here than it was to defrock me, since I did not care to be defrocked. So, Toussaint, Montana, is very far from power . . ."

Du Pré laughed.

"So I confess," he said, "and you give me penances you don't believe in."

"I have never given you terrible penances," said Father Van Den Heuvel.

"You hold services," said Du Pré.

"What I believe is mine," said Father Van Den Heuvel. "I have no need to chip away at the faith of others. It comforts them."

They saw Toussaint below. It was still light out and the tops of the Wolf Mountains burned from the setting sun.

They went in to the saloon.

Madelaine was at the bar, drinking pink wine and playing cribbage with Susan Klein.

"He is a doctor, geology," said Du Pré.

"Oh," said Madelaine, slapping down some cards and moving her pegs along.

"I am that," said Father Van Den Heuvel.

"He burned his weenie," said Du Pré.

"It fell into the fire," said the big priest.

"Weenie as in hot dog?" said Susan Klein.

"Uh, yes," said Father Van Den Heuvel.

"How about a big porterhouse?" said Susan.

She went back to the kitchen and soon meat sizzled on the grill.

Father Van Den Heuvel sipped a ditch.

"Geology," said Madelaine.

The big priest nodded.
"So why you don't teach it someplace?" she said.
"Few jobs in that," said Father Van Den Heuvel.
They sat silent.
Susan brought the steak.
The good Father fell to it hungrily.

CHAPTER 4

They sat at the bar late, and Father Van Den Heuvel looked so hungrily at a cheeseburger someone down the bar was eating that Madelaine went back and made one for him.

"You maybe think you should get married," said Madelaine. "Somebody who won't let you starve to death. That would be good."

"I can cook," said Father Van Den Heuvel.

"I can *fly*," said Madelaine.

"I can't get married," said Father Van Den Heuvel. "I'm a Jesuit, you know."

The Black Robes, Du Pré thought. They were ver' brave. Brulé Sioux, they are named for Father Brulé. He impressed them so much they ate him.

This is my body which is given to you . . .

Then Du Pré and Father Van Den Heuvel went to the little Catholic church and they unloaded all of the boxes that had come for the priest.

Du Pré left him happily opening boxes and uttering cries of glee at the contents.

Madelaine and Susan were alone in the bar, having a drink. Susan yawned.

"We go home," said Madelaine. "You lock up there."

The door opened and the fat man that Du Pré had seen earlier in the day came in. He was red-faced and bleary-eyed.

"You all have a telephone?" he said.

Madelaine looked at him.

"Pay phone is outside near the door," she said.

The man turned and went out again.

"Who the hell," said Susan Klein, "is that?"

Du Pré spread his hands wide.

The fat little man came back in.

"Phone don't work," he said. "I need to call"—he pulled a scrap of paper from his pocket—"Bill Hefnan."

"Bill Heffernan," said Susan Klein. "He's . . . Here, you can use this."

She handed the bar phone to the man. He dialed slowly.

"Mister Heffernan," said the fat man. "It's Pastor Flowers . . . I'm at . . ." and he looked at Susan.

"The Toussaint Saloon," said Susan.

The fat man repeated that and he listened for a moment and handed the telephone back to her. He went out the front door.

"Not long on manners, is he?" said Susan.

They shut the lights out and went out the front. Benny Klein was there in his sheriff's cruiser.

Susan went to the cop car and she got in and she and Benny kissed.

The fat man was leaning against the side of the orange rental truck. His family was still in the van. His wife had her head against the steering wheel.

Dim lights appeared down the road.

Heffernan pulled up. His old pickup ran rough and the lights brightened and dimmed with the speed of the engine.

Du Pré and Madelaine got in the huge SUV and Du Pré drove to her house. He parked the monster out in front and he and Madelaine went in.

She made raspberry leaf tea and they each had a strong cup.

Du Pré took a long shower and then he came to bed, and Madelaine was already asleep.

He turned out the light.

———

He woke early, his bladder full, and he went to the bathroom and then he went to the kitchen to make coffee.

He heated water to boiling and poured it into the French press and he waited a moment and then he put the plunger down. He poured a cup for himself and he drank it, the heat and the bitter flavor waking him more. He poured a cup for Madelaine and he put cream and sugar in it and he carried it into the bedroom.

Madelaine smiled at him.

"Good service," she said. "You got to go with the priest."

"What?" said Du Pré. "I got things I am doing out at Bart's."

"That fool is going to go into the mountains," said Madelaine, "and you know him. He will die he goes alone."

"He maybe die he goes out of his house," said Du Pré.

"He shuts his head in the car door," said Madelaine. "You want him walking up the trail alone? Maybe you get him two mules, they can kill him."

"I can't spend time keeping him from killing himself," said Du Pré. "I don't have time for nothing else . . ."

"Du Pré," said Madelaine. "We both know what will happen, and then it will be our fault."

"How about I just kill him," said Du Pré. "We don't have to wait and it is sure anyway."

"Geologist," said Madelaine.

"Yah," said Du Pré. "He thinks there is gold and platinum in the Wolf Mountains."

"Lots of people think that," said Madelaine. "Some even find some, though not very much."

"He says there are giant goobers full of gold under the mountains," said Du Pré. "I maybe give him a shovel, tell him dig, when you get there you let me know."

"Du Pré," said Madelaine, "you got to go with him. Let him hurt himself enough he don't want to go back."

Du Pré went back out to the kitchen and he poured some more coffee and he drank it and he went back in the bedroom.

Madelaine was brushing her black hair with the silver streaks in it. She did a hundred strokes every morning.

"Maybe take Chappie," said Madelaine. "He is not doing much but drinking ditchwaters and walking on that leg."

"I don't even know that Father Van Den Heuvel wants to go," said Du Pré.

"He got some stuff in those boxes," said Madelaine. "He will want to go now."

There was a knock at the door.

Du Pré went to it and he opened it and he saw Father Van Den Heuvel in new clothes. Heavy twill pants and shirt, high boots, a straw hat. He had a geologists's pick on his belt in a leather holster.

"Shit," said Du Pré.

"And good morning and may the Lord bless and keep you, too," said Father Van Den Heuvel. "I was wondering if perhaps you could pack me into the mountains. There is a formation back there on the maps that I would like to look at."

"Shit," said Du Pré.

"Du Pré," said Madelaine, "stop standing there stupid, saying *shit*. It is too late for that. Good morning, Father, you would like some breakfast?"

"Sure," said Father Van Den Heuvel.

Madelaine went to frying bacon. She waited while it sizzled and popped and then she cooked eggs in another pan. She sliced bread and put it in the big toaster and she put on water for more coffee.

They ate bacon and eggs and toast and they drank two more pots of good strong coffee.

Father Van Den Heuvel pulled out a map and he unfolded it. It was a Geodetic Survey map. He pointed at a place where the contour lines crowded close to each other.

"Goat Cliff," said Du Pré.

"You know it?" said Father Van Den Heuvel.

"Yah," said Du Pré.

"I want to go and look at it," said the priest.

Du Pré sighed.

"OK," he said.

"How long does it take to get there?" said the priest.

"Long day, day and a half, take it easy," said Du Pré.

"You are taking Chappie," said Madelaine. "He is asleep in the little trailer back there. He wakes up sometimes screaming, so he won't sleep in here."

"OK," said Du Pré.

"When could we go?" said Father Van Den Heuvel.

"Now," said Du Pré. "Sooner you kill yourself, sooner I can go back to work."

"Kill myself?" said the priest.

"Have more coffee," said Madelaine. "Now you go wake up Chappie, tell him to come in here."

Du Pré went out. He stopped to piss out the coffee he had been drinking. He tapped on the trailer door. There were scuffling sounds inside and then Chappie came to the door. He had his leg on and a shirt and nothing else.

"Your mother wants you come along me and the priest, go look at goobers," said Du Pré.

"Goobers?" said Chappie.

"Priest wants to go and look at rocks," said Du Pré. "Take us maybe three days we go this afternoon, he don't want to stay too long."

"I don't want to go," said Chappie. "My leg—"

"You are going," yelled Madelaine from the back porch.

"Shit," said Chappie.

"Shit," said Du Pré.

They nodded vigorously in agreement.

"I got everything," said Du Pré. "You just need clothes. I got a couple new bedrolls ain't been used."

"OK," said Chappie.

He hadn't put on his eyepatch. Where his eye had once been there was a flat place and a red scar.

Du Pré went back to the house.

"Why don't you take them?" said Du Pré.

"Quit whining," said Madelaine.

"Shit," said Du Pré.

"It should be interesting," said Father Van Den Heuvel. "Gabbro is interesting stuff."

"Goobers," said Du Pré.

"Du Pré," said Madelaine, "cut it out."

"OK," said Du Pré. "Gabbro, me, I remember that from college. Sounds like my name."

"Gabriel," said Madelaine, "don't sound like *gab-bro*."

"Coarse-grained igneous rock," said Du Pré.

"I didn't know you went to college," said Father Van Den Heuvel.

"I didn't know you were a doctor of geology," said Du Pré. "Wish I still didn't."

Madelaine was filling bags from her pantry and fridge.

Chappie and the priest and Du Pré loaded the food and booze into the big SUV.

"Do you ever win?" said Father Van Den Heuvel.

Du Pré shook his head.

"Never," he said.

CHAPTER
5

"They're gone to Your-ope," said Booger Tom. "That gal, who is so beautiful every time I think of Bart with her I about puke, hauled pore ol' Bart's fat ass clear across the pond to stare at pitchers. I tol' him things would be slicker'n snot on a doorknob till she got round to improvin' him. He just looked at me with an expression common to poleaxed steers and made a sorta mooin' sound."

The old cowboy twitched his long white mustaches.

"Well," said Du Pré, "you have been putting bluing, your mustaches, since she came."

"I ain't neither," said the old cowboy. He bristled.

"Bart's a ver' lucky man," said Du Pré. "Pidgeon, she is a good person."

"I liked him better when he was diggin' ditches," said Booger Tom. "Feller that rich is generally worthless but he was showin' promise. Just 'fore he left he took a crowbar to a electric motor had the gall to shock him. Durn near burned down the machine shed."

"I am taking that Father Van Den Heuvel up to look at Goat Cliff," said Du Pré.

"Him?" said Booger Tom. "Shit, he couldn't ride from here to there without fallin' off twelve times. Any here to any there."

"I need a good horse for him," said Du Pré.

"Ya need two," said Booger Tom. "Put a hammock in the middle. One got seat belts on it."

"Also one for Chappie," said Du Pré.

"Chappie," said Booger Tom. "Madelaine's kid? One that little asshole in the White House sent off to E-rack and come back mostly, but without some parts."

"Him," said Du Pré.

"Trapper fer the Jesuit and ol' Ralph fer the sojer. Trapper's that fat son of a bitch over there, one showin' his teeth at us. Ralph is the sorrel standin' over there thinkin' deep thoughts about his next snack."

The old cowboy picked up a catch rope and he and Du Pré went to the pasture. The horses all came over to the pole fence. They hung their heads over the top rail and whickered at Booger Tom.

Booger Tom picked up a bucket filled with carrots and apples.

"All right, ya welfare-chiselin' sonsabitches," he said, giving each horse a treat. "You are gonna have ta work a little."

The horses crunched their treats.

Du Pré opened the gate and eight horses filed out and followed Booger Tom to the big barn. Booger Tom opened the swing gate and the horses filed in, Trapper taking a grab for Booger Tom's thick felt Stetson as he passed. Booger Tom slapped the horse on the nose and Trapper snickered and went on.

"I'll skin ya and ya can spend the rest a your career coverin' baseballs," he said as the horse passed.

"They'll be here in an hour or so," said Du Pré.

"How's Chappie doin'?" said Booger Tom.

"Drinkin'," said Du Pré. "Not eating much."

"Feller gets shot up that bad," said Booger Tom, "takes a bit to settle with it."

Du Pré nodded.

"He could job out here," said Booger Tom. "Bart's easy with the payroll."

"I can ask," said Du Pré. "His wife she is gone, Chappie is lost. Has a look on his face sometimes like he is someplace but doesn't know it or like it."

"Ya," said Booger Tom. "I know the look."

"When he is in the hospital," said Du Pré, "he finds out his leg is paid for by some foundation. Government is too cheap to do it."

"Don't get me started," said Booger Tom, "on the danged government."

They saddled three horses and they hung packsaddles on the other five. By the time they were done Madelaine and Chappie had arrived with the food and some gear.

Du Pré and Booger Tom loaded the pack string.

"Where is that priest?" said Du Pré.

"He said he forgot something," said Madelaine. "He would meet us here."

"He is driving here?" said Du Pré.

Madelaine nodded.

"Christ," said Du Pré. "I go and fish him out of the ditch now."

Chappie set to adjusting the stirrups on the saddle he would ride.

Du Pré took one of the ranch pickups which had a winch on the front bumper and he drove back toward Toussaint.

About halfway there he saw Father Van Den Heuvel standing on the road next to the car he had been driving, which was nose down in a spring creek that flowed through a culvert under the macadam.

The old tan car was steaming.

Du Pré pulled up and he looked at it.

"Wilbur will come and get it and fix it," said Du Pré.

"There was a rabbit in the road," said Father Van Den Heuvel.

Du Pré nodded.

He got into the back of the car and he handed bundles and a bedroll to the big priest who put them in the back of the truck.

"Should we call Wilbur?" said Father Van Den Heuvel.

Du Pré shook his head.

"Madelaine will send him," said Du Pré. "We need to go. It is a day, half another. We have the half now we go soon."

"I have never been up in the Wolf Mountains," said the big priest.

Du Pré turned the pickup around and he drove back to the ranch. They got out and carried Father Van Den Heuvel's gear to the pack string and distributed it and then they stood for a moment, Du Pré and Booger Tom smoking.

Chappie went to his horse, put his hands on the saddle horn, hunched down for a moment, and then got on, swinging his artificial leg over and using his hand to guide the foot into the stirrup.

Du Pré held Trapper while Father Van Den Heuvel clambered up. He missed the stirrup the first three times.

Trapper swung his head around to look at the idiot who was trying to get on him.

"I'm sorry," said Father Van Den Heuvel to the horse.

Trapper shrugged.

"Four, five days," said Du Pré to Madelaine. He kissed her.

"Don't find gold," said Madelaine. "It always brings trouble."

Father Van Den Heuvel laughed.

Du Pré led the string and Chappie and the big priest came along behind. A cowboy at work in the upper pasture opened the gates for them and then they began to wind up the foothills to the trail that went alongside the west wall of the canyon. Water and time had cut a deep trench in the old stone, and the creek roared and hissed down below.

Du Pré looked at the trail. Too stony to hold tracks and he would have to get down to see what had passed by lately.

There were a few clouds to the west. They were moving now.

Du Pré sniffed the air.

Rain by morning, he thought.

But just up high, may miss us.

His horse set a good pace and the string was well packed and the horses knew Du Pré knew what he was doing and that practical jokes would have to wait until camp.

They are back there plotting, Du Pré thought.

I take horses recommended by that old bastard I should be worried.

A golden eagle kited down the canyon and shrieked, trying to startle something it could eat from cover.

A big old raven sat on a rock by the trail and watched the string pass. Du Pré looked at its black eye.

At least I don't see three of them, he thought.

They started to wind up the switchback trail that led to the ridge trail that went up on a knee of stone set out from the mountain. They would then cross the face and go through a pass and down to a high basin, one with good grass and water. A fine place to camp.

Du Pré dozed in the saddle. His horse knew where to go and the string was eager to get there and be rewarded with oats and molasses and good new grass.

He nodded, and dozed, and he woke when they began to rise on the knee ridge.

The clouds to the west had thickened into a wall.

For chrissake, it is going to *snow*, Du Pré thought.

The horses walked steadily. Now and then there was a thud or a clank from the packs as something too hastily stowed settled.

Ravens called and swooped down, circled around Du Pré and the pack string.

There were a dozen of them.

Something dead up ahead, Du Pré thought.

He came up over a little rise and saw a mangled elk carcass gone to rot and maggots lying on rocks a few feet off to the side.

. . . bear dragged it there . . .

The smell of rotting flesh billowed out from the carrion. The horses shied a little as they passed, but they did not break stride.

The trail turned to go across the face of the mountain. It was narrow in places and a fall could be fatal. Du Pré fingered his Saint Christopher medal and he prayed for Father Van Den Heuvel.

They went across the dangerous ground without trouble and Du Pré went through the narrow cleft between spines of rock that topped the pass.

The high basin spread before him.

The creeks meandered in the silts collected by beaver dams. A cow moose and calf stood in one pond, water weeds hanging from their mouths.

Du Pré got to the big grassy meadow, an old lake long since filled in with peat and soil. At the far end there was a camp, a pole corral for horses, a tall fire pit that had an iron grate over the top.

The last party to have been there had left kindling ricked up between two small trees and a pile of short lengths of lodgepole pine.

Du Pré stopped and he got down.

The string stood there patiently.

Chappie looked very pale. Du Pré went to help him get down but Chappie waved him away.

"I have to do this," he said.

Du Pré went to strip the packs from the backs of the horses.

Trapper stood and Father Van Den Heuvel sat on him.

The big horse neighed once, and lifted his hind end high.

Father Van Den Heuvel went over Trapper's head, doing a half turn and thudding to earth on his back.

Trapper looked very pleased with himself.

"I'm all right," said the big priest. "I think I had it coming."

CHAPTER
6

They rose early and went on and got to Goat Cliff about three in the afternoon. There had been snow, just a skiff, and when Du Pré got up to make the fire the horses were frosted like doughnuts.

The meadow had steamed when the sun warmed it and they had ridden most of the way in cold white fog that got much colder in the stands of trees.

A mountain lion screamed once as they passed a huge tree the cat used as a territorial marker. Claw marks as high as the cat could reach from the ground showed fresh in the old gray wood, a scar from a lightning strike.

Du Pré and Chappie made camp while Father Van Den Heuvel hammered on the cliff face with his geologist's pick. From time to time he would yelp as a fragment of stone punctured his skin.

Once he came back to have Du Pré dig a chip of rock out of his cheek. Blood welled out of the hole but Du Pré could feel the point of his knife grate on the buried rock and he lifted it out.

"You could wear a helmet and face mask," said Du Pré.

"Then I couldn't see," said Father Van Den Heuvel. "I wonder if anyone ever did an assay on this. It could be barren, I suppose."

Those old prospectors went about everywhere and assayed

about everything, Du Pré thought, but then they did not know how to heap-leach metals out of crushed rock.

Du Pré found a package of steaks in the cooler and he made a fire. Chappie had gone to a nearby pond and he had pulled up enough cattails to cut the edible shoot from the base.

They had grilled steaks and boiled cattail shoots and a salad of lamb's-quarters and peppery watercress.

"Grenville Dodge," said Father Van Den Heuvel. "He carried watercress seed and he tossed it in any creek he came to. The pioneers died of scurvy often enough and he thought they could eat the watercress. But most of them did not know what it was."

Grenville Dodge the army engineer, Du Pré thought. I wonder if he *was* here.

"He came here leading an expedition to look for fossils," said Father Van Den Heuvel, "but the Wolf Mountains are igneous. Very mysterious, some of these ranges. They just all came up about fifty million years ago. Popped up like corks in water. Something going on down there, but we don't really know what, other than it was hot. Heat is what lifted up the mountains."

Chappie was pulling at a bottle of whiskey, but at least he had eaten a steak and starches and a few mouthfuls of greens.

"What other mountain ranges?" said Chappie.

"All of the island ranges," said Father Van Den Heuvel, "the Elkhorns and the Little Rockies, the Snowies and the Belts, the Bearpaws and even the Beartooths. They are older than the ranges to the west."

Chappie nodded.

"I read a good book about all that," he said. "Interesting."

"I have many more if you wish to read them," said Father Van Den Heuvel.

He went back to his chipping at the rock face, though this time he did so in a different place.

All the material he had collected went into canvas bags which were tied off and piled on an old stump.

"Must have been warmer and wetter here when that tree seeded," said Father Van Den Heuvel. He had put up his hammer for the day. There was only an hour or so of light left.

The big priest scraped away at a broken end of wood, where the tree had snapped in a gale long ago.

"All pitchy," he said. "This tree could be some thousands of

30

years old. They don't rot, and this spot is high enough so it would not have been flooded after the glaciers left."

He shaved off a few small curls of wood.

He put a match to them and they flared up brightly, popping as the pitch gasified and burned.

Du Pré had cut an alder stock, loosened the bark by holding it over the fire, and slid it off. He bored a channel and he cut some holes in the bark and slid it back on and he whittled a mouthpiece and then he let it set a while and then he played the flute he had made. It had a sweet and melancholy tone, the fingerholes were about right and he had a reasonable scale.

Chappie kept at his whiskey, yawned, went to bed. He took off his prosthesis and he set it beside his bedroll.

Du Pré woke in the night. The horses were whinnying. He pulled on his boots and he took a flashlight and rifle and he went to the meadow. The stock was hobbled and all bunched together.

He shone the light round the meadow, saw a dark lump. The lump moved.

Du Pré fired over the bear's head.

The animal ran into the timber and crashed though the thick trees. The sound died away.

Du Pré turned and looked back at the camp. A flashlight beam was waving around wildly.

"Don't shoot!" yelled Du Pré.

"I don't have a gun," said Father Van Den Heuvel.

Du Pré walked back to the camp.

He shone his light on the horses. They had gone back to grazing.

Father Van Den Heuvel was standing near his bedroll holding a flashlight.

Chappie was asleep. He murmured something. Then he screamed.

He flailed around for a moment, woke up gasping and clawing at the blankets.

"It is all right," said Father Van Den Heuvel, kneeling by Chappie.

"Bad dreams," said Chappie. "Goddamn bad dreams."

He sat up, flipped the blankets back, pulled the socket of the prosthesis over the stump of his left leg.

He got up and he walked off into the dark.

"Bear," said Du Pré. "He was not doing much but looking. Horses didn't like it, though."

"Bear," said Chappie. "I was in Iraq, I dreamed of bears and now I dream of explosions. The one got me was weird. I never heard anything, it was too close. I just saw a shimmer of air. That was it, and next thing I knew I was in a hospital with a bunch of tubes in me."

He sat down on a log, fished a bottle out of his duffel, opened it, had a slug, offered it to Du Pré and then Father Van Den Heuvel.

Du Pré had some. The priest didn't.

They went back to sleep.

In the morning the priest went off with a collecting bag and his pick and he moved along the cliff face. There were piles of scree shed off by freezing water at the base of the cliffs.

Du Pré watched the big clumsy man struggle up the piles of rocks to the face. Then he heard the pinging of the pick on rock.

Chappie ate part of an egg and then he got up to go off and relieve himself.

"Yay!" yelled Father Van Den Heuvel. "I think I found it!"

Du Pré walked over to the rocks and he climbed up to where the priest was.

Father Van Den Heuvel pointed to a gray-black formation, a triangle thrust up into lighter-colored stone.

"I think that may be it!" said Father Van Den Heuvel.

He pounded on the rock, but it merely showed whitish scars where the steel pick hit.

The priest looked at the rocks under his feet.

"Nothing here," he said. "This all came from above."

Something clacked high overhead and Du Pré looked up to see a big chunk of rock falling toward them. He pulled the priest away and down the pile of rocks; they lost their footing and fell and rolled. Du Pré dove into a cleft just as the chunk of rock hit the pile. There was a cracking boom and then a splatter of chunks and chips.

The air stank of sulfur.

Du Pré waited until the last rattling stopped.

He edged out of the cleft.

Father Van Den Heuvel was on his hands and knees, looking at something.

"Wow," he said. He held up a dark red stone set in grayish rock.

"Garnet," said Du Pré. "Whole cliff up there is full of them."

"This is a fascinating place," said Father Van Den Heuvel.

They went back up to the grayish incursion that so excited the priest.

Du Pré left Father Van Den Heuvel there, banging away on rock that did not care to give way.

He walked downhill along the cliff face until he found another upthrust of the gray-black rock.

This one was broader than the one the priest had found and it reached higher.

Du Pré looked at the spall heap below the cliff.

He found two huge chunks of stone, and he rolled them down the pile to the grassy soil at the edge of the basin.

He looked again for a smaller chunk but he didn't see any.

He walked back up to the priest.

"I got two big pieces," said Du Pré.

Father Van Den Heuvel was bleeding from multiple small wounds in his face.

They went down the pile and over to the two chunks Du Pré had found.

"That's it," said Father Van Den Heuvel. "Can we get them back down? I don't think we can break them apart."

Du Pré looked at the smaller one. There was a crack in it near a knob of stone that jutted out from the mass. He held out his hand for the pick.

Father Van Den Heuvel gave it to him.

Du Pré tapped lightly at the crack and the stone knob parted from the mother rock.

It weighed perhaps five pounds.

"This," said Du Pré, "we can carry."

"You just *tapped* it," said Father Van Den Heuvel.

"Yah," said Du Pré.

He looked crestfallen.

"I don't know if it is gabbro," he said. "I'll have to assay it."

"You got an assay furnace?" said Du Pré.

"I hoped perhaps you could help me make one," said the priest.

"Means I make it," said Du Pré.

"I know," said the priest.

"Catfoot had one," said Du Pré. "I find it."

"Your father?" said Father Van Den Heuvel.

"Yah," said Du Pré. "He maybe assayed this rock anyway. He was all over the mountains. Lived up here."

"I would have liked to know him," said Father Van Den Heuvel.

CHAPTER 7

Du Pré took the last packsaddle off the last horse and he turned it out in the pasture. Father Van Den Heuvel was loading their gear into the big SUV. Chappie and Booger Tom were sharing a pint while commenting on the priest's efforts.

"I didn't know you bastards worked," said Booger Tom. "I thought you passed collection plates and molested children."

"Go bugger a goat," said Father Van Den Heuvel. "I'll give you absolution in advance. Hell, I'll up it to three goats. That should get you through the weekend."

"Yer dangerous," said Booger Tom. "Now I know why they done sent you out here."

Du Pré walked over to the porch where Booger Tom and Chappie were and in a moment the big priest came, too. His face was swollen from festering wounds he had given himself pounding on rocks.

"Thanks," said Father Van Den Heuvel. "I have lots of specimens. Now all I need is that assayer's furnace."

"The barn back of Raymond and Jacqueline's," said Du Pré. "It is there someplace."

Du Pré and Chappie and the priest got in the SUV.

"How's the cruiser?" said Booger Tom.

"Wilbur, he is putting in the new head gasket," said Du Pré.

"Wilbur," said Booger Tom. "How is that pore Bible-thumpin' son of a bitch? I allus worry about men married to women three times bigger than they is."

"He's putting in my head gasket," said Du Pré, "is how he is."

"Wilbur could use a new head gasket," said Booger Tom. "Well, good ta see ya. That woman who is makin' Bart's life so much better than he wanted and him is back tomorrow."

Du Pré nodded.

"She is good folks," he said.

"I know," said Booger Tom. "I just think it is such a waste, her being sweet on that guinea bastard. She coulda had me, you know."

"She isn't stupid," said Du Pré.

"No," said Booger Tom. "Nothing more dangerous than a smart, beautiful woman."

Du Pré put the SUV in reverse and he backed and turned and drove off down the long road to the county cross-bench gravels.

They shot along the bench for a few miles and then went down a cut to the back road to Toussaint.

Du Pré dropped Chappie off at the trailer he lived in, not far from the saloon. Then he and Father Van Den Heuvel drove to the little white Catholic church.

Du Pré pulled up to the back door that led to the priest's small apartment.

"Good Christ," said Father Van Den Heuvel.

Someone had used white spray paint on the door. They had drawn a crude Star of David.

Du Pré and Father Van Den Heuvel got out.

"This," said the big priest, "is interesting."

Du Pré scratched at the paint with his fingernail.

"Cheap stuff you get any hardware store," he said. "Who is this stupid person did this?"

"Oh well," said Father Van Den Heuvel. "I had been meaning to paint the door for the last ten years or so."

"Get some mineral spirits and that will take this off," said Du Pré.

"I think I have some," said the priest.

He went in and came back out with a can of thinner and a rag.

"I go and look for that assay furnace," said Du Pré.

He drove on to his old place where he had grown up, Catfoot

and Mama there. Now they were both dead and so was Du Pré's wife and all three were in the little cemetery at the edge of town.

Pallas and Lourdes were at the barn combing the tangles out of the manes of their horses.

Stewball and Moondog. Bart had spent a fortune on them and then he had just given them to the girls. The horses' coats gleamed from good feed and brushings. Moondog had a white mane and tail, black everywhere else; Stewball was a blue roan. Thoroughbreds in a land of quarter horses.

Du Pré stopped for a moment, then he went into the big shed that was stuck on the side of the barn. There were wooden boxes and cardboard ones, and stacks of old lumber and machine parts, a Model/A engine, and God knows what else.

Du Pré thought for a moment.

He lifted some cardboard boxes off a wooden one and he lifted the lid up on that.

The assay furnace sat there, and a rack of porcelain cups to melt the samples in.

The thing was heavy, so Du Pré got a dolly and he wheeled the box outside and up on the loading ramp, then he backed the SUV up and he slid the big crate down into the back end.

The springs sagged but not too much.

He went back and found the gas tank—acetylene, propane did not burn hot enough—and the hose and fittings for the furnace.

The two girls, mounted, were clearing the fence at the far end of the pasture by a good three feet.

Stewball and Moondog stayed around because they wanted to.

He drove back to the priest's. He looked round and found an old hardstand, bricks set in mortar, a flat place on the ground.

Father Van Den Heuvel was scrubbing the white paint off the door.

He put down his rag and he came.

"This is heavy," said Du Pré.

The big priest nodded. He reached in the back, got hold of the handles on the wooden box, and lifted it out and set it down easily.

Du Pré raised his eyebrows.

"I lift weights," said Father Van Den Heuvel. "It's hard to jog in a cassock. Very practical garment, a cassock, good heavy wool and easy to move in."

Du Pré nodded.

Father Van Den Heuvel was around six foot six and broad, so he would weigh well over two hundred and fifty pounds.

"I weigh two-seventy-five," he said, "and that crate *was* heavy."

Du Pré hooked the hoses and valves and control up to the furnace, then he picked the striker up out of it and he sparked it while he turned the valve stem. A blue flame caught, and it roared.

"Still had acetylene," said Du Pré. "I think the oxygen tank is about out."

"I can do this," said Father Van Den Heuvel.

Du Pré looked around for things that could burn, but there wasn't much but a little grass.

He went over to the door. The white paint was gone mostly, but pale smears now covered the door and the jamb.

He shook his head.

"It would be some kid," said the priest, "some ignorant kid. He probably thinks I *am* a Jew. The important thing is the hate, then you find someone to fit it."

"I don't like it," said Du Pré. "You have been here, long time, and now this. People around here, they are not like this."

"Oh, I disagree," said the big priest. "There is a lot of anger and ignorance and frustration here. This is not the land some of these people knew. The economy is dying and with it their hopes. No, I have heard a few things, and they are very sad."

Du Pré nodded.

"You will be all right?" he said.

"Fine," said Father Van Den Heuvel. "If not, you will see a tower of flame."

"I don't want to see that," said Du Pré.

He drove back to Bart's ranch to find him and Pidgeon carrying suitcases into the house.

Bart saw Du Pré and he set his suitcase on the porch. He walked over. He looked a little tired.

"You have a good trip?" said Du Pré.

"Lovely paintings," said Bart. "I was in the Louvre once before but I was drunk. I didn't remember much of it."

Paris.

"I was there, long time ago," said Du Pré. "On leave, the army."

He had spent a week in Paris, gone to the museums, and gotten the clap from a whore. A most successful vacation from barracks life in Germany.

Pidgeon came back out. She smiled at Du Pré, came to him, kissed him on the cheek.

"He wanted to buy me a painting," said Pidgeon. "I told him no. He's putting the money in the school here, well, the high school in Cooper."

"New computers and books for the library and an addition to the library," said Bart. "She found out how much the painting was and drove a hard bargain."

"I'm middle-class," said Pidgeon. "I think beautiful things should be in museums so many people may enjoy them. If I had a painting that good on my wall I would feel like a turd."

She laughed.

"You ever talk to that Harvey?" said Du Pré.

Pidgeon nodded.

"He has a couple of beauts. One guy killing prostitutes in Florida, and not the poor girls on the street. Expensive call girls. They are careful, but he steals identities and they go to met clients they have been with before. Game player. It is as much about fooling the cops as it is killing the women. Then there is some creep hitting second-floor bedrooms, gets in off the roof, killing women home alone while their husbands are away. He tortures them for hours before he kills them. Just the usual, if you do the kind of work I do."

"You could quit," said Bart.

"Not if I can stop one of these bastards, I can't," said Pidgeon.

"So she is leaving me," said Bart, looking mournful.

"Just three days," said Pidgeon.

"We feed him," said Du Pré.

Pidgeon nodded.

"I already talked to Madelaine," she said. "Called her from the plane. You were up in the mountains."

"Father Van Den Heuvel is a geologist," said Du Pré.

"Oh, really," said Pidgeon.

"I still don't know why he is here," said Du Pré.

"He's a troublemaker," said Pidgeon. "They send troublemakers here. Jedgar Hoover used to send agents to Butte."

"Somebody spray-painted a Star of David on Father Van Den Heuvel's door," said Du Pré.

Pidgeon scowled.

"You tell me if there is any more of this shit," she said. "I don't suppose you took a photograph of it before he cleaned it up?"

Du Pré shook his head.

"Next time there is something like this, you do that," said Pidgeon.

CHAPTER

8

Du Pré tended bar while Madelaine and Susan and a couple of other women ran the big platters of prime rib out to the tables. It was Friday night, and people from the ranches came in to have someone else cook for a change and to see the neighbors.

The bar had every stool full of hands or single people. The tables were left for families, though there were no signs saying so.

Du Pré made everyone ditchwater highballs no matter what it was they ordered by way of liquor and he pulled draft beers from any tap in quick reach, on the grounds that it all came out of the same vat at the factory.

"God damn it, Du Pré," said one weathered man, "I want a god-damned martini."

Du Pré put some whiskey and ice and water in the cocktail shaker and he shook it and slopped it into the highball glass.

"Great martini," said the man. "See, I bitch enough I get good service."

The place was packed and about eight-thirty Bassman and Père Godin showed up to play music with Du Pré.

The prime rib had all been served and the dishes all washed and Susan went back to tending the bar and the two other women stayed in the kitchen to cook.

Du Pré went out to Bassman's van. Bassman lit a spliff the size of a broomstick and he inhaled the sweet smoke and he held it down in his lungs.

"Père Godin has two more kids," said Bassman. "Somebody is gonna shoot that old bastard. We think he has seventy-seven kids now. Old fart, he smiles and they lay down and spread their legs."

"He is good at it," said Du Pré. "Seventy-seven kids is a lot of kids."

Bassman drew heavily on his huge joint again.

Du Pré had some whiskey and he rolled a couple of cigarettes.

The green van with the Texas plates pulled into the field by the saloon and the little fat man got out. He was alone.

He walked stiff-legged into the saloon.

"Who is that?" said Bassman.

"Bible-thumper," said Du Pré. "I dunno what he wants here."

Then they heard him shouting about sin and being saved.

Then they watched as he flew out of the doorway, landing fifteen feet away.

Susan Klein came out. Her face was red.

"You are eighty-sixed, mister," she said. "You cannot come in here and insult my friends. You stay out of here."

The little man got up, looking very pleased with himself. He brushed some dust from his clothes.

Benny Klein pulled in just then, stopping near the little man.

He got out.

"Benny!" said Susan. "You tell this bastard never to come here again."

Benny looked from his wife to the little fat man.

"Ah, shit," said Bassman, stubbing out his joint.

Benny was talking quietly to the little man, who was listening, sort of.

He said something.

Benny looked at him.

"Get Benny turn away," said Bassman.

They walked over.

The little man had pulled a small book from his back pocket.

"Hey, Benny," said Du Pré, nodding toward the corner of the building, "need a word with you."

Benny turned to join Du Pré.

There was a wet slap and a howl of pain and surprise, and they turned to see Bassman standing over the little man, who was face-down on the ground with Bassman's foot on his back.

"Benny!" said Bassman. "You come here there are drugs I think."

Benny hurried over.

Bassman picked up the little fat man by the collar and Benny pulled a huge partially smoked joint out of the man's shirt pocket.

"Marijuana," said Benny. "You are under arrest, you have the right to remain . . ."

Du Pré and Bassman watched as Benny arrested the little man, stuck him in the back of the cruiser, and then came up to them.

"You just never know who will use drugs, do you?" said Benny.

"It is a scourge," said Bassman.

"Terrible," said Du Pré.

"I guess I have to drive to Cooper," said Benny. "After I eat the prime rib that Susan saved for me. I will probably stay for a couple of sets, too."

The little man was screaming and pounding on the back window.

"I'll park someplace away from the saloon," said Benny. He went off and Du Pré and Bassman went in to find Père Godin talking to a woman named Linda who had left her husband.

"Somebody gonna kill him, that old man," said Bassman.

"Maybe tonight," said Du Pré, looking toward the door.

They tuned up and Père Godin came away from his latest conquest and he picked up his accordion and they started with *Baptiste's Lament,* then they played some dance tunes, *Boiling Cabbage, Sugar in the Bowl,* and people got up and began to dance on the tiny floor.

They played one set and Benny stood against the wall, prime rib grease shining on his chin, smiling and tapping his foot.

Benny stayed through the next set and then he went out and he came back in a moment, his face troubled.

"You are all right," said Du Pré. "Guy kick out of your car?"

Benny shook his head.

"I just let him go," he said, "and I told him he could never come here again. I think he was a bit scared by then. I don't think a bust for dope would help with his reputation."

Du Pré nodded.

"And he did not really deserve that this time," said Benny.

Du Pré nodded.

"But I talked with the dispatcher and she said she got a nine-one-one call and she can't find out where it came from."

Du Pré nodded. Other counties had systems that gave addresses of calls automatically but Cooper County could not afford that.

"Somebody, a woman or a kid maybe, just said help, help, help three times and then the connection was broken or they hung up," said Benny.

It was nearly midnight and many people had left or were going. They had to be up at dawn for the unending work of raising cattle and wheat on the High Plains.

Benny and Susan sat at a table holding hands while Du Pré and Bassman and Père Godin played a short last set. Linda looked adoringly at the old goat with the accordion.

Then they quit and packed up the instruments and the sound system and Du Pré and Bassman hauled the stuff out to Bassman's van.

It was rocking on its springs.

"That old bastard," said Bassman. "Not that we can do anything."

"Seventy-eight," said Du Pré. "You can stay with us, you can any time."

Madelaine gave Du Pré a huge grin when he came back in.

"Him something, eh?" she said. "Bassman lose his happy home."

Benny looked at his pager, got up and went out.

Du Pré had a whiskey and then he had another. He yawned.

Susan turned the lights up. A couple of hands trying to be seriously drunk were gulping shots in the corner.

"You boys sleep it off here," said Benny.

They shuffled out to sleep in the back of the pickup they had come in.

"Du Pré," said Benny, "I got a weird one. Dispatcher got another call. It was a kid, she thinks. She talked to the kid a little bit. Kid didn't know where she was. But she was scared she was going to be killed."

"A joke maybe?" said Du Pré.

"Dispatcher didn't think so," said Benny. "She has it on tape. But it is over to Cooper."

Du Pré nodded.

"OK," he said.

"I think I know everybody around here," said Benny, "and then I find out that I don't."

Du Pré went back in the saloon.

"I got to go Cooper," he said.

Madelaine nodded.

"Take the SUV," said Du Pré. "I ride with Benny."

Madelaine shrugged.

"Not that far," she said.

Du Pré and Benny went out to his cruiser and Benny got in the passenger seat and Du Pré drove at one-ten most of the way to the county seat.

They parked near the front door.

They went in.

The dispatcher was a plump middle-aged woman, the widow of a rancher.

She fiddled some dials and she pressed a switch.

"Emergency," said her voice.

"Help," said a child's voice, thin and anguished.

"Where are you?" said the dispatcher.

There were some sobs.

"I don't know," said the voice.

"Who are you?" said the dispatcher.

There was a flurry of voices and the line disconnected.

"The second one," said the dispatcher.

She flipped another switch.

"Emergency," said the voice.

"They are going to kill me," said the child's voice. It sounded like a girl's.

"Where are you?" said the dispatcher.

"I don't know," said the child.

"Honey," said the dispatcher, "just stay calm."

"I'll try," said the child.

"Are you in a house?" said the dispatcher.

"Yes," said the child.

"Can you see anything?" said the dispatcher.

The line went dead.

"If we had better phones," said Benny, "we could get a number off the damn thing."

"Too far away from anything," said the dispatcher.

"If she calls back," said Benny, "let me know."

45

CHAPTER 9

Du Pré went into the barn where Pallas was brushing Moondog's coat. The horse whuffled with pleasure. Pallas frowned and she picked apart a knot in his mane.

"Him one spoiled son of a bitch," said Du Pré.

"Yah," said Pallas. "But if I do this maybe he don't buck me off." Du Pré snorted. The horse loved Pallas.

"I got this tape I want you to listen to," said Du Pré.

Pallas looked at her grandfather.

"The nine-one-one people get two calls from some girl asking for help, says she may be killed, she is afraid, but she does not stay on the telephone and we don't have a way of finding the number. Benny is talking to the phone company, maybe they can help," said Du Pré.

Pallas nodded.

Du Pré pulled a small tape recorder from his pocket and he pressed the red button.

Pallas listened intently.

She motioned for Du Pré to play it again.

"Cell phones don't work here yet?" she said.

Du Pré shook his head.

"Satellite phones, but we don't got enough people for them to build a cell phone thing," said Du Pré.

Pallas went to her bag, took out her cell phone, punched in some numbers.

She looked at the screen.

"Drive me toward Cooper," she said.

Du Pré and Pallas got in the big green SUV and he drove off east toward the county seat.

They got to the hill above the town and Pallas motioned for Du Pré to stop.

She handed the phone to Du Pré.

"Nine-one-one," said the dispatcher. "What is the problem?"

"Nothing," said Du Pré. "I was just testing this phone." He hit the off button.

"They have put in a tower here," said Pallas.

"Benny did not know about it," said Du Pré.

"It is Sunday," said Pallas. "Maybe they don't announce it is ready until tomorrow. Anyway, I bet it is a cell phone, old one, account is closed, but you can always call nine-one-one on them. I bet this call came from the very edge of the range of the tower. That would change some depending on time of day and stuff."

Du Pré nodded.

Pallas looked off toward the Wolf Mountains. They had clouds in the high clefts that led to the basins.

Pallas was thinking.

"I get on the computer," she said. "There is a lot I don't know about cell phones."

She walked toward the house and she went in.

Du Pré rolled a smoke and he lit it and he stood with on foot on the bottom rail of the pole corral, watching an eagle float across the face of the mountains.

Pallas came back in a few minutes.

"I don't know a lot more," she said. "But the best I could do was that this is an old cell phone, that it could work from as far as forty or fifty miles if the phone was on a hill or on top of a building, so the call was made from maybe someplace in eight thousand square miles."

"Eight thousand square miles," said Du Pré.

"Yah," said Pallas. "Big place we live in."

Du Pré nodded.

"Thank you," he said.

"I will find out what I can find out when I think of what it is we want to find out," said Pallas.

"OK," said Du Pré.

"So I will ride, maybe see you later," said Pallas. She grinned at her grandfather.

He helped her saddle Moondog and he watched as she rode out of the barn. She whooped and headed for a fence and the horse soared over it.

Bart pulled in in his battered old ranch truck. He got out. He was wearing his frayed and stained overalls, the ones he wore when he was running his backhoe or dozer or dragline.

He looked at Pallas and Moondog, heading up toward the Wolf Mountains.

"She needs that horse nearer to school," said Bart.

Du Pré laughed.

"Madelaine skin me you do that," he said.

"I," said Bart, "will save you from the terrible Madelaine. I feel bad. I should have thought of it."

Du Pré nodded, rolled a smoke, gave it to Bart, made another for himself.

"She is something," said Bart. "Whole wide world before her."

"I hope she finds as much of it as she needs," said Du Pré.

"All of us, Gabriel, all of us," said Bart.

"You are digging ditches today?" said Du Pré.

"Cleaning out one that fell in," said Bart. "It had a bad lay and I told Burton it needed to be wired, but he didn't want to spend the money."

They nodded to each other and Du Pré got in the big SUV and he drove toward Cooper.

Benny was at the little sheriff's office, looking mournfully at stacks of papers on his desk.

The dispatcher looked up as Du Pré came in.

"Any more calls, that girl thought she would be killed?" said Du Pré.

"No," said the dispatcher. "Just one for a heart attack. The EMTs went there but the guy was all right. Just had a chest pain and got nervous."

"I had a chest pain I would be nervous," said Benny.

One of the deputies called in, a crackling spate of words. Du Pré could not make out any of them.

Du Pré sat on the corner of Benny's desk.

"Pallas says it is probably an old cell phone, can't call any number but nine-one-one, and it is someplace in eight thousand miles."

"Oh," said Benny.

"That Pastor Flowers from Texas," said Du Pré. "Him, his family only people moved here, last couple of days."

Benny nodded. "I will . . . ," he said.

They looked at each other.

"Wouldn't work and might get the girl killed," said Du Pré.

"How about checking up on the kids?" said Benny. "They should be in school." Du Pré nodded.

"Now," he said, "all we got to do, find a social worker."

"They are scarce here," said Benny. "But there is the school principal. One of the things he has to do is see that the kids are either in school or being homeschooled."

Du Pré nodded.

"Let's go," said Benny. "I—"

"It's Sunday," said Du Pré.

"So we will call him at home," said Benny.

He looked up the number and he dialed and he asked for Mr. Lennart.

He listened.

He put the telephone back.

"His wife said he went to Ella Drue's to fix a door she broke or something," said Benny.

They went out and drove east of town to a big white ranch house set in cottonwood trees, down in a small flat valley, out of the wind.

There was a new Cadillac parked in the garage and an old van full of tools parked in front of the yard gate.

Lennart was inside, setting some new hinges on a door that led from the kitchen to the mud room on the back porch.

He set a couple of screws with a battery drill driver.

"Hope you ain't takin' him till he fixes m'door," said Ella, a white-haired woman nearly eighty now, wiry and strong, dressed in worn denims and boots and a stained crushed hat.

"No," said Benny. "The heavens may fall but you get yer door fixed first."

"Coffee?" said Ella.

Benny and Du Pré nodded.

"What's up?" said Lennart.

He was in his early thirties, blond and square-built, and he had a wife and three children. The small salary a principal's job paid was not enough for them.

"We got a problem," said Benny. "We're gettin' calls from a girl who says she is afraid she will be killed but we can't find her. Only people moved here recent was that Bible-thumper from Texas. He has kids."

"Oh," said Lennart, "so you want me to go and talk with him."

"Don't know what else to do," said Benny.

"Texas?" said Ella. "We got more a *them?*"

Benny ignored her.

"I could go in the morning," said Lennart. "I have to teach a math class at nine but I could go around ten."

"You could go today," said Ella. "The hell with the damned door."

"They'll be in church," said Lennart. "That is what he does."

"I heard they was looking for a new parson," said Ella, "them Baptists. Last one was flat crazy and spent all his time tellin' them they was going to hell."

"That is what Baptists *do*," said Lennart. "All last year they were yelling at me to stop teaching evolution in the science class. They steal all the books in the library that they don't like, and won't give them back, and I have had kids in my office bawling in terror, because their classmates tell them they are going to hell, too."

"I bet he's homeschooling," said Benny.

"Maybe," said Lennart. "That way the kids are as ignorant as the parents. It is a great time for ignorance in this country. I'd buy stock in it if I were you."

Du Pré and Benny laughed, and Ella hooted.

"I'll go this afternoon," said Lennart. "Where do they live?"

"I don't know," said Benny.

"Wilbur knows," said Du Pré.

"Wilbur knows something?" said Ella. "That's new."

"Ella," said Benny, "I got to ask you keep quiet about this."

"You always were a dumb son of a bitch," said Ella. "If the whole county knows about the girl and the phone calls and all, someone who knows something might *call* you."

"How'd you know about it?" said Benny. "I mean, we just come."

"It's a small place," said Ella. "I got lots of friends."

CHAPTER
10

"So," said Madelaine. "You find that girl yet?"

"No," said Du Pré. "Pallas, she say that the girl is out there, eight thousand square miles."

"Pallas find her," said Madelaine. "That is one smart kid."

Du Pré nodded.

"Bart, he is going to send Moondog back there for Pallas," said Du Pré.

"That girl have a horse there she will not study so much," said Madelaine. "I will talk to that Bart."

Madelaine was putting on her light jacket, the one with the quillwork on it. There was a design on the back, a mother coyote and four pups. The mother was showing the pups a bee's nest.

"I am going to get Chappie up, make sure he eats breakfast," said Madelaine. "I meet you at the saloon in maybe an hour. Maybe you are there he don't eat."

Du Pré nodded. A mother trying to help her son.

"I go and see if Father Van Den Heuvel burn down the church yet," said Du Pré. "I maybe go to confession, too."

"Father Van Den Heuvel would not hear your confession," said Madelaine. "He don't believe in it any more than you do."

"You go him," said Du Pré.

"I believe what I believe," said Madelaine. "I don't need either of you do my believing for me."

She went out and up the street, putting her feet down firmly. When she walked on hard floors Du Pré could hear the tapping of her heels even in a crowd and know that it was her without looking.

He went out and got in the big SUV and he drove over to the little Catholic church. The service there was early, so Father Van Den Heuvel had most of the day to work with his rock samples.

Du Pré heard the roar of the assay furnace.

He went out behind the church. Father Van Den Heuvel, wearing a long leather welder's coat and a face mask, was peering down into the crucible that the furnace flames were heating.

The sounds were loud.

Father Van Den Heuvel took some tongs and he reached down into the fire and he clamped the tongs on the crucible and he lifted it up and he began to swing it over to a porcelain pad so it could cool.

Something happened and he dropped the crucible and then the tongs.

Molten material sloshed out of the crucible when it hit the ground and it set the dry grass on fire. Wisps of smoke curled up here and there.

Father Van Den Heuvel yelped.

Du Pré looked at the man's feet. A thin wisp of blackish smoke curled up from the toe of the big priest's right boot. He reached down and untied the laces and he started to pull the boot off and he fell over backward on to the hot material in the smoldering grass.

"Yowww!" said Father Van Den Heuvel. He slid the boot off and he scrambled up and he shed the leather coat. He stood panting on cold earth.

Du Pré looked at him, eyebrows raised.

The priest pulled off his right sock.

He had a burn the size of a silver dollar on top of his arch. The burn was deep.

"Ah, shit," said Father Van Den Heuvel.

The skin was visibly swelling and blistering.

Du Pré helped him to a chair and he went in the house and got some ice in a small plastic bag and he came back and he handed it to the priest, who clapped it on his burn.

Father Van Den Heuvel winced.

Du Pré stomped out the few clumps of burning grass.

He went to the assay furnace and he shut the valves and the flames died and the roaring stopped.

"You distracted me," said Father Van Den Heuvel.

"Sure," said Du Pré.

"Actually," said the big priest, "to be fair, I didn't notice you until you helped me to the chair."

"Time like this, who wants to be fair?" said Du Pré.

"God damn it," said the priest. "I bet I have to have a skin graft. That is one deep hole."

Du Pré nodded.

He bent down to look.

"Skin is not charred," he said. "You just have to wear a moccasin with the top off awhile."

"I pray for grace every day," said Father Van Den Heuvel. "Of course, I don't actually believe in a god of any sort, so perhaps that is presumptuous."

Du Pré laughed.

"You do all this get sent here?" he said.

"Actually," said Father Van Den Heuvel, "I had hoped for Wyoming. I like fossils and they have more of them there."

"We got lots here," said Du Pré.

Father Van Den Heuvel nodded.

"Perhaps," he said, "I should go over to that. You know, as I think of it, if there is a metal-rich layered gabbro deposit where I think there is, it would just cause a lot of trouble. Money always does cause that."

"This grant," said Du Pré, "where you get it?"

The big priest flushed red.

Du Pré laughed and laughed and laughed. He had to sit down on the back steps and wipe his eyes with his kerchief.

"Mesa Resources," said Father Van Den Heuvel, "those nice folks that bring cyanide to you."

"Christ," said Du Pré.

"Actually," said Father Van Den Heuvel, "I think I had best lie to them and say the assays were disappointing. I will have to send samples, though."

Du Pré nodded.

"And that is complicated," said Father Van Den Heuvel. "They will want samples which are obviously gabbro."

Du Pré nodded.

"I'll figure it out," said Father Van Den Heuvel.

"It is in the wilderness area," said Du Pré. "We were not supposed to be doing that up there."

"Pursuit of knowledge is OK," said Father Van Den Heuvel.

"Fine," said Du Pré, "long as we find good knowledge."

"I better get something on this," said the big priest.

Du Pré found some petroleum jelly and a big square bandage in the house, and an old snow boot that he slit so the top would not bind Father Van Den Heuvel's foot.

He dressed the wound.

"Ah," said Father Van Den Heuvel, "could you pick up a bit of that stuff I was reducing? I need to get it analyzed."

Du Pré found several lumps of blackish rocky foam. He touched them carefully but they were already cool.

He handed them to the big priest. Then Du Pré unhooked the gas tanks and he carried them to the SUV. He came back with the splitting maul it carried. He smashed the fire bricks in the assay furnace and he bashed the brass gas fittings to a mess of torn metal.

He looked at his handiwork.

"OK," said Father Van Den Heuvel, "I get the point."

"Me," said Du Pré, "I should not have done this."

"Thank you," said Father Van Den Heuvel, "for saving my life."

"I come when I have the truck with the winch arm," said Du Pré, "get this crap out of here."

Father Van Den Heuvel stood up. He winced.

"Shit," he said. "I know better but I still do it."

Du Pré laughed.

Du Pré fetched his flask and gave it to Father Van Den Heuvel.

They each had a pull.

They each had a cigarette.

"How's Chappie?" said Father Van Den Heuvel. "I worry about him."

"You and Madelaine," said Du Pré. "Me, too."

"That goddamned war," said the priest. "These people are nuts."

Du Pré nodded.

"I'll see how it goes," said Father Van Den Heuvel. "I can make it to the clinic if I have to."

Du Pré shook his head.

"Call me," he said.

Father Van Den Heuvel looked at him.

"You didn't come here to fix a burn I had yet to give myself," he said. "I'm sorry."

Du Pré told him about the telephone calls and the conclusions that Pallas had come to.

"Oh, God," said Father Van Den Heuvel.

"Yeah," said Du Pré.

"That poor child," said Father Van Den Heuvel.

"So," said Du Pré, "Lennart, that school principal, Cooper, he is going to see the fat man from Texas them Baptists brought here."

Father Van Den Heuvel nodded.

"It could be them or a lot of other people," said the priest. "There is a great deal of hate and anger now. The country is full of it. All the little people who were left behind by the modern economy. They are terrified and humiliated. Makes them dangerous."

Du Pré nodded.

"Let me know if there is anything I can do," said Father Van Den Heuvel.

"You had breakfast?" said Du Pré.

The big priest shook his head.

"Come on," he said, and he waited while Father Van Den Heuvel limped to the SUV and got in.

Du Pré drove down to the Toussaint Saloon and he waited for the priest to get to the front door before he went in.

Madelaine was on a stool behind the bar, Chappie in front. He had a platter in front of him and he was chewing grimly.

Father Van Den Heuvel limped over to the bar, clapped a huge hand on Chappie's shoulder.

"We need some help," he said.

CHAPTER
11

Du Pré and Father Van Den Heuvel sat at a table and they ate from big platters. Madelaine had cooked bacon and eggs and hash browns and hot popovers and she had put the platters on the table and pointed.

Chappie laughed a little.

"She is not done, my ass yet," he said.

Father Van Den Heuvel ate like a famished man.

"I usually drop the eggs," he said, "between the fridge and the pan."

Du Pré nodded. He put hot sauce on his eggs.

Madelaine had her mouth close to Chappie's ear and she was saying something. Chappie's head was stock-still.

She finished and she came over to the table where Du Pré and Father Van Den Heuvel sat.

"Chappie," said Madelaine, "has great emptiness in his life. He is searching for answers. As long as he can stand it, he will get them from that fat little fool from Texas the Baptists hauled up here."

Du Pré and the priest nodded.

"Maybe it is a kid playing a joke," she said.

"That is fine," said Father Van Den Heuvel, "if it is also true."

Chappie limped over to the table.

"If I ever forget again that there are people in more trouble than I am," he said, "I will be very angry with myself."

"Don't beat on yourself," said Father Van Den Heuvel.

"Now that I am worried about that girl," said Chappie, "I am not worried about myself. But before I do this I want to go to confession and take communion."

Father Van Den Heuvel wiped his mouth and he stood up.

"Hurt yourself?" said Madelaine, looking at the snow boot.

"I do not," said the big priest, "want to talk about it."

"Fine," said Madelaine. "Soon as you are gone Du Pré will talk about it."

"I have my car," said Chappie. He and the priest went out, slowly.

"God damn that stupid man in the White House," said Madelaine. "I am getting mad at him."

"So Chappie goes to that church," said Du Pré.

"I think even they would smell a big rat it was you or Father Van Den Heuvel," said Madelaine. "Chappie is all shot up and drinking too much, so maybe they will believe him."

"Maybe," said Du Pré. "Why are we sure that it is these people? They are not good people, but maybe they aren't the ones with the girl in danger."

"My, Du Pré," said Madelaine. "You always think of more things than I do."

"*Non,*" said Du Pré.

"Pallas, she is not happy in the school," said Madelaine, "so I say she don't have to be there, and she say she would not be happy here, either. She said she is having a time when she is not happy and it don't matter where she is so she will stay in the school. Smart kid. She was always the smartest of them. I hope it don't cause her a lot of trouble."

Du Pré laughed.

"It will," he said.

"Yes," said Madelaine.

"Father Van Den Heuvel drops the crucible, burns his foot," said Du Pré, "so I bust up the assay furnace. I should never have let him have it."

Madelaine nodded.

"He should study rubber toys," she said, "things don't got points or edges or are hot."

"When does Chappie go, church?" said Du Pré.

"Six," said Madelaine. "They have service at six, so many of them have chores in the morning."

"Where is Susan?" said Du Pré.

"She and Benny went to Miles City see a movie," said Madelaine. "They have not been out of town since last year."

Du Pré nodded.

"I am going out, Benetsee's then," he said.

"Him gone a long time this time," said Madelaine. "Someday he don't come back."

Du Pré nodded.

Old man, very old man, still walks everywhere, spooky old man.

He got up and some people came in, laughing, and two cowboys went over to the pool table and balls crashed down on the tracks. They *pocked* together and a cowboy racked them, and then they went to the important business of selecting cues.

"Tell old man," said Madelaine, "come to dinner tomorrow. Susan will be back and I will cook."

Du Pré went out and he got in the big green SUV and he drove up on the bench and then west to the dirt track that led back to Benetsee's ramshackle cabin.

There was no smoke, so the old man was probably not there, but Du Pré went in anyway. He parked near the porch. It had been swept, and when he got out he could smell pine pitch. So he had been there, at least long enough to bust some wood.

Du Pré knocked on the door of the cabin.

Nothing.

He went down the little incline to the flat by the creek where the sweat lodge stood. The flap was up. But there was a smell of burning, and when Du Pré went to the fire pit where stones were heated and he put his palm over the ashes, warmth touched his skin.

Du Pré looked round for tracks, found where Benetsee had gone to the creek after sweating. He went along the bank and could not find the place where he had gotten out.

He looked down into the deep pool. There was a shadow moving on the bottom, perhaps from a cloud overhead, a shimmer almost not seen, and then the golden sands and darker stones rippled under the flow.

"Old Man!" yelled Du Pré, "I bring you tobacco and wine! I need, talk to you!"

A kingfisher flew down the stream, *skraaaacking* as it passed.

Du Pré went to a weathered old stump and he sat, waiting.

Something yellow-gray flashed in the brush across the creek.

Coyote.

"Getting closer old man," said Du Pré softly.

He smoked a cigarette.

He felt something was behind him.

Benetsee was sitting on his back stoop, grinning. His teeth were gone save for a couple of stumps.

Du Pré sighed and he got up and walked up the little incline and he shook his head as he passed the old man.

He went to the SUV and he got a big jug of screwtop wine, and he went into the cabin and found a mostly clean tin cup. He came out the back door and sat beside the old man.

Du Pré poured a full cup of wine for him, and Benetsee swallowed it, and Du Pré poured two more and he drank them, too. Du Pré rolled him a smoke and he lit it and he passed it to him.

Benetsee drew the smoke deep into his lungs and he blew it out and then he nodded at Du Pré.

"Now what?" he said. "I come back, maybe rest, but that fool Du Pré, he comes, I don't get rest."

"Girl keeps calling the sheriff's office," said Du Pré, "says she is afraid she will be killed, hangs up, we can't find her."

Benetsee nodded.

"Can't see black hearts," said the old man. "Too dark."

Du Pré waited.

"You find the gold the mountains?" said the old man.

"Gold," said Du Pré.

"But he won't tell nobody," said Benetsee. "He is good."

"That is what he said," said Du Pré. "He is a Catholic priest but he don't believe in it."

Benetsee nodded.

"So he won't say anything about the gold," said Du Pré.

"Somebody does someday," said Benetsee. "It is not going someplace else."

This old man knows where there is gold you cannot see in rock sat on by whole mountains, Du Pré thought.

"It is not a big thing, maybe," said Du Pré. "Maybe it is some kid fooling."

Benetsee nodded.

"You think that," he said. He looked at Du Pré with his black eyes twinkling.

Old man always laughing at me.

"No," said Du Pré. "I don't think she is playing a joke."

Benetsee nodded.

"You help?" said Du Pré.

Benetsee shook his head.

"You can do this," he said. "If I am dead what do you do? You do it yourself. So, think I am dead if it will help."

Du Pré nodded. He took a packet of cigarettes from his pocket and he set them next to the wine.

"Maybe she dies," he said.

"Maybe she does you don't think good," said Benetsee.

"Why you not help me?" said Du Pré.

"You have enough," said Benetsee. "You don't need my help."

Du Pré got up.

"Madelaine says you, come eat tomorrow," said Du Pré.

Benetsee shook his head.

"I got to go someplace," he said. "Tell her thank you."

Du Pré walked round to his SUV and he got in and he pounded on the steering wheel for a while.

A raven flapped up from behind the house.

Another.

Another.

"Damn," said Du Pré.

Three ravens is death for somebody.

Du Pré got out and walked round the cabin.

Benetsee was gone. So was the jug of wine.

He goes for more time now.

Du Pré looked at the sky, very big, and it was pressing down on him.

CHAPTER
12

"Witches," said Chappie. "He went on about witches. How he'd seen witches with long blond hair driving red sports cars."

Madelaine and Du Pré looked at him.

"He said he can hear the Devil walking around at night," said Chappie, "and the witches he sees during the day. Then he quoted that Bible verse, *Thou shalt not suffer a witch to live.*"

"Poor little thing," said Madelaine. "Those witches probably cause his tiny little pecker to twitch."

"The rest of it was pretty incoherent," said Chappie, "other'n America has gone godless, abortionists and lesbians and *homosexuals* are defying the word of God, and he hoped that last week's offering would be bested by this week's."

Lennart, the principal from Cooper, stood up.

"Fits," he said. "They told me they are homeschooling the kids. Which *fits*. They had the kids in the house. I thought I saw a curtain twitch. The wife doesn't do anything but nod when he talks. Loving parents. These days, if you don't have an education and often enough if you do, you work for nothing and you get nothing for a life of work. Nothing complicated about it. And it is legal for them to do this. Now I am going home to my family and get some rest. Tomorrow I am going to try and teach a few things to the kids who do get to come to public school."

Chappie had another tall ditchwater highball.

"I'd like to go back to Iraq," he said. "At least there I wasn't *bored*."

They all laughed.

"So," said Chappie, "tomorrow night I get Bible study."

Madelaine patted his hand.

"Builds character," she said.

"Mama," said Chappie, "I got enough character. I got character up the ying-yang. I got more character than I need. I'm going back to school."

Madelaine looked at him.

"I was there with all these people I know," said Chappie, "and I could be one of them. I left after high school. They *scared* me."

Lennart went out and Chappie yawned.

The telephone rang.

Madelaine went round the bar and she picked up the telephone.

"Du Pré," she said.

Du Pré took it from her.

"Yah," he said.

He listened.

"I be there right away," he said.

"What?" said Madelaine.

"A dead girl," said Du Pré. "That was the dispatcher. That young kid Benny just hired, he is out on a call, break-in at a ranch. On the way back he stops by the road, maybe take a piss, and there she is."

Chappie and Madelaine looked at Du Pré.

He lifted his hands, dropped them, turned, and went out.

He drove west, toward the north-south road, and he turned off on a county road that wound along an ancient lake bed before climbing up to the benchlands.

He saw the blue lights turning slowly.

Du Pré drove up to them and he left his headlights on.

The young deputy was sitting in his car, door open and feet on the ground. His face looked very lost.

"You OK?" said Du Pré.

The young cop shook his head.

"But I'll do m'best," he said.

He had thrown up. A whiff of vomit rose up when he stood.

"She's over here," said the deputy.

Du Pré followed him.

She was in the barrow pit, near a tiny dry streambed that had water in it only a few weeks a year. She was lying on her back, naked, her face turned to her right.

Du Pré shone the light he carried over her.

She was very young, a girl, and very thin. Her ribs showed and her legs were so thin her knees looked swollen.

Du Pré played the light over the ground but he could not see anything.

The ground was gravelly, poor for tracks.

"Benny will be back a while," said Du Pré. "You go and call your dispatcher and have her call Pidgeon at Bart's, tell her what happened and where I— No, you just go to Bart's, get her and come back."

"Sure," said the young deputy. "You mean Bart Fascelli?"

"You know his place?" said Du Pré.

"Worked with ol' Booger Tom some," said the deputy. "I mean, I worked and that old fart criticized me, how it goes . . ."

"I stay here," said Du Pré.

The deputy went to his cruiser and he drove off, lights flashing, picking up speed.

Du Pré went back to the SUV. He fished out his flask and he had a pull and he rolled a smoke and sucked the tobacco into his lungs.

"Old man you know she is already dead we talk," he said.

Du Pré stubbed the cigarette out on the door handle and he went back to the place above the girl and he squatted on his haunches.

Ourfather . . . whoartinheaven . . . hallowed be . . .

She looks so young and so small, Du Pré thought, just left here like a sack of garbage. Someone somewhere knows who she is.

And I will find whoever put her here.

Flashing red lights showed down at the blacktop and the ambulance turned and made its way up to Du Pré.

He stood in the road and the ambulance stopped and the man and woman in it got out. Neighbors who had gone through the EMT program, who drove an ambulance and tried to help the ill for no pay.

"Du Pré," said the man.

"Whatcha got?" said the woman.

They were trying to be casual.

"Dead girl," said Du Pré. "I called for that Pidgeon to come. Be hours before the Highway Patrol makes it, their people."

"Was she . . . ?" said the woman.

Barbara, that is her name, Du Pré thought.

Du Pré held his hands up.

"She is naked," he said. "I don't see any wounds but she is on her back. She was just dumped here."

The ambulance crew looked at each other.

"Well," said Barbara, "we'll wait for the cops."

"Be twelve hours maybe," said Du Pré. "Go on home. I stay here, make sure she is not moved, the people get here look this over."

"Can't help at all?" said the man. But he looked relieved.

Du Pré shook his head.

They got back in the ambulance and they turned round. About halfway to the road they speeded up, the lights began to flash, and they turned west and raced off.

I hope that one is living and they keep them that way, Du Pré thought.

He had more whiskey, another smoke.

He smelled a skunk, turned on his big flashlight, took out his 9mm.

The skunk was beyond the fence, standing and sniffing the new carrion by the road.

Du Pré yelled and the skunk turned and lifted its tail and after a moment it bobbed off.

That kid is so young.

She the one called?

This world can be a ver' bad place.

Du Pré had some more whiskey, another smoke.

He stood up.

"Shit," he said.

He slammed his hand into his palm.

He could see flashing blue lights now, far to the east, visible when the car was on top of hills, disappearing when it went down into the little valleys.

Du Pré took a leak and cursed while he did so.

65

He waited until his hands stopped shaking.

Stupid stupid stupid.

The deputy roared up in his cruiser, and as soon as it stopped he and Pidgeon got out.

She was dressed in jeans and a calico shirt and hiking boots.

"Doo Pray," she sang out.

The deputy stayed by his car.

Du Pré led her down to the body. They stopped a few feet away.

"Could I have the flashlight?" said Pidgeon.

Du Pré gave it to her.

She knelt and used the beam to throw the earth into high shadow.

"Nothing there," she said. "You see anything?"

"No," said Du Pré.

"Me, either. You recognize the girl?" said Pidgeon.

"No," said Du Pré. "Not that I know all the kids here, Cooper, like that."

"I don't think it is a sexual homicide," said Pidgeon. "Could be, the autopsy will tell us that. But I don't think so."

Du Pré waited.

"Staties coming?" said Pidgeon.

"I don't know," said Du Pré. "They should be."

"This poor kid," said Pidgeon. "She is so thin."

Don't matter to her anymore, Du Pré thought.

"I bet she isn't from here," said Pidgeon. "I bet she is unidentifiable, and I bet this turns into a real mess."

Du Pré nodded.

Pidgeon played the light over the dead girl again.

"Nothing but her," she said. "They might find fibers or something useful."

Du Pré rolled a smoke.

Pidgeon knelt and put her face close to the girl's chest.

"Soap," said Pidgeon. "She smells of soap. She was washed."

Pidgeon stood up.

"Shit," she said.

CHAPTER
13

Du Pré stared into the big box back of the rental truck Pastor
Flowers had driven. It was clean and had nothing whatever in it.

"Company's paying me to fix the carb," said Wilbur. "I tol' them
it wouldn't even make it to Billings. Got to take it there anyway.
These days there is so many more folks moving to Montana than
out of it you got to pay more and take it one of four places, no
more cheap movin'. This damn thing cost over two grand for ten
days move their stuff up from Texas."

"Where are they?" said Du Pré.

"We rented the old Gable place for 'em," said Wilbur. "Hadn't
had anyone in it for maybe fifteen years but it cleaned up pretty
good."

Du Pré nodded.

He walked back to the SUV and he got in.

"So," he said, "what you want to do now."

"Nothing with this," said Pidgeon. "The truck will be here for a
while. I have the plate numbers and we can find it easily. Nothing
quite fits. There might have been some evidence in it but probably
not. We can't search their place without a warrant and we have no
evidence sufficient to get one."

Du Pré nodded.

"So," said Pidgeon, "we wait on the autopsy."

"A week maybe," said Du Pré.

"A week probably," said Pidgeon.

"We do not know even how she died," said Du Pré.

"We'll know more soon," said Pidgeon. "Now I need to go on home and see about Bart. He gets upset when I do this sort of work. He has a kind heart and the world hurts it terribly."

Du Pré nodded. He backed and turned and drove off toward the spur road that went up on the bench to Bart's ranch.

Bart was drinking tea in the kitchen. He brightened a lot when he saw Pidgeon. She went to him and kissed him on the forehead and then the lips.

Du Pré looked out the window.

Father Van Den Heuvel and Booger Tom were out in the round corral. Father Van Den Heuvel was listening intently to Booger Tom, who held the reins on Trapper, the trail horse. The priest got up on Trapper. The horse stood there with an unbelieving expression on its face. Then its ears went all the way back.

Booger Tom was making tracks for the fence and he ducked through it.

Trapper shrugged Father Van Den Heuvel off.

"I need to see Booger Tom," said Du Pré. He went out without looking back.

By the time Du Pré got to the corral Booger Tom was back inside it gentling the horse, whose eyes were showing a lot of white.

Father Van Den Heuvel was searching the ground for his spectacles. He found them, uttered a small cry of triumph, and he put them on. One lens was cracked.

Father Van Den Heuvel got up.

Trapper pulled against the reins that Booger Tom was holding, and then lunged at Father Van Den Heuvel. He bit the big priest on the arm.

"Git outta here!" yelled Booger Tom.

The priest ducked through the poles and the horse calmed down.

Booger Tom stripped off the saddle and blanket and headstall and he opened the gate and Trapper ran out to join the other horses in the pasture, neighing his tale of imbecile humans.

Booger Tom threw the saddle over the top rail, and he hung the headstall on a post.

"Father," said the old cowboy, "it ain't common, but there are some folks horses hate. I don't know why but they do. Now, usually them horses just hate that feller somewhat. I never seen a situation like this, though, where horses really hate a feller. They really hate you. They hate you on sight and they hate you on smell more. I dunno what to do about it."

Father Van Den Heuvel hung his head.

"Trapper seemed all right," said the big priest. "I mean, I rode him up there with Du Pré."

"Trapper has had time to consider matters," said Booger Tom. "He hates you even more than them other horses. You saw him. I went out with a catch rope to git him and he usually is about the easiest horse to git, and he weren't havin' none of it. I give up. I get near and he starts cussin' me and tellin' me he'll kill me I git that rope on him, drag him over to you."

Father Van Den Heuvel nodded.

"I suppose," he said, "that I had best just walk to where I want to go."

"I got one more idea," said Booger Tom, "Hooper and Noodles."

Du Pré turned away so Father Van Den Heuvel wouldn't see him laughing.

Hooper and Noodles, them, two mules got dispositions like badgers and only Booger Tom would not have shot them long time gone.

"And who," said Father Van Den Heuvel, "are Hooper and Noodles?"

"Allow me ta make an introduction," said Booger Tom. He started over to the big horse barn. Something kicked the metal wall and pooched it out. There was a very loud bray.

I got to see this, Du Pré thought. Maybe I have to tell Father Van Den Heuvel's family how he died.

"Cut it out, ya bastards," yelled Booger Tom as he went into the barn.

There was a thudding sound and one of wrenching metal, too.

Booger Tom switched on the huge overhead lights.

The two mules were in a pen not far from the big doors. They were both dark brown with tan markings, and they both looked really mean.

"There's some apples there," said Booger Tom, pointing to a bucket. "Whyn'cha see they'll eat one. Watch yer fingers, especially with Hooper. He's the one on the right."

Father Van Den Heuvel bent and he got two apples and he went to the gate and he held the apples out.

Hooper and Noodles looked at him balefully.

Hooper and Noodles looked at each other, and they brayed.

Having made a decision, they walked calmly over to the apples and they looked for a long time at Father Van Den Heuvel. Then they each reached out delicately and they each took an apple from a hand. They munched while reflecting.

God damn, thought Du Pré.

Father Van Den Heuvel got two more apples and the mules took those, and then he got two more and he let himself through the gate.

The mules backed up, but just enough to let the gate swing, and then they came over and took the apples. Father Van Den Heuvel stood between them, a hand stroking each huge neck.

The mules nodded heads, brayed, nodded heads some more.

Booger Tom nodded to Du Pré and he jerked his head toward the door and they went outside.

"I'll be damned," said Du Pré.

"Sure bet," said Booger Tom. "Ain't that a daisy? It was you or me, them old bastards would be lookin' to kick us to death. Actually, yesterday, this thought done occurred to me. So I hazed them on in. I give them oats and molasses and they tried to take my head off. I can't get on with 'em nor can you, but that crazy priest can, it seems."

Du Pré nodded.

"Mules is mules," said Booger Tom, "and I think the three of them might be real happy together."

Du Pré laughed.

"They's all three misfits," said Booger Tom.

Du Pré nodded.

"What about that girl you done found?" said Booger Tom.

Du Pré shook his head.

"She was dead," said Du Pré. "No marks, no clothes, no nothing there. Just her. No wounds or bruises we could see. State people come, take the body, go over the ground, nothing. Pidgeon said she had been washed."

Booger Tom nodded.

"No tellin' how long she was dead?" he said.

"Not long," said Du Pré. "It has been warm."

People, they are not very good keepers.

"Tracks?" said Booger Tom.

"Ground is stony there," said Du Pré. "Old glacial pan, outwash."

"Bart's in a twist," said Booger Tom. "He's feared of Pidgeon digging around in this shit. He's afraid she will get hurt or maybe killed."

"There are not that many people here," said Du Pré. "We have photographs, someone clean them up, the computer, she must belong to someone."

"Not somebody here," said Booger Tom. "We would have heard. You know about them new folks over to the old Bateman place?"

Du Pré looked at him.

"They come in a few days ago," said Booger Tom. "Ted spotted them when he was a-flyin' his patch, lookin' for strays."

"Who?" said Du Pré.

"I don't know," said Booger Tom. "Just that there was some cars and trailers and trucks and such there and folks moving stuff in the house."

"More crazies?" said Du Pré. "It was quiet here a while."

"I dunno," said Booger Tom. "Only thing there is in Toussaint is the saloon and the little old Catholic church and Wilbur's garage . . . Post office is in Cooper now."

Du Pré nodded. Toussaint hadn't had its own post office for a few years now.

"Anyway," said Booger Tom, "I thought you'd like to know."

Du Pré nodded.

"Du Pré," said Booger Tom, "you be careful now."

Du Pré looked at the old cowboy.

The old man's face was set and serious.

"Don't get to the place you don't give a damn," he said. " 'Bout yourself I mean."

Du Pré nodded.

Father Van Den Heuvel came out of the barn looking pleased.

"Could I ride one of them?" he said. "Are they saddle-trained?"

"It was tried some," said Booger Tom. "The results was not all they coulda been."

"I'd like to try," said Father Van Den Heuvel.

"How do you get all the air outta a mount?" asked Booger Tom.

"Blow in their nostrils and make them sneeze," said Father Van Den Heuvel.

"Bright young feller," said Booger Tom. "Pays attention."

"Pray for me," said Father Van Den Heuvel, heading back into the barn.

CHAPTER
14

Du Pré waited in the office and in a few moments Lennart came in, looking a bit harried.

"Mister Du Pré!" he said. "How may I help you?"

"There are some more new people," said Du Pré. "No one knows anything much about them, they got some kids, you have any new kids here?"

"Just one," said Lennart. "Fourth-grader, Susie Koch. Her father is part of the crew working on the new bridges."

Du Pré nodded. The county had finally found the money to rebuild a number of old bridges that were about to collapse.

Lennart looked perplexed.

"I am troubled," he said. "It seems when anyone new comes if they don't act like we expect, we bother them. I am not sure I like it."

"There was a dead girl in a ditch," said Du Pré. "I am not sure I like that."

"Oh my God," said Lennart. "I had not heard."

Du Pré shrugged.

The girl had been taken off for an autopsy and quietly at that. The news people might come or not. News had a very short shelf life.

"It's just wrong to assume that it is these new people," said Lennart.

"I am not," said Du Pré. "You are looking for something you look at what has changed. There are people I know here, been in Deer Lodge Prison, drunk driving, assault, maybe burglary they were young. Bored kids here, nothing to do, nowhere to earn money, they are young, pull shit like that. We don't have young girls tossed in ditches much. So I am worried."

"All right," said Lennart.

Du Pré got up.

"I feel like we are persecuting people for their religious views," said Lennart.

"Me, I do not care what they believe," said Du Pré. "I care what they do."

They shook hands and Du Pré went out to the SUV. He looked at the big, expensive machine.

"I am rid, your sorry ass today," he said. He patted the hood.

He drove back to Toussaint to Wilbur's garage. His old cruiser was sitting out in front.

Wilbur was deep in the guts of a Ford truck.

"It's done," said Wilbur from inside the engine compartment. "You might try driving a little slower. Head gaskets always blow when you break the sound barrier."

"How much?" said Du Pré.

"Eight hundred'll do it," said Wilbur. "Them gaskets on them things cost a lot. Everything costs a lot these days."

Du Pré pulled out his wallet, took eight one-hundred-dollar bills out of it, and he left them on the dash of the Ford.

Wilbur was talking to himself.

Lord Jesus, help me loosen this bolt.

Du Pré shook his head as he walked out.

The old cruiser started easily and purred, and Du Pré backed up and he turned and went toward Madelaine's.

She was in the yard grubbing away at a flower bed.

The poppies were coming up tall, their gray-green hairy leaves spreading for the sun.

"So," said Madelaine. "You get rid of your yuppie car?"

"Yah," said Du Pré.

"Good," said Madelaine. "Drive one of them too much you start wearing gold chains and listening rap music."

"I escape," said Du Pré.

"Someday you might not," said Madelaine.

Du Pré nodded.

The sun was hot. Madelaine stood up, brushing dirt from the knees of her pants.

"Iced tea," she said. "Lilacs are coming on, smell really good though they are not full bloom yet."

Du Pré walked round to the back yard while Madelaine went through the front door. He sat under the lilacs on the bench he had made and in a moment she came out with tall glasses of iced tea.

She sat down, looked at the ground, plucked up some mint, crushed it in her hand, and dropped it into her tea.

"You don't like mint?" she said.

Du Pré shook his head.

"So," said Madelaine. "You find the people kill that girl yet?"

"*Non*," said Du Pré.

"You will," said Madelaine.

Du Pré nodded.

"Benetsee, he says he will not help," he said. "Him die soon maybe."

"Him die when it is a joke on you," said Madelaine, "is when him die."

"Yah," said Du Pré.

"You see him, he was all right?" said Madelaine. "He don't come to eat."

"Old man is all right," said Du Pré. "How is Chappie?"

"Him, he is having a good time. Got lots of people wanting to save his soul. He is gone to Bible study. They watch these videos. Then they talk about the videos. Then he gets to go to the saloon, talk about the videos, how he sent away for some prosperity oil he is supposed, apply to his checkbook," said Madelaine.

"Prosperity oil," said Du Pré.

"Yah," said Madelaine.

They heard hooves and then they saw Pallas on Moondog, running in the big field behind Madelaine's hedge of lilacs.

Pallas was sitting Moondog as casually as she would have sat on a chair.

Moondog slowed and stopped, turned, and started walking toward Du Pré and Madelaine.

The big horse easily jumped the three-strand wire fence, and he came into the yard slowly, almost as though he was not sure he was supposed to be there.

Pallas slid off, landed on the ground soft as a cat.

"Nice horse," said Du Pré. "Bart paid a quarter million for him I think."

"Great horse," said Pallas. "I don't know if I am good enough to ride a horse this good."

Du Pré and Madelaine laughed.

"You get me a picture of that girl yet?" said Pallas. "I can look on the computer maybe find who she was."

"Not yet," said Du Pré. "Only pictures, you could not see much of her face."

Pallas sat down on the bench.

"She was my age, wasn't she?" she said.

"Yah," said Du Pré. "Close anyway."

"So I am lucky and she is not," said Pallas. "I have people love me and she did not. She had people that killed her."

"Plenty of times," said Madelaine, "your people have wanted to kill *you*."

They all laughed.

"Yeah," said Pallas, "but they don't do it."

"You are sad," said Madelaine.

Pallas nodded.

"You know why?" said Madelaine.

Pallas shook her head.

"Just sad," she said. "Any girl has Moondog should not be sad."

The black horse pricked up his ears at his name.

He whuffled, cropped a little new grass. His muscles rippled under his gleaming black coat when he moved.

Pallas began to cry, silently, tears coursing down her cheeks.

Madelaine put her arm around her.

"You know where Benetsee's is?" she said.

Pallas nodded.

"You ride Moondog out there," she said. "We meet you there. There is something we can do."

Pallas nodded, stood up, went to her horse, mounted, and was gone.

Madelaine slapped Du Pré's thigh.

"I will bring food," she said. "You go on start a fire. She sweat she feel better, maybe that old man is there, he hears things."

Du Pré went out to his cruiser. He headed west and then north and he soon got to the rutted track that led to the old man's cabin.

He parked and he opened the trunk and found a jug of wine and some tobacco in a can that had cigarette papers taped to the lid.

He smelled smoke.

When he walked round the cabin and down to the sweat lodge he found a fire burning, ricks of split wood that the round stones were heating on. The fire was roaring.

Du Pré looked around but he could not see Benetsee.

He looked back and the old man was there, his face painted half white and half black.

He had one eagle feather in his hair.

He wore only a leather breechclout. His shrunken old body was crisscrossed with scars, some the puckered healings of bullet holes.

Madelaine came soon, carrying a wicker hamper.

She went behind some bushes and when she came back she wore a loose thin linen dress and she was barefoot. She held another for Pallas.

Benetsee pointed to a soaring hawk to the east, and in a moment Moondog leaped the little creek and he came into the flat very fast, and sat back on his haunches to stop.

Pallas got down and Madelaine took her to the bushes and they came back in a moment each in a linen shift.

Du Pré carried the stones to the lodge and he dropped them in the firepit.

Pallas and Madelaine got in and then Benetsee, and he pulled down the flap and Du Pré fiddled the edges so the door was tight.

Steam curled out of the cracks in the lodge, and Du Pré heard them begin to sing.

He sat on the log by the stream, smoking and sipping whiskey.

He went to Moondog after a bit and took off his tack and saddle. Without the bit the horse could drink, now that he was cooled.

"Prosperity oil for checkbooks," he said, flipping a butt into the stream.

77

CHAPTER
15

"She was starved to death," said Pidgeon.

She looked at the papers, glasses perched on the end of her nose.

"They went over her body carefully," said Pidgeon. "No trauma, no sexual battery, not any of that. Her potassium levels were so low, that is what probably killed her. She could have lived longer, but she just got her electrolytes so out of balance she died."

Pidgeon frowned.

She left the papers with Du Pré and she went inside the house.

He looked at them.

Nothing on the body but a few fibers, all of them ordinary and no two alike.

Du Pré sighed.

He looked out at the small pasture.

Father Van Den Heuvel was mounted on Noodles. Noodles did not seem to mind.

Hooper was standing away perhaps twenty feet, and seemed to be laughing.

Father Van Den Heuvel said something and Noodles started to trot around the pasture.

"Ain't that a sight," said Booger Tom. He had come from somewhere without making a sound.

The old cowboy's long white mustaches flipped in the breeze.

His bleak blue eyes stared out at the world through a mess of wrinkles.

Du Pré looked at his hands. Like most old cowboys, the old man's hands were far larger than they would have been if Booger Tom had been a stockbroker. They looked like old tree roots.

"How you know the mules and him would take to each other?" said Du Pré.

"I didn't," said Booger Tom. "But it was the last chance. I ain't seen horses so down on a feller for fifty years as they was on pore ol' Father Van Den Heuvel there. Last feller I recall them dislikin' that much was that danged actor feller come up to learn cowboyin' so he could make an ass of himself and a movie, too."

Actor feller, thought Du Pré.

"Which actor?" said Du Pré.

"Some danged New York feller wanted to act in cowboy movies," said Booger Tom. "I can't remember what he called hisself. Rimfire McGonigle or some such. I got better things to do with m'time than recall every jackass ever come out here be a cowboy."

Du Pré laughed.

"Let me guess," he said. "You worked in the movies."

"Yah," said Booger Tom. "Did a while. Money was good, but the people was so awful I couldn't stand it no more."

"He is going to go up there by hisself," said Booger Tom, nodding at the priest and Noodles and Hooper.

"Not a good idea," said Du Pré.

"If they kill him," said Booger Tom, "and they just might, we don't have to put up with him no more."

Du Pré laughed.

"So you are going?" he said.

"I would feel guilty they stomped him and left him there to die by inches," said Booger Tom. "This way I kin give him some euthynasia with m'Colt. It'll save him pain and us worry. How would we feel he come crawling outta there and lived?"

"He wants to go the place where all the fossil clams are," said Du Pré, "and those big ammonites."

"Shit," said Booger Tom. "There's them things up there size of

79

cartwheels. Wagon wheels. Too heavy to pack out on a horse or a mule."

Father Van Den Heuvel did a neat forward somersault and he landed on his back with a thud they could hear.

Noodles and Hooper thought this was enormous fun and they talked about it.

"Jokers," said Booger Tom. "I expect I better go and chew them out. Mules have a great sense of humor."

The old cowboy walked toward the pasture, his bowed legs swinging.

Pidgeon came back out and she lit a filtered cigarette and she sat down on the steps with Du Pré.

"I called the doc did the autopsy," she said. "He said the girl could have died of bulimia. Could have been done in by that."

Du Pré looked at her.

"But it was not on the report," he said.

"No way to conclude that it was that," said Pidgeon. "I still don't get why she was just dumped. Maybe her parents thought they would get in trouble."

"We don't know who she is," said Du Pré.

"No," said Pidgeon, "we don't."

Who throws a child away, leaves their body by the road after washing it? Du Pré thought. What is this?

"What'd Lennart find out?" said Pidgeon.

"There are two families at the Gable place," said Du Pré, "eleven children between them. They dress the girls in long dresses and bonnets, and he only saw one of them walking to the barn. Two brothers from Texas and their wives. Ardreys, their name."

"Why are they here?" said Pidgeon.

"Flowers," said Du Pré. "They followed him. The brothers are looking for work."

"Those phone calls bother me," said Pidgeon. "This whole business bothers me. I have spent my professional career studying pure evil. People who kill because it pleases them. Women are usually the victims. It is almost always sexual."

Du Pré nodded.

Pidgeon got up.

"Bart and I are going to New York and D.C.," she said.

"He is becoming well-traveled," said Du Pré.

"I have things I must see to," said Pidgeon. "I still am on the payroll as a consultant. The FBI still goes after the occasional bad guy, when they aren't grabbing perfectly innocent people and pulling out their fingernails."

Du Pré nodded.

"Don't get me started," said Pidgeon.

She went back in the house and she and Bart came out in a few minutes, each of them carrying a suitcase.

"You need a ride?" said Du Pré.

"No," said Bart. "Ted will fly us to Billings and the jet will meet us there."

Du Pré nodded.

"See you a week or so," said Bart.

Pidgeon clapped her hand on Du Pré's shoulder as she passed.

"Maybe I will know more," she said, "when I get back."

They walked to one of the SUVs in the big shed and they got in and Bart drove them away.

Du Pré got up and he walked over to the fence.

Booger Tom was whispering sweet nothings in Noodle's large ear. The mule seemed to be listening.

Father Van Den Heuvel was sitting on Hooper, who was listening to Booger Tom or at least seeming to.

"I have to go to Cooper tomorrow," said Father Van Den Heuvel. "I am to take some kids on a walk and talk about the rocks."

Du Pré nodded.

"Why don't you come?" said Father Van Den Heuvel.

Du Pré looked at him.

"Some of the kids there are from the new people," said the big priest. "It seems that Flowers decided to send his kids there after all."

Du Pré nodded.

"It might be interesting," said Father Van Den Heuvel.

"OK," said Du Pré. He went to his cruiser and he got in and he drove to Toussaint and he went into the saloon.

Madelaine was sitting on a high stool behind the bar doing some beading on a small bag.

She had on her reading glasses, and a special light gave a harsh white glare. She held the bag in the glare and she slid the needle through the leather.

Du Pré waited until she had finished.

"Medicine bag for Pallas," said Madelaine. "She has this she won't feel so lost maybe back there."

Du Pré nodded. He went into the kitchen and he took out a thick patty of beef and he put it on the grill and he cooked it medium rare and when he flipped it over he put two slices of cheddar cheese on top. He found a bun on a shelf, and a plate and some dill pickles in the fridge. He carried his lunch out to the bar and he made himself a ditch and he ate the burger and he drank the ditch while Madelaine poked her needle through the leather.

"Pidgeon thought maybe that girl died of bulimia," said Du Pré.

"Eat and throw up," said Madelaine, "because you are not pretty enough."

"Yeah," said Du Pré.

"Girls die of that," said Madelaine, "they just don't usually get tossed in a ditch by the road."

"Yah," said Du Pré.

Madelaine began to thread bright blue beads on her needle. She slid them down on to the thread and she set the row and began to backstitch between the beads to hold them in place.

"Father Van Den Heuvel teaches about rocks tomorrow, school in Cooper, they are going for a walk," said Du Pré.

Madelaine looked at Du Pré.

"Good for them," she said. "Why you are going?"

"Some of those kids will be there, Flowers's, the other people moved to the Gable place," said Du Pré.

Madelaine nodded.

"You don't like this much," she said. "You have had people, evil people, you hunt them and you are good, Du Pré. This time you don't really know."

Du Pré shook his head.

"Throw her in the ditch," said Du Pré. "That is bad."

"Yeah," said Madelaine. "But it is not like those bastards are killing girls, strangling them, stabbing them, you remember them."

"Yah," said Du Pré. "Pallas, she will be all right."

"I know she will," said Madelaine.

Du Pré sipped his drink.

"It is what it is, Du Pré," said Madelaine.

"I try, remember that," said Du Pré.

CHAPTER
16

Du Pré was up very early, at five, and the light was just beginning to rise. The lilacs had bloomed and their sweet cloying scent filled the house. Madelaine had sprays in vases and bottles in the living and dining rooms and the kitchen, too.

Du Pré lit a cigarette to cover the heavy odor.

He made a cup of coffee and he put cream in it and took it in to her. She smiled at him.

"Off with the little ones," she said. "I would come, too, but Susan had to go to the dentist and so I am it today at the saloon. Those old farts would die they couldn't get their red beers at eight in the morning."

"I die I don't get one," said Du Pré.

"You been an old fart since you were about twelve," said Madelaine.

"Yah," said Du Pré. "After this walk, then Father Van Den Heuvel and Booger Tom are going up into the Wolfs."

Du Pré made breakfast and a couple of roast beef sandwiches for lunch, one for him and one for the priest, who would forget to bring anything.

He kissed Madelaine, who was still sipping her coffee, and he went out to his old cruiser and he drove to Father Van Den Heuvel's.

There was another Star of David sprayed on the door.

Du Pré knocked and after a moment Father Van Den Heuvel peered out.

"You get another star last night," said Du Pré.

"Damn it," said Father Van Den Heuvel, "I don't want to have to paint the door again."

"Get a big dog," said Du Pré.

"I hadn't thought of that," said the priest.

He ate a couple of stale storebought doughnuts and he had some coffee. Du Pré had a plastic mug filled with coffee and whiskey.

Father Van Den Heuvel dressed in his work clothes and heavy boots, and he checked his pack for his geologist's pick and acid bottle and porcelain hexagons to scrape minerals across.

Du Pré had bottles of water in the car.

"Sunglasses," said Du Pré.

Father Van Den Heuvel found a pair that had only one earpiece.

"OK," said the big priest. "We meet at the school and then we go over to that patch of badlands east of the mountains."

Du Pré nodded.

They got in his cruiser and Du Pré drove to Cooper. There was a school bus in front of the school, the engine idling.

Kids were lined up and getting on. Some of the girls had on long dresses and bonnets.

Du Pré saw the green van with the Texas license plates.

"You better lead us," said Lennart. "I'm driving, but I am not sure where to go."

Du Pré nodded. He turned around and waited while the bus did, too, and then he drove to the blacktop east-west highway. He got up to sixty and stayed there because the school bus wouldn't go any faster.

The green van was behind the bus.

"I don't like this," said Father Van Den Heuvel.

Du Pré laughed.

"Maybe they want to know geology," he said.

"They worship ignorance," said Father Van Den Heuvel. "I doubt they want to learn anything."

It took an hour to go the fifty miles to the patch of badlands that stretched east and north from the flanks of the Wolf Mountains.

Du Pré went over a cattle guard and down a winding road that went along a dry riverbed. He parked at the end of the road, which did not end but seemed to fade away.

The sun was up and there were clouds around the forests on the mountains, dew cooking off to fall as dew again the next night.

Lennart counted the kids as they came off the bus, and the children all laughed and chaffed each other. The new kids acted like new kids, unsure of themselves and quiet.

Lennart called for the children to gather round.

"Stay together," he said. "We don't want anyone getting lost."

The wind moaned in the weird mud-and-rock landscape of the badlands.

"Father Van Den Heuvel is also a geologist," said Lennart, "and so I will let him speak."

The big priest began to talk, and he described the badlands, saying they were there because the Wolf Mountains gathered all the rain and here none fell. Long ago, he said, there was a sea here, and huge dinosaurs walked along the shores, and the land was much farther south, near the equator, and there were tropical trees like palms and cycads.

The Flowerses had come up behind the little group of kids their children were part of. Flowers began to pray and his children joined in.

The other children crowded around Father Van Den Heuvel, who ignored the Flowerses and led the kids along a dry creekbed.

He came to a thick yellow-brown band of rock and he took his pick and he broke a piece off. It was a solid lump of fossil oyster shells.

"How long ago were these oysters living?" said a serious boy, who alone among the students had brought a notebook.

"A hundred million years," said Father Van Den Heuvel.

"Wow," said the boy.

"The estimates aren't precise," said Father Van Den Heuvel, "but they are close. Does anyone know what caused this land to rise up and make the sea drain away?"

"God," said Flowers.

"Heat," said Father Van Den Heuvel, ignoring him. "Heat is what makes the land rise. Heat is what breaks whole continents apart and welds them together again. Heat and enormous amounts of time."

Lennart went back to talk with Flowers.

Flowers stood there with a look of smug stupidity on his face so idiotic Du Pré wanted to break his jaw.

Father Van Den Heuvel went on and all the children followed him except the new kids, who hung back listening to the argument that Lennart and Flowers were having.

Father Van Den Heuvel found a gray-green band of rock that had a reddish band above it. He pounded away with his pick until a big slab broke off, and when it fell it held the stencil of an ancient leaf, one that had been broad and veined, larger than any leaf here now.

"I think it is a giant fern," said Father Van Den Heuvel, "but we can take it back and I will have to look it up."

The priest was a good lecturer, and the kids paid careful attention.

So did Du Pré.

Mountain ranges rose and were worn away, seas rose and fell, Father Van Den Heuvel found an ancient riverbed cut by newer rivers, and he described how they were looking upstream from below the bottom of the water.

He found a tooth.

"Crocodile," he said, pointing to a groove. "See?"

The children nodded gravely.

Father Van Den Heuvel found an odd stone, round like a loaf of bread, which had a purple crust and a center of what seemed to be fossil mud.

"This was formed on a seabed," he said. "There are rocks just like this being formed right now on the ocean floors."

They went on, through the carved landscape.

They found more oysters, so many that Father Van Den Heuvel could break them apart and every child could have one to take home.

Du Pré glanced back at where Lennart and Flowers had been, but he could not see them anymore.

Father Van Den Heuvel came to Du Pré.

"I, uh, don't know how to get back," he said. "I think we have to be back at the school by noon."

Du Pré nodded.

"You see that mountain there?" he said, pointing to Sword Peak.

It was named for a huge scar that ran down its face, shaped something like a broadsword.

"Yes," said Father Van Den Heuvel.

"You keep your eye on that coming in, it will lead you out," said Du Pré.

"I was looking down," said Father Van Den Heuvel.

"Look up once in a while," said Du Pré.

He led the priest and the kids back along the trail, pointing out tracks here and there, fresh turnings of the scarce earth and small stones.

It was getting hot.

"Wait!" said Father Van Den Heuvel. He went to a knob sticking out of a yellow-gray band of crumbly rock.

"That is a hip joint, the ball," he said, excited. "That is a big one!"

He began to hack at the rock around it.

"*Non,*" said Du Pré. "I think you need, take more time with that."

Father Van Den Heuvel nodded.

"OK," he said, "but I will never find it again."

"I find it for you," said Du Pré.

The children were laughing and chattering behind the two of them as they walked back to the school bus.

Du Pré could hear chanting.

The wind was rising and he could not make out the words.

They came round the last little butte and they could see the school bus.

Lennart was sitting on the steps.

The children that had stayed behind were chanting.

You're goingtohell . . . You'regoingtohell . . .

The Flowerses were sitting in their green van.

"Good God," said Father Van Den Heuvel.

Lennart was stone-faced.

The chanting children stopped when Du Pré and Father Van Den Heuvel and their classmates walked up.

The kids that had gone with Du Pré and the priest began to file onto the bus.

Then the other children, the ones that had stayed behind.

Du Pré looked at one of the last girls to get on the bus.

She was a gangly girl, growing quickly.

Her dress did not fit her.

It was large and loose-fitting. The hem brushed the ground.

It was too small for Mrs. Flowers, though.

The girl looked once at Du Pré, and she flinched and got on the bus.

CHAPTER
17

The house trailer edged through Toussaint, pulled by a tractor.

It was an old one but in fairly good condition.

The tractor turned at the eastern edge of town and pulled the trailer back to an old concrete pad that still had a well and a drain line for sewage and a power pole.

The pad sat next to a big machine shed that dated from around the turn of the century. It was wood and poorly found, so it had hogged on its ridgeline and sagged and racked everywhere else. But the big sliding doors still worked, and with a little work the place would be usable at least in the warmer months.

"Ardreys are gonna set up a welding business," said Wilbur.

"Everybody here," said Du Pré, "does their own welding."

"They're gonna make portable sorting corrals and chutes and gates and such," said Wilbur.

Du Pré shrugged.

"We are getting that stuff from China now cheap," he said.

Wilbur looked annoyed.

"Well, they are gonna try anyway," he said.

"Who lives in the trailer?" said Du Pré.

"The older brother, Larry Dean," said Wilbur. "Younger one's Ben Dean."

Du Pré shrugged.

"I done owned this for years," said Wilbur. " 'Bout time it got used I'd say."

Wilbur and Marge owned a lot of the old buildings in Toussaint, none of which were occupied by anything but rodents and boxes of stuff the people who had left stored against the day they would come back for them but never did.

"We got to get this town movin' again," said Wilbur. "It could be like it was. Hell, there was over five hundred people here right after the war."

He means World War Two, thought Du Pré, and I remember them leaving when I was small, four or five.

"It could be like it was," said Wilbur. He nodded for a moment. Trying to convince himself.

"Hope it works out," said Du Pré.

He walked away toward the saloon a couple of hundred yards away.

Susan and Madelaine were there, sprinkling rosemary and green peppercorns over the huge slabs of prime rib that they would serve that night.

Du Pré went behind the bar and he made himself a ditch and he went back to the kitchen, which smelled of spices and beef blood.

"Wilbur rented the old machine shed to one of the Ardreys," said Du Pré. "They are going to have a welding business there."

"Who the hell are the Ardreys?" said Susan Klein.

"They come up from Texas with that idiot Bible-thumper," said Madelaine, "so I don't think them playing with matches is such a good idea."

Du Pré nodded.

"How long you think before they burn it down?" said Madelaine.

"Not long," said Du Pré. "Fire truck is close by at least."

The volunteer fire department had a fairly new fire truck and people who knew how to run it, but much depended on whether or not they were near enough to get the truck and get to the fire in time.

The telephone rang and Susan wiped her hands on her apron and she went to the telephone.

"Du Pré," she said, "Benny's on a wreck out on the main road. There's some sort of trouble up at the school in Cooper."

Du Pré nodded.

"What kind of trouble," said Susan.

She listened.

"Oh, for chrissake," she said.

She hung up.

"The science teacher's quitting," said Susan. "Lennart is frantic. He has a class to teach. Anyway, Benny wondered if you could go and see about it. The deputy's in Billings. His wife's having a baby."

The county only had Benny and one deputy now.

"Yah," said Du Pré.

He went out to his cruiser and he got in and drove away. The blacktop road that led to Cooper was deserted. The ranchers were doing the first cuttings of hay now, and so they were all in their hayfields from dawn to dark.

Du Pré roared up the road, slowing at hill crests and then speeding up when he could see clearly.

He pulled in to the parking lot at Cooper's Consolidated School.

A small SUV was backed up to the main entrance. The doors were all open.

A young red-haired woman came out of the door carrying a cardboard carton filled with books.

She put them in the back of the little SUV.

Du Pré walked to the door. He waited.

He rolled a smoke and he lit it and by the time he had smoked it down to a butt the young woman was back with another carton.

"Benny called," said Du Pré. "He said there was trouble."

The young woman's eyes were puffy. She had been crying.

"Trouble?" she said. "Shit. I've been here three years. I love it here. I love the kids and I love teaching and I found something in my mailbox this morning. I've done a good job and I would have liked to have gone on doing it."

Du Pré waited.

She pointed to a paper sack on the ground by the door.

Du Pré went to it.

He lifted a rag doll out of the sack. It was a red-haired Raggedy Ann. It had a paring knife thrust through its neck.

"Looks a little like me, right?" said the young woman. She pointed to her flaming red hair.

90

Du Pré nodded.

"I'm not supposed to smoke near the school," said the young woman, "but since I quit, could I have one of those?"

Du Pré nodded. He rolled a smoke and he lit it and gave it to her. She sucked in the smoke and she coughed.

"Mmmmmmgood," she said. "Good tobacco."

A gray-haired woman came out of the door. She looked upset.

"Sarah," she said, "I'm so sorry."

They hugged.

"I can't stand it," said the young woman. "I don't mind arguing civilly with the parents. They were worried that if their children began to believe in evolution they stood in peril of damnation. I'm Catholic, I don't despise faith. I told them that there shouldn't be any conflict. Religion was religion and science was science and they ought to complement one another. And they nodded and went away. But this—"

Lennart came out.

"Du Pré," he said, "I can only stay a minute. I have a class to teach."

Du Pré looked at him.

"What you want me to do?" he said.

"I don't know," said Lennart miserably. "Sarah, I am so sorry."

"You've been great," she said. "I just can't stay after this."

"Could you stay until I can find someone?" said Lennart.

"No," said Sarah, "I can't."

"Call Van Den Heuvel," said Du Pré. "Him do it."

Lennart brightened.

He went back inside.

"Are you a deputy or something?" asked Sarah.

"Yah," said Du Pré.

"I am scared to go and get my stuff from my place," said the young woman.

"I go," said Du Pré.

"You're the fiddle player," she said. "You are wonderful."

Du Pré laughed.

"Not much help right now," he said.

He looked around the grounds.

There was an odd metal dingus set on a pole near the western fence.

"What is that?" he said, pointing.

"For cell phones," said the young woman. "They haven't got a full system here yet, but we run some of our computer stuff off it. Those people working on the bridges put it in, so they could stay in touch. Happened that it was compatible with some of our stuff."

Du Pré nodded.

"You know how far it will reach?" he said.

"Thirty miles or so," she said. "More, depending on weather. Cloud cover helps."

She made two more trips and then Du Pré followed her to the white apartment building which had served as the teacherage for a century.

Du Pré went in with the young woman. She had obviously packed up her possessions the night before. He carried several boxes down and three big clothes bags. The SUV was packed to the ceiling and the passenger seat in front held a television and consoles for videos and discs.

There were still ten boxes, but they were all packed and addressed and taped shut.

The young woman came down with one last case, for cosmetics.

"Lennart said he would forward those boxes," said the young woman. "UPS, I guess. Could you give him this check?"

"I do it," said Du Pré. "I got to go, Billings a day or two, I do it then."

"I already made the check out to Lennart," she said.

"We pay for it," said Du Pré. "I am sorry."

The young woman looked at him.

"Thank you," she said.

"I am sorry for this," said Du Pré.

"I am, too," said the young woman, "but I can't take this."

Du Pré nodded.

"Boxes are all addressed," she said.

Minneapolis.

"Stay and fight," said Du Pré.

The young woman looked at him, tears in her eyes.

She shook her head.

"This is what they want you to do," said Du Pré. "They want you to go."

The young woman took out a handkerchief.

"Take a day maybe think," said Du Pré.

She looked up at him.

"Fuck them," she said. "Fuck those assholes. I am going to stay."

She snuffled for a moment and then Du Pré helped her carry her things back upstairs to her apartment.

CHAPTER
18

"A paring knife though the doll's neck," said Madelaine. "Who are these bastards anyway?"

"It's why I quit teaching," said Susan Klein, "and I never had anything like that happen. I got fed up with ignorant parents complaining to me about the history I taught or the books I assigned my English classes."

"I liked my English classes," said Chappie. "You were the best teacher I had."

He was sipping a ditch and eating salted peanuts. A small mound of shells sat before him.

"The final straw was when we got a grant to take the kids to Billings to see a ballet at the Alberta Bair Theater," said Susan. "You'd a thought I sold the kids to a brothel, the way some of the parents carried on."

"I thought it was just me," said Sarah. She sat next to Susan Klein, on a stool at the far end of the bar.

"Oh, no," said Susan Klein. "Giving shit to the teachers is the main sport in places like Toussaint, Montana."

"I'm sorry," said Sarah. "I shouldn't have given those assholes the satisfaction of upsetting me."

"It's Friday," said Susan Klein. "You have a nice slab of red meat tonight, dance a little, stay over, that way you can drink as much as you want, and by Sunday you'll be ready to go back."

"Sounds like a plan," said Sarah.

"There's three rooms out back in that long trailer," said Susan Klein. "One teacher to another, you can have one free. I rent them on occasion but usually only in the fall when the hunters come."

"Well," said Sarah, "I should have come down here sooner, but I was afraid it would cause talk."

"So," said Madelaine, "what!"

Everyone laughed.

Sarah got up and she went out the front door.

Chappie's eyes followed her.

"Ooooh," said Madelaine.

Chappie blushed.

Sarah came running back in.

"There's a dog out here," she said. "He needs help. He's real sick."

Du Pré got up. Sarah had gotten a couple of bar towels and she was wetting them.

An old border collie was lying down across the road, and when Du Pré came up the dog whined and wagged his tail a little bit.

Du Pré sniffed, smelled rot.

The dog had a big wound on his side, and it was suppurating and crawling with maggots.

Sarah came with the towels.

"Go and get some sugar," said Du Pré, "and a box big enough for him. We got to take him to the vet quick."

"Sugar?" said Sarah.

"Yes," said Du Pré. "Kill the maggots and it eats proud flesh."

He petted the old dog's head until Sarah came back with everybody behind her.

Du Pré and Sarah carefully lifted the old dog into the carton, which Susan had packed with old towels. The dog wagged his tail a little and then fell asleep.

They put the dog in the back of the cruiser and Du Pré and Sarah got in and Du Pré took off for Cooper.

Each time he crested a hill and the old car flew Sarah shrieked and then she would laugh.

When Du Pré pulled in to the veterinarian's the man was just getting into his truck.

95

"We got an emergency," said Du Pré.

The vet ran to the car, looked the dog over.

"Bring him in," he said. "And could you call the Martin ranch and tell them I will be late."

They brought the box into the surgery and Du Pré made the call to the Martins'.

The vet shaved the hair around the wound. He gave the dog two shots. The second anesthetized the animal.

Sarah handed the vet his surgical implements and she wiped up the maggots that fell on the table.

Du Pré sat outside, smoking.

An hour later the vet came out.

Sarah was still inside.

"He's an old dog," said the vet, "malnourished, a badly infected wound. I cleaned it up and filled him full of antibiotics. He's in a recovery box. I can't say for sure that he will make it."

Du Pré took out his wallet. He pulled out some bills.

"Call it a hundred," said the vet.

Du Pré gave him a lot more.

The vet shrugged.

"Poor old bastard," said the vet. "The owner oughta be shot."

"Yah," said Du Pré.

"I had best get out to the Martins'," said the vet. "I'm Vince McClary. You wouldn't recognize me, Mr. Du Pré."

"I am sorry," said Du Pré.

"When Dad had the stroke he quit and I came," said McClary, "but you don't have stock anymore, I guess."

"Not so much," said Du Pré.

"Music tonight?" said McClary.

"Jesus Christ," said Du Pré. "I am playing I forgot."

"So busy round here," said McClary, "I have trouble keeping track myself."

They laughed.

"What about the dog?" said Du Pré.

"When he wakes up," said McClary, "you can take him, make sure he's comfortable. If he tries to stand up he may fall. I can check him this evening. Like I said, he will either make it or not, and I can't tell you which."

The vet got in his big truck with the cabinets hung over the sides of the bed, and he drove off toward the huge Martin ranch.

Du Pré fished his flask out and he had some whiskey and a smoke and then he went into the clinic.

Sarah was sitting on a folding chair watching the old dog sleep.

"Him say we can take him," said Du Pré. "He may make it and may not. But he will be at the saloon tonight and he will check on him then."

They carefully slid the old dog into the box they had brought him there in. Sarah threw out the soiled towels and she put her ski jacket in the box so the old dog would have something soft to lie on.

They carried the sleeping dog out to the cruiser and they put him in the back seat. Sarah got in beside him.

"Not so fast on the way back," she said. "We got a patient here."

Du Pré laughed.

He drove slowly back to Toussaint.

They carried the old dog into the end room of the big white trailer out in back of the saloon.

Bassman's van was parked in front of the middle one.

Du Pré saw a book on the dashboard.

"Kim, she is here," he murmured.

Sarah knelt beside the sleeping dog.

"He will be all right here," said Du Pré. "He sleep another couple hours anyway." She nodded.

Sarah got up reluctantly.

She went to the back door of the saloon with Du Pré and they went on in and sat at the bar.

Susan Klein put platters with cheeseburgers and fries in front of them.

"Eat," she said. "I got a box of dog delicacies you can feed that poor old guy when he wakes up. But you eat."

Sarah ate quickly.

Susan Klein brought out a plastic bottle with a tube.

"Give him water first," said Susan.

Sarah nodded.

"Not too much water," said Susan.

"I don't know much about animals," said Sarah. "I hope I don't blow this . . ."

"Chappie!" said Susan, "this lady needs a little help."

Chappie blushed, but he got off his stool and he came over.

Susan introduced him.

Chappie and Sarah, laden with food and water, went out the back door together.

"Pretty slick," said Madelaine, looking at Susan.

"I am good," she said.

"I have bad dream Chappie gets tangled up with some girl that church," said Madelaine.

"I do what I can," said Susan Klein.

Bassman's girlfriend Kim came in then. She looked happy.

"Ah," said Susan. "Good to see you. And how is our favorite drug addict?"

"Good," said Kim. "He sends his love."

"And he wants some Budweisers," said Susan Klein.

She fished a six-pack of tall cans out of the cooler.

Kim grinned and she went out.

The door opened and a man came in, and he blinked as his eyes adjusted to the light.

"You seen an old dog around here?" he said.

"What kind of dog?" said Susan Klein.

"Old sheepdog," said the man. "He was over where we're workin' but I can't find him."

"Nope," said Susan Klein. "Haven't seen him."

"He shows up," said the man, "we're settin' that trailer back there."

"OK," said Susan Klein.

"Kin I buy a couple pops?" said the man.

"No," said Susan Klein, "you cannot. Now get the fuck out of here and don't come back, and that goes for any of the rest of you, too."

The man looked stupidly at her.

"Go now," said Susan, "or I call the cops."

The man backed out the door.

"I," said Susan Klein, "have had it with these folks."

CHAPTER
19

Du Pré pulled his bow across the strings for the last time and the people left in the saloon cheered. It was the fourth encore.

The woman Père Godin had seduced the last time he was here sat forlornly at a table in the back. Père Godin was somewhere else making a baby with someone else.

"That old bastard," said Madelaine. "Him get away with more than any other man I know."

"Me," said Du Pré, "I don't get away with anything."

"Right," said Madelaine. "I am glad you know that."

"I know that," said Du Pré.

Raymond was back home for the weekend and he and Jacqueline had been dancing all night. Pallas and Lourdes had been dancing with the cowboys who had come in for a few drinks and a number of couples in from the ranches left holding hands.

"Where is Chappie and that Sarah?" said Madelaine.

Du Pré grinned.

"Watching the dog," he said.

"I am worried about the dog," said Madelaine.

"Uh-huh," said Du Pré.

"Go check the dog," said Madelaine. "I am his mother, I cannot check the dog."

Du Pré went out back and across to the trailer. He knocked on the door and he waited. The lights were on. He heard the off-rhythm walk of Chappie.

Chappie opened the door.

"How's the dog?" he said.

"Come in and see," said Chappie.

Du Pré went in and found Sarah sitting on the couch with the old dog, who had his head in her lap. He lifted his head when he saw Du Pré and he wagged his tail. Then he put his head back down on Sarah's lap and he sighed.

"Miraculous recovery," said Sarah. "I do think he will make it."

The dog's eyes were bright and his breathing slow and steady.

"Madelaine wanted me to check," said Du Pré.

"He's OK," said Sarah. "Chappie has been a great help."

Chappie was putting on his jacket.

They all said good night and Du Pré and Chappie walked back to the bar together.

They went in the back door and Chappie went out the front after giving Madelaine a peck on the cheek.

She waited until the door closed.

She looked at Du Pré.

Du Pré held out his hands, palms up.

"Him got beat out by an old dog," said Madelaine. "That will piss him off." Du Pré laughed.

Bassman and Kim were at the bar, counting out the money that Susan had given them.

The woman Père Godin had wooed and won left then, slouching some.

"How that old bastard do that?" said Bassman. "Him going to get a load of buckshot from husband one day."

"How did you escape all those years?" said Kim, looking very sweet.

"I am talking about that old accordion man," said Bassman. "He make me look like a priest."

"People were asking if you guys would play again tomorrow night," said Susan. "I know you usually just play Friday."

"I got nothing on," said Bassman.

"Done," said Susan.

"What about me, I don't get a vote?" said Du Pré.

"No," said Bassman, Madelaine, Kim, Susan, Benny, Lourdes, and Pallas. Du Pré shrugged.

"Where is that Père Godin?" he said.

"Him, he not come here a while," said Bassman. "Till she have the kid."

"How do you know she is pregnant?" said Madelaine.

Bassman just looked at her.

He shook his head.

Susan put the lights up and the last customers finished their drinks and went out. There were a few whoops in the parking lot.

"You make them cowboys as happy as they get to be," said Jacqueline to her daughters. Pallas and Lourdes both smiled.

"We lock them in tonight," said Jacqueline.

"Deadbolts," said Raymond.

They all laughed and Raymond and Jacqueline and the two girls went out.

"Pallas," said Madelaine, "is going to be a real beauty. Lourdes, too, it will cause Lourdes trouble."

"How about Pallas?" said Susan.

"Not so much," said Madelaine. "Girls they are just about women. Whole new bunch of trouble."

"I dunno how we survived," said Susan.

The telephone rang and Benny went to get it and he listened a moment and he said something and he hung up.

He came back, looking troubled.

He nodded to Du Pré and the door.

"That was the Reverend Flowers," said Benny. "He said that one of their kids run off. One of the girls."

Du Pré looked at him.

"He wanted me to get out there and search for her," said Benny. "I said we did not do that unless there were signs of foul play. He started in about the Devil."

"If he is in this," said Du Pré, "she is probably a lot happier."

Benny laughed.

"Kids run away," said Benny. "They run when they are mad or sad or happy. They come back mostly."

"Sometime some didn't," said Du Pré. When the killers were stalking women.

Benny looked at him.

"You don't think . . . ?" he said.

"*Non,*" said Du Pré. "She is run probably and she will spend a cold night out there, noises will scare her."

"I wonder if she can drive," said Benny. "I suppose if there was a car missing . . ."

"Morning," said Du Pré.

He went back in with Benny and they helped with the last of the cleanup.

Bassman and Kim left and as soon as the last floor was mopped and the last dish stuck in the washer they all said good night.

Du Pré and Madelaine walked to her house, Du Pré carrying the old rawhide fiddle case with his fiddle in it.

They went in.

Du Pré yawned and Madelaine made raspberry leaf tea for their aches and pains and they drank it. Du Pré took a shower and then Madelaine drew a hot bath and she put the lavender salts in the water.

They coupled and then they slept.

Du Pré woke in the night, and he looked at the watch he had set by the bed.

Four o'clock.

I hear something but I do not know what.

He tried to drift off again but he woke again suddenly.

He slipped out of bed. Madelaine murmured and turned.

He dressed and carried his boots to the kitchen.

He got a flashlight and he pulled on his boots and put on his old worn leather jacket. He put his pistol in his belt.

The noise had come from the back where the trailer Chappie lived in was. Du Pré slid out the front and he went round the far side of the lilacs, feeling his way slowly so he did not have to turn on the light.

Chappie's trailer was dark.

Du Pré stopped still and he listened.

He heard something, muffled, perhaps on the far side of the trailer.

He edged forward.

He waited for a moment by the end of the trailer and then he heard the sound again.

102

Breathing, or perhaps soft sobbing.

He edged round the trailer, crouched over so there would not be a silhouette against the night sky.

A shadow sat next to the skirtings that closed off the area underneath the trailer.

Du Pré slowly lifted the flashlight and he pressed the switch and the beam blazed.

A girl leaped up from where she had been sitting on the ground.

She screamed and she turned and she ran. She ran toward the fence.

Du Pre' switched off the light.

"I will not hurt you!" he yelled.

He could see her struggling. Her dress must have gotten caught on the barbed wire.

He stayed where he was.

Cloth tore and then there was more sobbing.

"If you need help I will give it to you," said Du Pré. "What is it you are here?"

The girl sat down on the ground.

Du Pré walked up to her.

He squatted on his heels.

"What is it?" he said.

She just shook her head.

He could see tears on her cheeks, glistening from starlight.

"Come in we give you some tea, get warm," said Du Pré.

She shook her head.

"What is this?" said Madelaine.

She had come up behind Du Pré soundlessly.

Du Pré shrugged.

Madelaine went to the girl and she squatted down.

"You come in," she said. "We will not hurt you."

The girl sobbed and sobbed.

Madelaine clucked to her, lifted her up, put her arm around the girl's shoulders.

They walked very slowly toward the house.

Du Pré looked at the fence.

He looked at the ground where the girl had sat and the path she had taken when Du Pré had startled her.

He found nothing, and so he went in the back door of the house.

"And that Chappie, sly dog, he is not there," Du Pré murmured.

CHAPTER
20

"Christ," said Benny, "what do I do now?"

Madelaine was sitting on the couch with the girl, who had her hands folded in her lap. She was looking straight ahead and seemed to be frozen.

"Honey," said Madelaine, "you have to tell us who you are and what is wrong. We can help you if you do."

She sat catatonic.

Madelaine got up and she went into the kitchen and she made some tea. She brought it back and she set a cup in front of the girl who would not look at it.

The girl's face was scratched where she had run into things.

Her long dress was torn, muddy at the hem. She wore old lace-up boots. Her hands were red from work, and dirt showed in the creases.

"If we just knew who she was and how old she is . . . ," said Benny. He looked exhausted.

"At some point I got to tell her family she is alive," said Benny. "Look, honey, we can help, but we have to have some help from you."

The girl looked straight ahead.

She had compressed her lips into a thin line, and she kept her eyes closed.

Madelaine poured some tea for herself and she sipped it.

"Were you looking for Chappie?" she said.

Some emotion flickered across the girl's face.

"Chappie is gone for a little while," said Madelaine. "He is my son. Now if you tell me who you are, that would be good. If Chappie was here, he would tell you to."

But the girl had gone back inside herself and slammed her eyes shut.

Madelaine nodded at Du Pré and the two of them went outside.

"Chappie is with the teacher," said Madelaine. "Here is a nice mess. Maybe he is with some woman he just met, you know, while this one wants to see him and she don't trust no one else."

Du Pré nodded.

"Du Pré," she said, "you . . ."

"Yah," said Du Pré. "There are telephones, the rooms?"

Madelaine shook her head.

"No," she said. "Susan got tired paying year-round for them. Hunters can use the phone in the bar they need to."

"Ok," said Du Pré. "I go and see if Chappie unplug himself long enough to come."

"Ver' funny, Du Pré," said Madelaine.

"You are his mother," said Du Pré. "It is, delicate situation."

"You," said Madelaine, "are in that delicate situation."

Du Pré cursed and he went to this cruiser and he got a bottle and had some whiskey and then he walked to the trailer behind the saloon.

There were lights on in the room that the teacher was in.

Du Pré went to the door and he tapped lightly.

There was a silence, and then Du Pré heard light feet on the thin floor.

Sarah opened the door a crack.

"I am sorry, bother," said Du Pré. "I wondered if maybe Chappie was here."

Sarah looked at him.

"We have some trouble," said Du Pré. "We have a girl won't say anything, she is one of those people at the church Chappie has been going to."

"Oh my God," said Sarah. "She ran away?"

Du Pré nodded.

"I . . . was just worried that people would talk. Just a moment," said Sarah.

She shut the door and shortly it opened. Chappie stood there, blinking.

"A girl run away, we think, the Christers," said Du Pré. "She maybe come to your place looking for you. She won't talk, us."

Chappie nodded.

He shut the door and there was a low murmur of voices and then Sarah laughed.

Chappie came out soon enough.

He shut the door.

"How is the dog?" said Du Pré.

"I wish I was that fucking dog," said Chappie. "Now, you have a girl, one of those kids from that church bunch? Poor things. They all look like they get beaten twice a day and more if their bastard fathers feel like it. One of the older ones? There was one who kept looking at me there, but her mother slapped her once and she quit."

Chappie could walk but not very fast. It took him and Du Pré ten minutes to cover the distance to the little trailer behind Madelaine's that Chappie had been living in.

"She is in the house," said Du Pré.

Chappie nodded.

"I need a couple pills," he said. "My stump is really hurting." He went in and he was soon back out.

They walked to the back door and let themselves in and Chappie went ahead of Du Pré to the living room.

When he walked in, the girl gave a start, but she then went back to her rigid sitting.

Chappie pulled up a dining chair and he sat, stretching his artificial leg out.

"I don't know your name but I have seen you," said Chappie. "Do you want to go back home?"

The girl choked, gasped, put her hands to her face.

"If you won't help us," said Chappie, "we will have to do just that."

The girl shrieked and she jumped up and tried to go out the

back door. Benny moved to the door but Madelaine grabbed the girl and shoved her back down on the couch.

"All right," she said. "We take her to Billings, put her in the hospital. You, come on." She got up and she pulled the girl up from the couch.

Du Pré sighed and he went to the front door.

"*Non,*" said Madelaine. "You got to play tonight. We go in my car. Call, have Benny call."

"You need somebody else," said Du Pré.

"*Non,*" said Madelaine. "You see."

She pulled the girl round so she was facing her.

"We are going to a safe place," said Madelaine, "or you are going home. You come with me, you behave, or I take you back."

They went out. Madelaine grabbed her purse as she passed the rack by the door. They got into her little station wagon. Madelaine started the engine and she flipped on the lights.

It was close to dawn. There was a fingernail of pink on the eastern horizon.

Madelaine waved and pulled away.

"I feel a shit," said Chappie. "I should have gone."

Du Pré shook his head.

"Your mother is fine," he said. "She don't need us this time."

"Good," said Chappie. "I guess I'll go back and help Sarah."

Du Pré nodded.

"We send in breakfast?" he said. "Balloons maybe . . ."

"Go to hell, Du Pré," said Chappie. But he smiled when he said it.

Du Pré watched him go, walking steadily.

"So," said Benny, "I think I'd best wait until Madelaine calls to tell the worried parents. I ain't sure this is legal. I sure as hell don't want Madelaine arrested for kidnapping and I don't know whatall."

"*Non,*" said du Pré. "It would be ver' bad when she got out. Thousands dead, prolly."

"Wonder what that girl was so terrified of," said Benny.

Du Pré shrugged.

They shook hands and Benny drove off toward his place and Susan.

Du Pré went in the house. His bootheels thudded on the dead floor.

There was a wet patch on the couch. The poor girl had soiled herself, probably when Madelaine threatened to take her back to her parents.

Du Pré heard whoops and he went out the back door and he looked toward the pasture and wheatfield between Madelaine's and Du Pré's old place, where Raymond and Jacqueline lived now with most of their children.

Lourdes on Stewball and Pallas on Moondog were racing flat out, soaring over fences and the little creeks.

A coyote burst out of some brush and the girls gave chase, the horses finally running on either side of the coyote, and then both girls turned their mounts and the wild dog went over a hill and was gone.

Du Pré waved and they waved back and then they came straight at him. They leaped the fence behind Madelaine's and went round the lilacs and pulled up.

"Madelaine's car is gone," said Lourdes. "She went someplace?"

"Some girl showed up, maybe looking for Chappie," said Du Pré. "Madelaine took her the hospital in Billings."

"One of the new kids," said Lourdes. "They all look ver' unhappy."

Du Pré nodded.

"So you don't go?" said Pallas.

"Have to play tonight," said Du Pré.

"My grandfather he is a rock-and-roll star," said Pallas.

"So is mine," said Lourdes.

"He is ver' famous," said Pallas.

"I got a famous gran'père, too," said Lourdes.

"We are ver' lucky," said Pallas.

"Got an awesome gran'père," said Lourdes.

Du Pré shook his head and he walked away.

The girls whooped and rode on, and when Du Pré turned to look they were running along the top of the hill, two splendid horses with smooth and easy riders.

Du Pré made himself some breakfast. He had coffee with whiskey in it under the lilacs in the backyard.

The van with the Texas plates drove past, very slowly.

Mrs. Flowers's face was pressed to the window.

Du Pré did not move.

The van went on.

Du Pré sighed and he got up and he went inside and called Benny.

"What?" said Benny, half asleep.

"They are looking for her," said Du Pré. "They come bother you soon, they know where you are."

"Shit," said Benny. "You want my job?"

"No," said Du Pré.

"Right now, neither do I," said Benny.

Du Pré hung up. He went out the front door with his plastic coffee mug in his hand.

He heard an eighteen-wheeler.

Sonny, muttering to himself as he usually did, drove past.

There was a decal on the door of the tractor.

ABORTION IS MURDER.

It said.

CHAPTER
21

Du Pré parked across the road from Wilbur and Marge's store, and he sat for a moment. He drummed his fingers on the dashboard, on the metal that showed through the thin padding now broken away, split by winter cold and one or another bored dog chewing a likely rent.

Sonny's eighteen-wheeler was idling right next to the store, blocking the gas pumps' inside lane.

Du Pré sighed and he got out and he walked across the road. The smell of diesel fuel and rotting garbage prickled his nostrils. He dropped his cigarette on the ground and he stepped on it.

There was a huge NO SMOKING sign on the entry door of the store.

Du Pré turned the knob and he kicked the bottom of the door lightly. It had been dragging for years and Wilbur never got round to fixing it.

Bells on a spring-steel bracket jingled.

There was no one in the store.

Du Pré heard voices behind a door.

Voices praying.

He went back outside and he rolled a smoke. He lit it and he looked at the Wolf Mountains.

The highest peaks were still white, flashing in the sun. The air was clear now, but by late afternoon a haze of dust would blur the mountains and the white peaks would not gleam.

Du Pré looked at the tractor and the big trailer. They were both fairly old but well-kept.

A wooden cross hung from a clip on the roof of the cab.

Something bright fluttered at the bottom of the door.

Du Pré bent over, saw a woman's breast, half a face, blond hair teased and fluffed.

Girlie magazine.

Du Pré laughed once, a bark of mirth.

The door opened behind him and Sonny came out. He smiled at Du Pré.

"Mornin'," he said. "They find Raylee yet? We were praying that they did. Terrible what happened."

Du Pré nodded.

"What happened?" he said.

"She's been kidnapped," said Sonny. "She's probably dead by now. Live here all my life but a little of it, and we got a child killer. They git him, they better by God put him to death."

Sex and death, and he got a man on a gurney already.

"That damned Benny won't even search for her," said Sonny. "Ain't that something? I always thought he was one of them danged liberals."

"Where all you haul from?" said Du Pré.

Sonny looked at Du Pré for a long time.

"Here," he said. "Got some contracts for Cooper, haul some from the Martins' spread. They are the only one big enough to hire it out anymore."

Du Pré nodded.

"You know Benny," said Sonny. "Why don't you tell him?"

"Tell him what?" said Du Pré.

"We got a child killer out there," said Sonny.

Du Pré reached up to the latch and he opened the door of the cab. A long pile of skin magazines fell out on the ground.

Sonny yelped and he knelt and he gathered them up and he put them back in and he slammed the door.

His mouth worked.

He looked at Du Pré.

"Benny got no reason, think the girl is dead," said Du Pré. "You think up a lot of things pretty fast there."

Sonny blushed, opened his mouth.

The door opened and Marge came out, easing her bulk through the wide door frame.

"Martins just called," she said. "Wondering where you were."

"Call 'em back I'm on my way," said Sonny. "I got to go."

He edged past Du Pré, climbed up in the cab. The engine roared, gears meshed, the big tractor-trailer rumbled away, very slow, gaining a bit of speed with every shift up in the gars.

"That poor Flowers girl," said Marge. "Poor thing."

"I need, talk to Wilbur," said Du Pré.

"He's back in the shop," said Marge. She eased herself back through the door.

Du Pré went to the garage. He lifted the metal door and it rumbled up the tracks.

The radio was on, some angry-sounding man griping about the liberal media.

Wilbur was under the Ford truck, his old stained boots poking out of his greasy coveralls.

Wilbur slid himself out from under the truck.

"Car all right?" he said.

"Fine," said Du Pré. "Sonny thinks the Flowers girl is dead. Why does he think that?"

A wrench clanged on the concrete.

"Girls get abducted all the time," said Wilbur. He sat up on the dolly he used to get under vehicles.

"Lot of talk," said Du Pré. "Sonny wants to execute somebody."

Wilbur sighed.

He got to his feet.

"Sonny's had a real hard time," he said. "You remember he was drinking so danged much. Even had to do thirteen months in Deer Lodge he got his sixth DUI. Hell, he was settin' in the cell thinkin' about his life and he found Jesus and he done changed, didn't do them things no more he got out. He was almost dead. For a while if the phone rang at night, I'd think it was the police callin' say he was dead, piled up his truck someplace."

Du Pré nodded.

"Wife left him, he had bills all over, couldn't pay 'em," said Wilbur. "Me and Marge don't have much. Anyway, Sonny come back out of Deer Lodge and he had found the Lord. He'd a died he didn't, Du Pré."

Du Pré nodded.

"We done started the new church," said Wilbur. "All them others was too danged liberal, we wanted one kept to the Bible. Kept to the right ways . . . Long time we didn't have 'nough money hire a preacher. Sometimes Sonny'd preach. He preaches pretty good. Really understands the Bible, Sonny does."

Du Pré looked at Wilbur.

"You wouldn't understand," said Wilbur. "You're Catholic."

The man on the radio was griping about a woman senator who was a liberal.

"Oh, god damn it, Du Pré," said Wilbur. "Whole danged country's gone to hell. Got Meskins coming across the border in millions. Lotsa Meskins in Billings. Nobody reads the danged Constitution. We got a right keep and bear arms and there's people don't think that and it is right there. Second Amendment. Can't have no prayer in the schools. This country was founded on the *Bible*."

"The girl they found by the road," said Du Pré, "she was not from here, they don't know who she is."

Wilbur nodded.

"Ardreys," said Du Pré.

"They are strong in the Lord," said Wilbur. "You oughta hear 'em pray."

"Wilbur!" said Marge, loud, from the store. "Phone call."

Wilbur went off.

Du Pré stood, looked around. Parts for trucks and bins of hardware, all of them used, all salvaged. Wilbur was frugal, and would not waste much.

He came back in a few minutes.

"God-danged government," said Wilbur. "They come by here few months ago, said I had to get me a new gas tank. Had to dig up all the soil over the one buried out there, have it hauled away. Polution. New tank is fifteen thousand dollars and we don't even make money on the gas. We got to have it, if we didn't no one'd come here at all. Christ, I ain't got fifteen thousand get the new tank and I told them that and they said they don't care."

Du Pré nodded.

Wilbur looked round at his shop.

"We didn't sell gas you think people'd still come with their cars?" he said.

"I would," said Du Pré.

"Sonny didn't do nothing," said Wilbur. He was breathing fast.

Du Pré nodded.

"They said I had to have that new tank ninety days or they shut me down," said Wilbur.

Du Pré nodded.

"I am sorry," he said. "Maybe there is something to do."

He went out then and he got into his old cruiser. He turned the key and the engine turned and coughed and went dead.

"Oh shit," said Wilbur, from the doorway. "Dang it, Du Pré, I meant to change out that fuel filter and I plumb forgot."

Du Pré popped the hood latch and Wilbur lifted it up and he bent over the carburetor.

Wilbur unscrewed the wing nut and he lifted the cover off, and then he took the whole baffle up and he set it aside.

He took out a screwdriver and he pried up the filter.

"Dang," he said. "Look at that." The filter looked like it had cream in it.

"Water," said Wilbur. "How long since you changed it before."

"Fall," said Du Pré.

"Get some water in the gas, the winter," said Wilbur.

Du Pré nodded.

Wilbur went off with the little paper sleeve and he came back with a new one. He set it in the line, tightened a screw, put the carburetor back together, shut the hood.

"Try her," he said.

The engine caught instantly.

Du Pré gave it more gas and it roared.

"Sorry," said Wilbur. "Little thing but it is important."

"How much I owe you?" said Du Pré.

Wilbur shook his head and Du Pré nodded and he drove away.

CHAPTER

22

Du Pré tapped the wooden matches into the holes where the screws that held the top hinge of the window had rotted part of the sash away. He took his cordless drill and he reset the screws. He swung the window. It moved easily and seated well. He went inside and latched it.

She is asking me to do that for about the last year, he thought.

He puttered about fixing little things and he suddenly felt hungry.

He went out to his cruiser and he got in and drove to the saloon. He parked in front next to the van with the Texas license plates.

What the hell is he doing in here, sink of sin?

When he opened the door he could hear Flowers.

"You know where Raylee is!" said the fat man. "I know you know! She run off and come this way!"

Susan Klein looked at him.

"I suggest," she said, "that you call the sheriff."

"He's your husband!" said Flowers. "The Lord will burn you both in hell."

"Enough," said Susan Klein. "Get your fat ass out of my saloon. Go now or I *will* call the sheriff."

LuAnne was mumbling to herself, her pudgy hands writhing around one another like coupling starfish.

Flowers started to pray, loudly and incoherently.

Susan Klein came round the bar, pointing to the door.

"Out now," she said, "and don't come back."

Flowers kept mumbling but he turned and walked away, and his wife followed him. He threw the door open and went through and she scurried past it as it closed.

"Jesus!" said Susan Klein. "The man is so stupid he thinks the cops exist to help him abuse his daughters."

Du Pré nodded.

"No word yet from Madelaine?" said Susan.

Du Pré shook his head.

"Benny called the staties," she said. "Tonight they plan to raid the Flowers and those other crackers who came up with them. See if there is anything—"

"How did he manage that?" said Du Pré.

"Endangered children," said Susan. "The dead girl was not from here and that poor creature Madelaine took to Billings wasn't, either."

Du Pré nodded.

"You remember the mess fifteen years ago with the Ewings?" said Susan. "When he wasn't hollering Scripture he was molesting his eight-year-old daughter? That son of a bitch was one of the reasons I quit teaching."

"Yah," said du Pré. "His wife, she shoots him, more than one time."

"Yeah," said Susan. "Poor Joanie. She didn't like guns, so she takes two shots to knock him down and one more through his head, so he won't ever molest Janey again, and there is no way the coroner can rule that bastard's death accidental, so Joanie got paroled three years ago, and Janey was dead by then. Poor kid, went to live with an aunt and uncle and she drank so much the first party she went to she passed out and never did wake up."

"Yah," said Du Pré.

"It is always sex with these bastards," said Susan Klein. "They hate women and they are afraid of them and so—"

"You should calm down," said Du Pré. "They are gone."

"I wonder," said Susan, "If that poor girl found in the ditch was one of theirs?"

116

Du Pré shrugged.

"We'll know tonight," said Susan.

Sarah came in the back door, looking tired.

"How's the patient?" said Susan.

"Much improved," said Sarah. "Dogs heal quicker than people do, I guess. Now how do I keep him?"

"Keep him," said Susan Klein. "What you do is go and file a complaint, cruelty to animals, you have witnesses, and the deal for the Ardreys will be if they shut up and leave you and that poor dog alone no more comes of it, and if they don't a lot comes of it. Maggots in his wounds. Jesus."

"He's a nice dog," said Sarah. "I had a dog when I was a kid kinda like this one. He got run over."

"I lose a dog," said Susan Klein, "it breaks my heart."

Chappie came in then, looking tired.

Susan looked at the three of them.

"Lunch?" she said.

She went off to cook cheeseburgers.

"That girl was here looking for you last night," said Du Pré, looking at Chappie.

Chappie winced.

Sarah looked at him and then she looked away.

"Some kid," said Du Pré. "She is so upset she won't talk. So Madelaine take her to Billings, the hospital."

"How you know she is looking for me?" said Chappie.

"You are so handsome," said Du Pré. "Why else would she be here?"

Sarah looked at Du Pré.

"She is one, the Christers," said Du Pré. "Chappie, him been going, see what he can see."

Chappie shook his head.

"The women there all have trouble laughing," said Chappie. "And they all look afraid except a couple. The girls all look afraid."

"What is going on here?" said Sarah. "This is nuts."

Du Pré nodded.

The telephone rang. Du Pré went to answer it.

"Du Pré," said Madelaine, "she is in the hospital. She still won't talk, so they need permission, next of kin, do anything."

"Shit," said Du Pré.

"Or," said Madelaine, "there has to be a hearing, judge commits her."

"So," said Du Pré.

"So I call Foote, he calls somebody here, hearing is soon, but I have to stay because I brought her, say how she was found, that she didn't talk," said Madelaine.

"OK," said Du Pré.

"So," said Madelaine, "I will be here some and probably can't help Susan tonight."

"I tell her," said Du Pré.

"Court is starting, got to go," said Madelaine.

Du Pré put the phone back.

Susan came out with the platters and she went back and brought one for herself.

"Madelaine can't make it tonight," said Du Pré.

"OK," said Susan. "I can call a couple people."

"So," said Sarah, "I have to go to Cooper to file the complaint?"

"Yah," said Du Pré.

"I guess I'll take Ralph along," she said. "He seems chipper."

"Ralph?" said Chappie.

"Well," said Sarah, "my other dog was named Ralph, too."

"OK," said Chappie.

They went out.

Du Pré got up, put money on the bar, pointed to the seats where Sarah and Chappie had been sitting.

"They seem confused," said Susan Klein. "But I did notice that Chappie wasn't asking for a thick ditch first thing."

Du Pré nodded.

He drove out to Bart's place.

He checked the pastures and the barn, but Booger Tom and Father Van Den Heuvel were still up in the mountains.

Bart and Pidgeon were gone, too.

A light plane flew over low, waggled its wings.

Du Pré waved back.

He went through the house after he punched the code into the alarm system, and then he locked it back up, and he checked the stock in the pasture. They had plenty of feed and water and a loafing shed to lie in when the sun was high and hot.

A contract crew was haying in one of the huge fields of clover. They bound the clover into rolls that weighted a ton each. Then the rolls were stacked. They all had plastic covers around them.

Du Pré drove back down to the county road and then he headed west and he came to Benetsee's by a back way.

The cabin was cold and empty, and there had been no fires built near the sweat lodge in the back.

Du Pré heard whoops, and he turned and looked up at the benchlands.

Pallas and Lourdes were riding, Moondog and Stewball cantering easily. Sweat glistened on Moondog's rump.

The girls wound down a trail that ran near the creek tumbling down from the Wolf Mountains. They saw Du Pré and they waved.

He rolled a smoke, had a drink from his flask, waited.

The horses crashed through the thick willows and they jumped the creek and Pallas and Lourdes got down and led them to a hitching rail set next to the cabin.

The horses whuffled and looked back at the water.

"We walk you down a few minutes," said Pallas.

Stewball and Moondog fell to bickering, out of boredom.

"Him gone?" said Pallas.

Du Pré nodded.

"Sometimes he is here, stays months," said Du Pré. "Sometimes he is gone months, too."

Pallas sat down on the bench. Lourdes went to the far side of the little meadow and she picked some flowers.

"Him, Benetsee, him the land, yes, Gran'père?" she said.

"Land is land," said Du Pré. "Benetsee is soul of it maybe."

"Don't know, how old he is?" said Pallas.

"Always been here," said Du Pré. "Him old, Catfoot tell me, when Catfoot is little."

Pallas nodded.

"These people, go to listen to that silly man from Texas," said Pallas. "It is like they want magic. But they won't find it."

"Ghost dancers," said Du Pré.

"Yah, them," said Pallas. "Same thing, huh? They want what used to be."

Du Pré nodded.

"You want that, too, Gran'père?" she said.

"Sometimes," said Du Pré, "but then I got Benetsee, so it is all right."

CHAPTER
23

Du Pré looked at the house, dark and sleeping.

He looked at the police. They were all dressed in black, all wore armored vests, all carried machine pistols but the leader.

They stood in the shadow of an old shed, fifty feet from the house.

The leader had a microphone set in his ear.

He raised his hand and the other nine cops moved toward the house. Two took up positions on each side of the front door, others went to the sides or the back.

A light flashed and the front door opened and the black-clad men rushed in.

There were shrieks and screams and one by one sleepy children came outside, the girls in long nightdresses, the boys in underwear.

A woman in the same battledress talked to them.

The Flowerses stumbled out.

Flowers was wearing a thick terry-cloth bathrobe and he had slippers on his feet. His wife had a long nightdress on and a cap.

"Why are you doing this?" screamed Flowers.

"Shut up," said one of the cops.

Lights went on in the house, flashlights shone in rooms before the lights were turned on.

Du Pré stood in the shadows, smoking.

The cops were inside for about twenty minutes and then one by one they came out.

The woman in the black battledress had gone down the row of children, talking to each one in turn.

The kids stood looking at the ground.

It was cold, and they were barefoot. They lifted first one foot and then the other, trying to warm their toes.

The cops went through the outbuildings, the van, a medium-sized white metal trailer. They went off into the grove of willows next to the little stockpond behind the house.

The leader went to Flowers.

"You can go back in now," he said.

The Flowerses and their children filed back inside.

They all began to pray.

"Nothing," said the leader. "Not a thing. No kid in the closet. They all seem to be all right, yeah?"

"Wouldn't answer my questions," said the woman, "but maybe they were just scared."

"So much for that," said the leader. "Now we better get out of here."

The cops all got into three black SUVs. The woman got into a van.

Du Pré walked to his cruiser, started it, and drove off toward Cooper.

He got there before the cops did. They pulled in within seconds of each other. When they got out, they had on windbreakers but no vests and they carried no guns.

"Fuckin' bust," said a young cop. He had a very thick neck and chest.

They all looked young and very tough.

The leader was a little older. He had black hair shot with gray and a scar on his cheekbone that could have been made by a bullet plowing.

"Maybe they found something at the other places," said one of the cops.

"I hope so," said the leader. "When we pull one of these and don't find dick it don't look good."

Everything in Cooper was closed. They made bad coffee in the machine on the front counter, and drank it, reluctantly.

Du Pré went out and had some whiskey and a smoke.

Headlights showed on the road.

More of the black SUVs came, and finally Benny in his cruiser.

The state cops went inside.

Benny came to Du Pré's old cruiser. He got in the passenger side.

"Not one fucking thing," he said. "All we did is scare the shit out of some people. There isn't a thing. They looked at everything. Nothing. If that girl Madelaine took to Billings would talk, that would help."

"Nothing about the girl we found?" said Du Pré. "Dead one in the ditch?"

"Everybody is accounted for," said Benny. "That poor kid wasn't from the Flowerses, or the Ardreys. I wonder if we don't like these people much and so . . ."

Du Pré shook his head.

"Nobody else," he said.

"There has to be somebody else," said Benny.

A white rental car pulled in and a couple of people jumped out.

"Oh, shit," said Benny. "Reporters."

Du Pré laughed.

"Government thugs scare good Christians to death," said Benny.

"Yah," said Du Pré.

"You said not to do this," said Benny. "Thanks for not reminding me of that."

"Don't work out," said Du Pré, "is all."

"Yeah," said Benny, "and now I bet we end up with a lawsuit the size of the county budget for the next hundred years."

Du Pré nodded.

Someone tapped on the window.

"Sheriff Klein," said the young man. "I'm Steve McCown, from the Associated Press."

Benny nodded grimly. He got out.

Du Pré chuckled.

He started his old cruiser and he backed up and turned around and he headed back toward Toussaint.

When he got to the draw that the highway dipped down into, a mountain lion leaped out of the darkness right in front of the car, and then leaped away a fraction of a second before Du Pré's cruiser would have slammed into it.

"Shit," said Du Pré.

He drove on, and came to Toussaint to find Madelaine's car parked in front of her house and the lights on.

He got out and went in.

"Du Pré," said Madelaine, "where you been?"

"They raided Flowers, those other people," said Du Pré.

Madelaine looked at him.

He shook his head.

"They don't find nothing," said Du Pré.

"Girl is in hospital," said Madelaine, "two weeks for observation. She don't say anything they will have to let her go."

Du Pré nodded.

"Nothing," said Madelaine. "This poor kid is weeping away, her padded room there, and she won't talk. She is scared of something."

"Hell, maybe," said Du Pré.

"She is in hell," said Madelaine.

"Benetsee," said Du Pré.

"Him leave you all alone," said Madelaine. "Him not do that, he don't think you can find this out."

Du Pré nodded.

"These people are fools," he said. "But they are no more than that maybe."

"That is foolish," said Madelaine. "We got a dead girl and one can't even talk. That is more than fools."

"They don't got nothing to do with the dead girl," said Du Pré.

"No sign that Booger Tom, Father Van Den Heuvel?" said Madelaine.

"Maybe they are dead, too," said Du Pré. "Me, I have to go the mountains, haul their dead asses back down."

"You are not feeling good right now, Du Pré," said Madelaine. Du Pré shook his head.

"I see the girls riding Stewball and Moondog," he said. "They are all right."

"Yah," said Madelaine. "You do a good job, Jacqueline, Maria."

"I don't do much," said Du Pré.

He sighed, went to the cupboard, took out a bottle of whiskey. He made a ditch and he sat at the table. Madelaine had a glass of pink wine.

"Maybe the dead girl, she has nothing to do with this," said Madelaine.

Du Pré nodded.

"Maybe," he said.

"Maybe she is just killed, some bastard like those others," said Madelaine.

Du Pré shook his head.

"Those people don't wash who they kill," he said.

"Pidgeon would know better," said Madelaine.

"They are back soon," said Du Pré. "I . . . am . . . tired of this."

"So there is trouble now," said Madelaine. "County get sued. State, too."

Du Pré nodded.

"Pallas goes back, two days," he said.

"She seems good," said Madelaine.

"Yah," said Du Pré. "That Ripper, him dead meat."

They both laughed.

The telephone rang.

Madelaine looked at Du Pré.

He went to it, lifted it up, put it to his ear.

"Yah," he said.

"What the fuck are you *doing* out there?" said Harvey Wallace, Blackfeet and FBI.

"Raiding," said Du Pré. "Running families out of home, dead of night."

"So I understand," said Harvey.

"How do you know already?" said Du Pré.

"It is on the news," said Harvey. "CNN to be exact."

"Not too good," said Du Pré.

"You have anything to do with it?" said Harvey.

"I am there," said Du Pré. "Lead one bunch to one house. I tell them not to do it."

"Pidgeon told me about the dead girl," said Harvey. "She's digging away."

Du Pré waited.

"Some things down south have happened we wonder about," said Harvey.

Du Pré waited.

"So," said Harvey, "the Pidge will be back there soon, and maybe one or two others."

124

"OK," said Du Pré.

"Madelaine there?" said Harvey.

"Some guy wants you to dance," said Du Pré, handing off the telephone.

CHAPTER
24

"It's the god-danged government," said Sonny. He was cabling a trash container up on to the bed of his trailer.

Du Pré laughed.

"Used to be we just threw the garbage in a pit," said Sonny, "an' dozed it over when it was full. Now we got to haul it to a government-approved pit so they can doze it over. County had to come up with a lot more money."

"You are getting some of the money," said Du Pré.

Sonny shut the winch down. He threw some dogs at the rear of the trailer that held the heavy steel container firm on the rails.

Du Pré watched him drive away.

Trash is hauled hundred and fifty miles.

Madelaine came out of the back door of the saloon.

"Sonny hauled it away," she said, "so we can fill this one now."

The huge green trash container was twenty feet long and seven wide.

"Lennart called wanted you to meet him after school," said Madelaine.

Du Pré looked at her.

"I don't know what about," she said. "We were busy."

Du Pré looked at his watch.

"I go then," he said.

"He just called," said Madelaine. "You see about Sarah and that Ralph. Chappie, he is lonely and is drinking ditches before going, Bible study tonight."

Du Pré nodded.

"How is that?" he said.

"It will go like it goes," said Madelaine. She went back in the saloon.

Du Pré got in his cruiser and he drove toward Cooper. The little town was visible fifteen miles away from the top of one hill.

"Used to be lots bigger," said Du Pré.

He drove across the flat land to the east of the town. There were haying crews at work laying up the winter feed.

He drove up to the school just as the students were streaming out at day's end.

Six yellow school buses were parked and waiting to take the kids home.

Du Pré got out, rolled a smoke, watched the buses pull out one by one.

The van with the Texas plates that Flowers drove had been parked behind one of the buses.

"Shit," said Du Pré.

He went into the building.

He could hear voices down the hall.

He went toward the noise.

"There is no possibility," said Lennart.

"I got the proof right here," said Flowers. "Evolution is untrue. You won't even look at this, that isn't right. You wait, we'll elect people to the school board care more about education than you do."

Du Pré went in.

Flowers and his wife were sitting on folding chairs in front of Lennart's desk, nodding in agreement with each other.

Du Pré heard voices outside the office and then the doors opened.

Wilbur and Marge and several other people came in and stood behind their pastor.

"He won't do it," said Flowers. "I don't understand it."

Du Pré saw Sarah edge out of a classroom. She started for the door.

127

Du Pré walked away from the office and the rising complaints. He caught up with Sarah in the parking lot.

She was white-faced and shaking with rage.

"They won't stop, will they?" she said. "Now they are here with some bullshit that ass Flowers got claiming to find something called Intelligent Design in . . . the universe."

Du Pré nodded, rolled himself a smoke. She looked at it hungrily.

He handed it to her.

He made another for himself.

They smoked.

"How is the dog?" said Du Pré.

"He's fine," said Sarah. "Healing well. Eating like a pig. He is a handsome dog once he gets cleaned up. I give him olive oil and his coat is shiny."

"You are staying?" said Du Pré.

"Goddamned right," said Sarah. "I just get so angry. These people disrupt classes, they lie to the kids, and I have to try to repair it. They are so damned smug, like they had a personal hotline to God."

"Lennart called for me," said Du Pré.

"He wants to know if Father Van Den Heuvel can come and teach next week for me," said Sarah. "I have to go home. My father is having heart surgery and my mother is frantic and she isn't well either."

"Why call me?" said Du Pré.

Sarah grinned.

"He needs reinforcements," she said. "Now, I have had enough of these morons and I am going to go home and collect Ralph and he and I are going for a nice long walk."

Du Pré nodded.

She got in her little sedan and she drove way, toward the white-painted teacherage.

Du Pré walked toward the door of the school.

"Shit," he said, opening it.

Several people were talking all at once in the principal's office.

Lennart was behind his desk.

There were piles of papers and books on it.

"If we were to do as you ask," said Lennart, "we would violate the law. Every time you people get this going, it costs the school district a lot of money, which is not then available to educate children."

Du Pré looked at the faces.

They were all set.

"We got to go," he said to Lennart. "We got that appointment."

Lennart nodded and he locked his desk and he began to shoo people out of his office. They moved reluctantly, and it took a few minutes for him to haze them out and lock the door.

When they walked out, Flowers was leading the group in prayer.

"Thanks," said Lennart. "I didn't know what to do."

They got into Lennart's van.

He gripped the steering wheel tightly.

"I want to quit," he said. "I love it here. The kids are great. I love teaching. I don't love the parents, some of them anyway."

"Go up there," said Du Pré, pointing to a butte that sat near the fronts of the Wolf Mountains.

Lennart started the van and he drove off, up the gravel road that led to the canyon of Cooper Creek.

He turned off toward the butte on a dirt track.

"We walk maybe," said Du Pré.

Lennart looked back toward the school.

The people were still there, now out in the lot.

"I wondered if perhaps the priest could teach science next week," said Lennart. "I have enough to do and our usual substitute . . ."

Du Pré looked at him.

"She teaches English and Spanish," said Lennart. "She was a missionary in Central America . . ."

"Him do it," said Du Pré.

"I've called," said Lennart.

"Him, Booger Tom up in the mountains," said Du Pré. "They be back two, three days."

"God, I hope so," said Lennart. "He won't be put off if they come back, will he?"

Du Pré shrugged.

"He is pretty tough," he said.

"Sarah, she almost quit," said Lennart. "It is hard enough to find science teachers in the first place, and then to have them harassed by religious nuts . . ."

"What you want me for?" said Du Pré.

"I know Benny is busy . . . ," said Lennart.

He looked at the ground.

"We've been getting telephone calls," he said. "Just calls. They wait while we say *hello? hello?* and then they hang up."

Du Pré looked at him.

"I am about ready to quit, too," said Lennart. "I am worried about my wife and kids. The oldest one starts school next year."

Du Pré nodded.

"Was it always like this?" said Lennart.

"No," said Du Pré.

"Anyway," he said, "I doubt there is anything anyone can do about the calls. I tried the telephone company, and they are sending me a trap that records the numbers people call from."

Du Pré nodded.

"I'm OK, I guess," said Lennart. "I signed a contract for next year already, and I was thinking of not doing it."

Du Pré nodded.

"What is so crazy," he said, "is that the people who are here howling at me to teach religion in place of science, many of them homeschool their children."

"Jacqueline, my daughter, she does that," said Du Pré, "but she has all this computer stuff Bart got her, got tapes and movies of professors explaining things. Kids love it, they are doing all right."

"That isn't," said Lennart, "what these people are using."

"They are not violent," said Du Pré.

"Then what about the girl found dead?" said Lennart. "What about her? Or the other one who is in the mental hospital? These people can be dangerous, Du Pré."

Du Pré nodded.

"I don't know if I can do this another year," said Lennart.

Du Pré fished out his flask from his back pocket. He sipped some whiskey, offered it to Lennart, who shook his head.

"It is bad," he said, "but you don't want to run, you let them win."

"I have to go home," said Lennart.

Du Pré nodded.

CHAPTER 25

Du Pré looked through the binoculars.

Booger Tom was leading the pack string, and Du Pré could not see Father Van Den Heuvel.

"Christ," he said, snapping the folding frame shut.

They were three or so miles away. Not close enough to know and not far enough away to bother saddling a horse and riding to.

Du Pré walked through the big pasture, the horses milling curiously around him. When they came too close he waved his hat at them and they ran off.

He opened the gate that led to the upper pasture and he waited.

Booger Tom grinned wolfishly.

Father Van Den Heuvel was facedown over a saddle.

His face was turned toward Du Pré.

He looked mournful.

The string passed.

Du Pré walked along beside the priest.

"I fell," he said. "It is very embarrassing."

Du Pré looked at the priest's butt. There was a big tear in his trousers, and blood.

"I think," said Father Van Den Heuvel, "I am going to need stitches."

"Tossed him off in the dump," said Booger Tom. "I think one a your old whiskey bottles got him. Lucky he's still got his nuts."

"The pain from this is nothing to what I have endured from him," said Father Van Den Heuvel. "I could almost manage to believe in hell, just so I could hope that old bastard was in it."

Du Pré nodded.

"Didn't happen till this mornin'," said Booger Tom. "That's when a mule allus gits ya, when ya think everything is fine with the buggers. Can't trust a mule."

"I didn't fall off because the mule threw me," said Father Van Den Heuvel. "I fell off because I fall off things. I am so clumsy."

"You need to go, the clinic?" said Du Pré.

"I suppose," said Father Van Den Heuvel.

"I kin stitch him up," said Booger Tom. "Time you git thar it will be gittin' late to do it."

"Shit," said Father Van Den Heuvel. "He's right."

Du Pré nodded.

Booger Tom and Du Pré helped the priest down and he hobbled into the house Booger Tom called home, a roomy cabin with a big skylight over the table.

"I'll take care of the stock," said Du Pré. Father Van Den Heuvel was slowly stretching out across the plank table.

Booger Tom was humming.

"I got m' stitch kit here," he said, "but you could maybe get one of them ampicillin bottles from the fridge in the horse barn and a sy-reenge, and the smallest needle that there is there. I don't think any of them is that small."

Du Pré went to the horse barn and he found the antibiotic and a syringe and a needle, large, but not as large as all the others.

He took them back to Booger Tom.

Booger Tom was painting the big wound in Father Van Den Heuvel's right butt cheek with a yellow disinfectant.

Booger Tom took some tweezers and he pulled some glass shards out of the wound.

Father Van Den Heuvel was silent.

Du Pré saw his lips moving.

He was praying, maybe.

"Motherfuck!" said Father Van Den Heuvel.

Right. Praying.

"I go take care of the stock," said Du Pré.

"Have him all jake in no time," said Booger Tom.

As Du Pré left he heard the first scritch of gut being drawn through Father Van Den Heuvel's flesh.

He stripped all the tack off the horses and the mules.

Hooper and Noodles kept looking at the house where the priest was.

"You like him, eh?" said Du Pré.

He turned the horses out in the pasture to run with the others and he led Hooper to the big stall and Noodles followed. They both ate oats hungrily, from the nosebags that Du Pré hung on them.

He carried all the tack into the shed, set the saddles on trees, put the bridles on pegs and the blankets over the pole fence to dry.

Du Pré went to his cruiser and he got some whiskey and he drank and smoked until Booger Tom came out of the big cabin.

"Damn, I am good," said the old cowboy. "He's gonna have a fancy diamond-stitch ass there. All the whores will love it."

Du Pré snorted.

"Is he awake?" said Du Pré.

"Sure," said Booger Tom. "Havin' your ass stitched up ain't all that restful."

Du Pré found Father Van Den Heuvel standing, white-faced, holding on to a door jamb.

"If they ever find Bin Laden," said Father Van Den Heuvel, "they should give him to that old bandit."

"You are teaching science, the school next week," said Du Pré.

"I'm dying," said Father Van Den Heuvel, "or I would."

"The Christers are troublesome," said Du Pré. "They want religion taught there."

"I could do that, too," said the priest. "I might even consider pointing out that for Christians they spend a lot of time persecuting people. Illiterate sons of bitches, they make trash out of the Gospels."

Du Pré nodded.

"I got whiskey, the car, I take you home," he said.

"I hope," said Father Van Den Heuvel, "you have a great deal of whiskey."

Du Pré waited while the priest hobbled painfully out to the

133

cruiser. Du Pré got a fresh bottle of whiskey from the trunk and the big priest drank half of it in one long swallow.

"I pity them, actually," he said. "A bunch of losers. They are the people who stayed on and did not think much of life, at least not enough of life to think about it at all. Now they want petty tribal magic to make everything right, and wreak vengeance on all those they don't like. They hate themselves and so hate everyone."

Du Pré nodded.

"I am gassing on," said Father Van Den Heuvel. "I apologize. Now please take me home so I can whine by myself."

"There's no charge," said Booger Tom. "Saved ya a trip to the doc, and he ain't sewed up near as many folks as I has cows."

"Thank you," said Father Van Den Heuvel.

"Oh, not yet," said Booger Tom. "I'll be by tonight round midnight give you another shot of that ampicillin. Good stuff."

"Oh, God," said Father Van Den Heuvel.

"I tried to give myself one oncet," said Booger Tom. "Chased my ass with that needle from Miles City to Spokane, gave up, had to ask fer help."

"God," said Father Van Den Heuvel.

"Got to," said Booger Tom. "I done all this fancy needlework, can't let ya die of the ass rot now. You git two more shots tomorrow and then we'll see."

"Kill me," said Father Van Den Heuvel. "You have a gun." He looked at Du Pré.

"What a friend we have in Jeeee-zussss," sang Booger Tom, in a voice that sounded like goat farts in a tin shed.

Du Pré helped the big priest into the back seat, so he could ride on his hands and knees.

He drove to town and stopped by the little Catholic church.

Father Van Den Heuvel backed out of the seat and he went inside, bent over.

Du Pré carried in another bottle of whiskey for him.

"Oh, God," said the big priest. "I may live, damn it."

"I tell the school?" said Du Pré.

"Sure," said Father Van Den Heuvel.

Du Pré sipped some whiskey from his flask.

Father Van Den Heuvel had a giant slug from the bottle.

"You can't get drunk when you want to," he said, looking at the window.

"The principal, he is getting hang-up calls," said Du Pré.

"Sure," said Father Van Den Heuvel.

"They are giving a lot of trouble," said Du Pré.

"They are very sad people," said the big priest. "They mistake religion for faith."

Du Pré looked at him.

"The old man, Benetsee," said Father Van Den Heuvel, "is a very holy man, a very spiritual one. It shines from him."

"You like him," said Du Pré.

"Very much," said Father Van Den Heuvel.

"Him, gone, I wish he was here," said Du Pré.

"Perhaps he holds up the earth on his shoulders," said the big priest. "Some say twelve men do that. Anyway, there isn't anything holy about these people."

"There are ver' many of them," said Du Pré.

Father Van Den Heuvel nodded.

"Modern communications," he said, "spread ignorance as well as information, and I don't know where this will end."

Du Pré had some more whiskey, rolled himself a smoke.

Father Van Den Heuvel nodded and Du Pré rolled one for him.

"I will be happy to help," he said.

"Maybe you feel better by then," said Du Pré.

"Better or not," said Father Van Den Heuvel, "it beats lying around here thinking on my own pain."

Du Pré went out to his cruiser and he drove up to the saloon.

It was late in the afternoon. Some of the ranch folk were coming in for beers and burgers, to take a break from the work.

There was laughter inside, and a couple of cowboys playing pool whooped when one of them made a hard shot.

Du Pré sat at the bar.

Madelaine brought him a ditch.

Du Pré drank it.

"Father Van Den Heuvel he is back?" said Madelaine.

Du Pré nodded.

CHAPTER
26

"It all hinges upon the girl in the Billings hospital who so far refuses to talk for whatever reason. Way things are going, she will refuse to talk because she is a paranoid schizophrenic, and at that point the county ought to just spare itself the agony and pay up," said Tapley, the county attorney.

"Jesus," said Benny Klein. "I called the state because we don't have the people to deal with a stupid situation like this. Fer chrissake, we had a dead girl in the ditch out thataway and then this one run off from them people."

"According to the lawsuit," said Tapley, "the Flowerses were aware of the mental problems their eldest daughter had and they were doing what they were supposed to do. When our jackbooted government thugs kicked down the door in the dead of night, they were gambling that when they got in they would find evidence of criminal acts. They did not. So they are hiding in the sewers of Helena and telling the Flowerses' folks with the writs that it was all our fault."

Du Pré looked at the cigarette smoking in the ashtray on the county attorney's desk.

First hopeful sign, he thought.

He rolled a smoke and lit it.

"So whatta we do?" said Benny.

Tapley sighed. He picked up his butt.

"About all that we can do," he said, "is countersue the state. The Ardreys also are party to the lawsuit. The jackbooted government thugs who raided their homes did not find evidence of criminal acts, either."

"This is all crap," said Pidgeon. "Those kids won't talk because they are terrified of something. Scared to death. You had the telephone calls, you had the dead girl, you had poor little Raylee Flowers running like a rabbit. There's something to this we just can't find it yet."

"As I said at the beginning," said Tapley, "it all depends on what Raylee has to say. Where do they get these goddamned names?"

"Hookworm," said Pidgeon. "Very strange place."

"We are underinsured," said Tapley. "Commissioners were cutting corners."

"Is this real," said Benny, "or just some goddamned lawyers smellin' money?"

"It's real," said Tapley. "And they smell money, too. See, in America everyone is protected by certain rights set out in our Constitution. Now, legally, our position is poor because we are."

Pidgeon snorted.

"Thanks for coming," said Tapley. "I have explained the situation, and now I have an appointment. I am to shoot gophers with my grandson."

"Lotta gophers this year," said Benny.

"We don't get very lucky," said Tapley, "that fat Bible-thumping idiot will own the gophers, too."

"I just asked fer some help," said Benny.

Tapley looked at him.

"You want to know what happened? I will tell you. Our Congress put up money for riot and raid training for police. This training was provided by the military. We have a very fine military, but they tend to obliterate whatever is in their path and discuss methods later. They give our police all this fine training. The police get all sorts of new toys—vests, nifty black costumes, machine guns, laser-guided whatnots . . . ," said Tapley.

Benny looked down into his cup of cold coffee.

"And then like small boys everywhere *they want to use the toys*," said Tapley. "Like my grandson, who was recently given a twenty-two. For his birthday."

"How old?" said Pidgeon.

"Six," said Tapley.

"Jesus," said Pidgeon.

"He wanted an AK-47," said Tapley. "Count your blessings. We have a somewhat different culture out here, ma'am."

Pidgeon looked at Benny.

"Don't worry," she said. "We'll find something."

"Good," said Benny. "Then I'll ask for the Hundred and First Airborne so we can fuck it up real good."

"Always cheerful," said Pidgeon. "Like I said, we have some other avenues we are pursuing."

"Meaning the FBI," said Benny.

Pidgeon shrugged.

"Oh, good," said Benny. "We can have another Waco."

"We are not," said Pidgeon, "going to have another one of those. Because we are not having the staties in on this again and believe me, after Waco, there were some very hard questions asked."

"What if the state comes anyway?" said Benny.

"And give the Flowerses' attorneys a sure thing?" said Pidgeon. "No, they won't touch it now. Not even if we asked them, which we won't."

They walked out of Tapley's office and he shut the door and he locked it. The county building was silent. People came to work in it when there was work, which was not very often.

Pidgeon and Du Pré walked out to his old cruiser. Du Pré opened the door for her and after she got in he shut it.

He got in and started the engine. It purred.

"Could I drive?" said Pidgeon.

"*Non*," said Du Pré. "You drive too fast."

He went to the main road and then he turned left and headed for Toussaint.

A few miles before they got there he slowed.

He turned on a spur road that led to the town dump.

"Going to check on what's new in the swap section?" asked Pidgeon.

There were a few discarded appliances, some batteries stacked near the edge of the drive-up. A huge green metal container sat below, mostly filled with bags of garbage.

There was an old rocking chair sitting by the batteries. It was missing some slats on its back. Du Pré looked at it.

Pidgeon got out of the car.

She bent over the rocking chair.

She pulled a penknife from her pocket. She scraped at the paint.

"This chair has really good lines," she said.

She scraped off white paint and yellow paint under that and under that brown paint.

A thin lozenge of wood appeared.

Pidgeon wet her forefinger and she rubbed it. She stared at it.

"I think it's rosewood," she said.

Du Pré looked at it.

"Maybe," he said. "Arms anyway."

He put the chair in the trunk. It sat on the stuff that was there already, and he held the trunk lid down with a bungee cord.

They drove on.

Bart's SUV was parked in front of the saloon. Du Pré pulled in beside it and he shut off the car.

"Could I pay you to fix that chair?" said Pidgeon.

Du Pré shrugged.

"Bart is not your craftsman," she said. "He does fine work with a backhoe no matter what it is he is working on. He tried to fix a hinge on my jewelry box . . ."

"Yah," said Du Pré.

They went in.

Bart was sitting at the bar, and he smiled when he saw Pidgeon.

"Hi, hon," said Pidgeon, kissing him.

"How'd it go?" said Bart.

"The county attorney is a very droll fellow," said Pidgeon.

"I could call Foote," said Bart.

Pidgeon shook her head.

"Won't come to that," she said. "If Du Pré and I get to the bottom of this."

"I thought you quit," said Bart. He looked scared.

"Took a leave," said Pidgeon.

"I wish you'd quit," said Bart.

"I can't," said Pidgeon. "There are a lot of really bad people out there. Time to time it seems I am the only one can figure out how to get 'em."

Bart nodded. He sucked on his soda morosely.

"Don't sulk," said Pidgeon, "I'll whop you."

Susan Klein put a ditch in front of Du Pré. He sipped it.

Father Van Den Heuvel came in. He was walking very carefully.

"How's the embroidery on your ass?" said Pidgeon.

"Levity," said the priest, "is unkind. It hurts and it itches."

"I'd really hate to have Booger Tom doing surgery on me," said Pidgeon. "That old goat can do about anything, though."

"An old cowboy at the end of life," said Father Van Den Heuvel thoughtfully.

Pidgeon looked at him, eyes narrowed.

"Often," said the priest, "when death crowds close, people turn to the solaces of religion."

"You son of a bitch," said Pidgeon. "You know, I am really beginning to like you."

Bart looked at Du Pré, who was looking carefully down into his ditchwater highball.

Susan Klein was laughing and trying not to.

"You wouldn't," she said.

Father Van Den Heuvel smiled in a wintry way.

"Chappie couldn't stand it anymore," said Pidgeon.

"There is a possibility," said Father Van Den Heuvel, "that Booger Tom might think very poorly of the notion. It might make him vengeful."

"Not," said Pidgeon, "until after he does it. Booger Tom is a very fair-minded man. He would wait until he had cause."

They all looked at Bart.

"What?" he said.

"We need to have Booger Tom join the Christers," said Pidgeon.

Bart's eyebrows shot up.

"I don't think he would like that," he said.

"He works," said Pidgeon, "for you."

"I would not touch this with a barge pole," said Bart.

"OK," said Pidgeon, "I'll do it."

"Christ," said Bart.

CHAPTER
27

Du Pré spread the paint remover on the parts of the rocking chair. The stuff was like petroleum jelly, thick and cloudy.

The old paint began to wrinkle and move.

Someone stepped across the doorway of the woodshop.

Du Pré glanced that way.

"You didn't have nothin' to do with that there ree-quest that gorgeous woman who un-accountably favors that asshole Bart just made of me, now did you?" said Booger Tom.

"*Non,*" said Du Pré.

"I thought not," said Booger Tom. "As we has known each other fer a long time. Thing I come to ask is after I kill all of them, will you be whinin' about the fact that I did?"

"*Non,*" said Du Pré. "I did not say anything, you know. So they will just have to live with their idea."

"I allus thought you was a smart son of a bitch," said Booger Tom. "If you was wonderin', I already figgered out that wafer-gnawin' son of a bitch in the granny dress is at the bottom of it."

Du Pré took a scraping tool and he slid a line of dissolved paint away from one of the rocking chair arms.

"Now," said Booger Tom, "I wouldn't be near mad enough to kill all of 'em if I didn't do it, you see, so I guess I will go on over and listen to them Bible-thumpers. I has done so in the past, which is why I have such a low opinion of Christianity."

"I have nothing to do with it," said Du Pré.

"That priest might make a fair mule man," said Booger Tom. "He's hopeless with horses, but mules and him, they seem to communicate some. Noodles pitched him into the garbage dump outta good humor. I saw it. You know how a mule grins just before he kicks you clear to Idaho or he manages to git yer hat and start eatin' it while you can't get at him to get it back."

"Yah," said Du Pré.

"Though I dunno exactly what I am supposed to look for," said Booger Tom.

"Those girls," said Du Pré, "the others there, they will be afraid of somebody. Maybe there is somebody there is not from here."

"You kin be born here and not be *from* here," said Booger Tom.

Du Pré went to the garden hose and he twisted the nozzle and he washed the old paint and stripping gel away.

"You kin make good bombs outta this stuff," said Booger Tom, reading the label on the can.

"Yah," said Du Pré.

"I been here a long time," said Booger Tom. "Used to was people had hope and now I don't think they got that much. I kin feel sorry fer them but I don't understand this business. Who would kill a little girl?"

Du Pré shut the hose off.

There was still thick paint here and there on the wood, but it was rosewood, a rich red-brown veined with lighter tones.

"So you don't got no ideas?" said Booger Tom.

Du Pré shook his head.

The old cowboy wandered away, looking at the ground as he walked.

Du Pré put the chair pieces out in the sun to dry.

He went up to the main house and he knocked on the door.

Pidgeon opened it.

"Is he going to do it?" she said.

Du Pré nodded.

Father Van Den Heuvel was perched on a straight chair, all his weight on the piece of his butt that wasn't full of stitches.

"We thought," he said, "given his reaction, that he would not."

"He do it," said Du Pré. "Then he hunt you all down, kill you one by one."

"Is that all?" said Pidgeon.

"*Non,*" said Du Pré. "The chair is rosewood. I have to get some more stripper. It is ver' expensive."

"I wonder who made the chair?" she said.

Du Pré shrugged.

Du Pré went out to his cruiser and he drove to Toussaint. He parked at the saloon and he went in and found Madelaine beading. She had the tip of her tongue at the right corner of her mouth and she was squinting.

"Old age, it is hell," she said. She set the stitch and she pulled the thread through the soft leather.

"Booger Tom, he is getting that religion," said Du Pré.

"Chappie is ver' sad," said Madelaine. "That Sarah girl is not interested, him. She was very nice, but firm. So poor Chappie he is out in his trailer now drinking his whiskey, thinking about life."

Du Pré nodded.

"He got to go, the VA tomorrow. See about his benefits, his job training. He was going to be a electrician maybe, but he can't climb like he would have to."

Du Pré made himself a ditch.

"Lot of things he can do," said Du Pré.

"If he want to do them, is all," said Madelaine.

"I maybe go with Booger Tom, the church," said Du Pré. "Say he cannot drive after dark."

"Oh, yes," said Madelaine, putting another stitch in.

"They don't trust me there anyway," said Du Pré. "But I got an excuse."

"You are worried," said Madelaine.

"Maybe it is not them," said Du Pré. "Maybe it just is that we want it to be them."

Madelaine nodded.

"Wait outside, though," she said.

Du Pré looked at her.

"Somebody knows something," said Madelaine. "You are near but not inside maybe you see something, maybe somebody says something to you, they are outside. Toilets are outside that place, I remember."

Some cowboys came in then, sat at the bar, and Madelaine put down her beadwork and she drew them beers.

Du Pré went out to his cruiser and he got in and he drummed his fingers on the steering wheel.

He started the car and he drove toward Benetsee's, and up the rutted track.

The old man had been there. Du Pré went to the sweat lodge. There were still coals in the firepit.

He went to the front door of the cabin.

There were some tracts there, Jehovah's Witnesses.

Du Pré snorted.

It was getting to be time for the evening service.

Du Pré drove back to Bart's and he found Booger Tom in his cabin. The old cowboy had shaved, washed, combed his hair and mustaches. He wore a clean white shirt and a new bandanna and a brushed suede vest and polished boots and twill pants. He had a brand-new hat, very pale gray, with a horsehair band.

"I drive you to church," said Du Pré.

"I kin drive myself," said Booger Tom.

"Madelaine says I drive you, you cannot drive at night. I wait outside for you," said Du Pré.

Booger Tom thought a moment.

"Makes sense," he said.

They got in the cruiser and Du Pré drove off toward the little white church, a clapboard box built perhaps a hundred years before. There were two white-painted outhouses in back.

They were early, and Du Pré and Booger Tom sat on the hood of the cruiser smoking and looking up at the Wolf Mountains.

"I been round here a long time," said Booger Tom. "You know, lately I been thinkin' about here. C'mon, I want t'show you somethin'."

They walked to the little graveyard off to the left of the church. It was poorly tended, and rank with grasses.

Booger Tom reached over the sheep wire and he pulled up a plant.

"Bluestem," he said. "Got yer bunchgrass there and yer wheat-grass, too. You know what this is?"

Du Pré looked at him.

"This was what was here 'fore we all come," said Booger Tom.

"This is the prairie. It is here, and some along the old railroad lines, in some places never got used up. I think it is just waitin' to come back. Waitin' for us to go. Very patient, the prairie."

Du Pré looked at the old cowboy.

"Good grass comes back," he said, "maybe the buffalo will be here again. Buffalo. We done killed all of them, starve the Indians, and we run cattle. Hell, now I hear there's ranches runnin' water buffalo. Them Asian buffalo with the funny horns."

Du Pré looked up at the Wolf Mountains.

An eagle flew across their faces.

"Not much more than a century," said the old cowboy, "probably be some sort of park for rich idiots ride around on in their machines, but it will be much like it was. It is too tough a place for city people."

"Sometimes," said Du Pré, "it has been too tough a place for me."

A pickup truck pulled in, a rancher and his wife got out. They waved to Du Pré and Booger Tom and they went inside.

"I guess," said Booger Tom, "I had best suck it up. Havin' to listen to fools never been one of my strong suits."

More and more trucks and cars appeared on the road.

The Flowerses' van with the Texas plates pulled in.

Flowers and his wife and their children got out. The kids filed meekly into the church.

Flowers and his wife waddled up the steps and inside.

"No help fer it," said Booger Tom. He went over to the church and he went inside.

There was singing, though no organ.

Du Pré had some whiskey.

He could hear Flowers's fat voice, though mercifully not the words.

A breeze came up.

A truck came very quickly up the road, a roostertail of dust behind.

Sonny.

Sonny jumped out of his truck and he ran to the door.

Du Pré looked at his hands.

He had old paint on them.

Sonny waited until the singing got loud and he let himself in.

145

Du Pré looked at the battered old truck Sonny had driven to the church.

He walked over and he looked through the open window.

There was a pistol on the seat, a big revolver.

And another skin magazine.

CHAPTER
28

The congregation filed out of the church, quiet and inward.

Du Pré smoked, sipped whiskey.

Booger Tom was the last man out. He was walking with Sonny, who was talking rapidly to him.

They stopped.

Sonny pounded his fist into his palm.

Booger Tom nodded.

The Flowerses came out, beaming, self-satisfied.

Flowers looked round the parking lot, saw Sonny and Booger Tom, and walked over to them.

Sonny went on talking, Flowers rocked back and forth on his heels.

He looked very smug.

Few seconds Booger Tom get mad and hit him, Du Pré thought.

Booger Tom listened, nodding, and he said something and then he shook hands with Sonny and Flowers.

He pointed to Du Pré.

The three came over to where Du Pré sat on his car.

The rest of the congregation was driving off, or about to.

Booger Tom got to Du Pré first.

"Got a gun?" he hissed.

Du Pré kept his face blank.

"You got to think about yer immortal soul," said Sonny.

Flowers nodded. He would not look at Du Pré.

"I got some prayin' to do," said Booger Tom. "Alone."

"I'd be happy to pray with you," said Sonny.

"Best do it alone," said Booger Tom. He got in the cruiser.

Flowers started to say something but didn't.

Du Pré got in and he started the engine and he waited until Flowers moved out of the way before he drove off.

"Ya didn't have to do that on my account," said Booger Tom. "Ya coulda run over both of them."

Du Pré laughed. He offered Booger Tom the flask.

The old cowboy had a long pull.

"M'parents was Bible-thumpers," said Booger Tom, "so soon as I could fork a horse I left. Old man used to git drunk and whip everybody Saturday nights. Sunday he'd be in church beggin' the Lord fer forgiveness."

Du Pré rolled a smoke while he accelerated.

"Sonny thinks of hisself as a preacher," said Booger Tom. "He wants to baptize me."

"Oh," said Du Pré.

"I hate baths," said Booger Tom. "They leave me weak and very feverish."

Du Pré backed off on the gas as a hill rose before them.

"That fat fool they drug up here from Texas," said Booger Tom, "went on forever 'bout how women is how the Devil gits in the door. After that he complained about the two hundred fourteen dollars seventy-three cents in the collection. Said it failed to *increase,* after which he quoted some Bible verses about *increase.*"

Du Pré turned the cruiser on to the long road that wound up to the benchlands and Bart's ranch.

Booger Tom rode in silence.

"We done knowed each other a long time, Doo Pray," said Booger Tom, "and what I am supposed to find there I cannot think of. It's our neighbors, most of 'em not very bright and all of them scared. There ain't anything there. And I ain't going back there."

Du Pré nodded.

"I dunno what is happenin' with them girls. You got a dead one and a crazy one. You hear anything about her?" said Booger Tom.

Du Pré shook his head.

"They may have nothin' to do with nothin'," said Booger Tom.

"Dead girl was not raped and not beaten," said Du Pré. "They think she maybe starved to death, got sick from no food."

"Whatever these fools is up to," said Booger Tom, "it ain't starvin' girls to death. Hell, I know most of 'em. Wilbur and Marge and Sonny'd give ya the shirt off their backs and pay fer the tailorin' it didn't fit. This idiot they got preachin' is stupid as they come, but he don't strike me as any more than that. It is prolly no more'n some bastard dumped a body here and Flowers has a teenage kid got the vapors."

Du Pré nodded.

"Now that we got social workers carry machine guns an' raid folks' houses the dead of night," said Booger Tom, "how long do you think it is 'fore people get killed. *I* wouldn't bust in to no house here after that. No, sir."

"Yah," said Du Pré.

"I also ain't all that happy with spyin' on m'neighbors," said Booger Tom. "I doubt they is sacrificin' virgins on a rock up Cooper Creek."

Du Pré turned in to the long road that went to Bart's house.

He pulled in and Pidgeon came out of the house, bundled up in a thick sweater. The wind off the mountains was cold.

"The hospital is releasing the girl tomorrow," said Pidgeon. "She did talk, a little, anyway. She denies being mistreated."

"She's scared," said Booger Tom. "Scared to death." He pulled the DVD out of his coat pocket. He looked at it like it had been live once and dead too long to find about one's person.

"The Reverend Armstrong Dealey," said Booger Tom. "Sonny shoved this on me. Says the man is very strong in the Lord."

Pidgeon snorted.

"I ain't goin' again," said Booger Tom. "I know it is a free country but I ain't goin' to go and listen no more. I don't want it said of me I thought badly of people 'cause of their religion, but these folks who is reasonable you see 'em change into somethin' else they go through that door. I can't explain it, but it gives me the whips and jangles."

"Their religion," said Pidgeon, "has provided a dead girl."

Booger Tom nodded. "Mebbee."

"You want this?" he said, waving the plastic case the DVD was in.

Du Pré took the case. There was a poorly printed photograph of a man in a silvery-gray suit, his long black hair combed and oiled into a pompadour, holding a Bible in his right hand, high, as though he meant to swat a bug with it. His mouth was open and his eyes were closed.

"I done had enough of the religious for one day," said Booger Tom. "You going to stick that in the box there I do believe I will go out to my cabin and read somethin' I kin learn from."

The old cowboy left.

Bart came in, looking sheepish.

"I hit something on the computer," he said, "and everything disappeared."

Pidgeon nodded.

"I can perhaps fix it tomorrow," she said.

Bart looked very uncomfortable.

"Oh, Christ," said Pidgeon. "No!"

"I was having trouble with mine," he said. "I just wanted to check a stock sale, they had some Santa Gertrudis—"

"On my computer," said Pidgeon. She massaged her eyebrows with the long fingers of her left hand.

"I thought it would be OK," said Bart.

"Sweetie," said Pidgeon, "keep your fucking hands offa my computer. It's not a goddamned backhoe."

"Ah," said Bart.

Pidgeon looked at Du Pré, and the box in his hand.

He gave it to her.

She walked to the TV set and she put the disc in the tray and she pressed the button on the control.

Bart and Du Pré and Pidgeon sat, looking at the screen.

The credits were brief.

A massed choir in white robes bellowed out a hymn. They were on a huge stage.

The Reverend Dealey strutted out from stage left, in his glimmering silver suit.

He put little reading glasses on, and he peered down at something on the lectern.

The choir bellowed on.

A band largely composed of electric instruments was loud, one player off-key and -rhythm.

The choir shut up suddenly and the band stopped, all but the lost picker.

"America has lost the godly way!" yelled the preacher.

"Yes!" yelled the choir.

Pidgeon shut off the sound.

"This craphead," she said, "will rant on about godless politicians, the home-sexual agenda, and so forth and so on. Just look at that fat fuck."

The preacher waved a Bible, turned one way and then the other, his mouth working rapidly.

"Sonny, eh?" said Pidgeon. "This is very interesting. Dealey keeps popping up here and there. Not in person. In these things, or in printed tracts."

"He come here?" said Du Pré.

"Nope," said Pidgeon. "These days you can use modern communications. Dealey lives in a fortress out of which he seldom ventures."

Du Pré nodded.

"I go," he said.

The preacher was red-faced and looked enraged.

"Thanks for this," said Pidgeon. "Haven't seen this one."

Du Pré went out and he drove to Toussaint.

Susan and Madelaine were finishing up the nightly cleaning. The place smelled of bleach and Murphy's oil soap.

They finished and Susan made Du Pré a drink and she poured wine for herself and Madelaine.

"I think I might sell this place," she said. "Benny and I could leave. Move to Canada."

"Yah," said Madelaine. "Pretty strange here now."

"Just have to find folks to shit on fer Jesus," said Susan. "What is happening to my friends and neighbors?"

"Bad times," said Madelaine.

"We've had 'em before," said Susan. "Got through them."

Du Pré nodded and Madelaine patted Susan's hand.

151

CHAPTER
29

"Thanks," said Father Van Den Heuvel, backing out of the rear seat of Du Pré's cruiser.

He bent over when he got to Du Pré's window.

"I can't drive very well with my ass half gone," he said. "I don't drive that well in any case."

"I come and get you, what time?" said Du Pré.

"Four," said Father Van Den Heuvel. "I don't have to coach basketball."

"You play basketball?" said Du Pré.

Father Van Den Heuvel looked at him.

Du Pré backed up and he drove off toward Toussaint. The American flag in front of the Cooper School snapped in the breeze.

Du Pré looked to the west. It was clear now, but there was weather over the horizon.

He drove down a back road and then across the bench road to the dirt track that led to Benetsee's cabin. The old man was not there. But Du Pré saw fresh tracks which came from the east. Someone on horseback had been there that morning.

Du Pré squatted down and he looked at the track. He put a

forefinger in the cup of the print and he looked at the smear of damp dirt on his skin.

He got up, took off his hat, waved it at his face. It was warm and it was going to get hot by noon.

He went to the sweat lodge and he found coals at the bottom of the fire pit where the stones had been heated. He held his hand over the stones in the lodge and there was warmth radiating from them.

He walked along the bank of the stream, smelling the mint crushed under his boots.

"Old man," he said, "you are something."

He shook his head and he laughed.

He went back to his cruiser, took out a jug of wine and a packet of tobacco and papers, and he put them in the kindling box by the front door.

Then he drove to Toussaint.

Madelaine was in the saloon, on her high stool, beading.

She did not look up when he came in.

She drew the thread through and she put down the doeskin bag.

"Pallas, she is staying another week," said Madelaine.

Du Pré nodded.

"She don't have to go back at all," he said.

"She knows that," said Madelaine. "She insists on flying with Moondog and the cargo plane is not here for . . . nine days."

Madelaine looked at Du Pré.

"What is it?" she said.

Du Pré shrugged.

"Oh, that," said Madelaine. "Pallas has been going to see Benetsee. So you are bent that he won't talk to you. Maybe he don't need, talk to you, he trust you."

"I need, talk to him," said Du Pré.

"Medicine person," said Madelaine, "aren't like us, you know."

"Old bastard," said Du Pré. "He help me figure this out, he would."

"Catfoot teach you to swim," said Madelaine.

He put me on a horse, ride into the river with my horse on a lead, I fall off and grab the horse's mane, I am swimming, one arm, then two.

"Yah," said Du Pré.

"You got nothing to do," said Madelaine. "Fix that rocking chair for Pidgeon."

"I am waiting, the wood. Wood to fix it is seven hundred dollars. One piece of wood. I better make it right first time," said Du Pré.

"Seven hundred dollars," said Madelaine. "How big is this piece?"

Du Pré gestured, the length and breadth and thickness.

"Gold would probably be cheaper," said Madelaine. "Why so expensive?"

"They cut all them rosewood trees down," said Du Pré. "They grow slowly and there are not very many of them."

"It is about right," said Madelaine. "Pidgeon she sees something, the dump, and it costs seven hundred dollars to fix it, probably the thing is not worth that."

"Ver' pretty wood," said Du Pré.

"So that Father Van Den Heuvel is teaching science," said Madelaine. "I hope his lesson don't include mixing chemicals."

"I know I go back," said Du Pré, "school is still there he did not."

The front door opened and a young man in a suit came in. He was carrying an attaché case and some electronic dingus.

He waited a moment to let his eyes adjust.

Then he walked up to the bar.

"Good afternoon, ma'am," he said. "I am looking for a . . . Gabriel Du Pré."

Du Pré looked at him.

"Him dead," said Du Pré. "They take him the hospital this morning."

"And where is that hospital?" said the young man.

"Billings," said Du Pré.

"How sad," said the young man. "And since you are Gabriel Du Pré, I must serve you with this summons." He handed an envelope to Du Pré. Then he turned around the electronic dingus. Du Pré's face was on it, a photograph from one of his records.

Du Pré tore the summons in half.

The young man shook his head.

"Won't help," he said. "You have a court order to appear and be deposed."

"*Non,*" said Du Pré.

"You can be jailed for contempt," said the young man.

"Fine," said Du Pré, "but I don't talk. Here is your papers."

The young man backed away.

"I can't take them," said the young man.

"You take them," said Du Pré, "or I arrest you, littering, and you go to jail here."

The young man took the papers.

He went back out the door.

"Pret' smart," said Madelaine. "Go to jail over some papers."

"I am not going, jail," said Du Pré.

"They want you, the lawsuit against the county," said Madelaine.

Du Pré nodded.

"We got a lot of trouble here," said Madelaine.

"I don't care about that," said Du Pré. "I care about that dead girl."

"Yes," said Madelaine, "I know.

"Don't know what happened to her," said Du Pré.

Madelaine nodded.

"Pallas," said Du Pré, "she is going to see that Benetsee."

Madelaine nodded.

"She is sad all the time," said Madelaine. "She has been some better now."

They heard a horse outside and some boots landed on the wooden porch and a moment later Pallas swept in.

She was rosy-cheeked from her ride. Her long black hair was braided in a single long braid and she wore a new hat, dark blue felt with a horsehair band.

"Your grandpa is jealous," said Madelaine. "Benetsee talk to you but he won't talk, Du Pré."

"He say that," said Pallas. "Him got stuff he is doing."

Du Pré rolled a smoke.

"What are you up to with him?" he said.

"I have things," said Pallas. "I have things I have to do. He makes thing better for me. I wake up crying for a while, Grand-père, it was not good."

Du Pré nodded.

"Him say anything about the dead girl?" he said.

Pallas shook her head.

"He say there is something wrong with his stove," said Pallas. "Wanted to know if you could fix it."

Du Pré nodded.

"His stove is about five hundred years old," said Du Pré, "maybe older."

"That was what he said," said Pallas.

"So," said Madelaine, "Lourdes is in school and you are riding horses."

"I have work to do," said Pallas. "Got a computer you can work anywhere."

"Stove," said Du Pré.

He got up and he went round the bar and he kissed Madelaine and he went out to his cruiser and he drove out to Benetsee's.

"Stove," said Du Pré.

The cabin was open, Benetsee never locked it.

The woodstove that heated the small cabin was also the cook-stove, an old Monarch, with a hot water reservoir built around the chimney. A pipe from the reservoir went out over the sink, and a red cast-iron pump stood on the drainboard, which brought sweet well water.

Du Pré looked at the stove.

He took a section of newspaper and he lit it with his lighter and he put it in the firebox.

One of the cast-iron slabs on the side of the box was cracked.

Cracked badly. There were pieces of it missing.

"Shit," said Du Pré. "Where I find another one of those?"

He took the broken slab out and he put it in the trunk of his cruiser.

He walked round back of the cabin.

There was another fire in the pit where the stones were heated, but when he called Benetsee's name there was no answer.

A kingfisher flew past, going downstream, a bright fish in its bill.

Du Pré walked back to his cruiser.

He drove out to Bart's and he went to the welding shed with the slab. He tried to braze over the hole but the brazing would not stick. He dropped some on his boot and scorched the leather.

"Shit," said Du Pré.

When he picked up the slab it separated.

Du Pré looked at the metal.

It was old cast iron and well shot with pure carbon.

"Never get this," he said.

156

He looked for a piece of slab steel he could cut but there was not a piece both big enough and thick enough.

The slab of iron was cool enough to touch in a few minutes.

Du Pré heard scrabbling under the plank floor.

A badger stuck its head up through a hole, and looked at Du Pré with its black eyes.

CHAPTER
30

Du Pré went to the saloon. Susan Klein was there, and when he came in she handed him the papers he had torn in half the day before.

"Telling a judge to stuff his order up his ass," said Susan, "is a really dumb thing to do. Benny would no doubt have to arrest you. You are not going to do that to Benny."

Du Pré nodded.

"Go talk to Tapley about it," said Susan. "But my guess is you will have to talk to these people."

Du Pré rolled a smoke.

"You read the papers?" he said.

"Of course I did," said Susan. "Your deposition is a week from Thursday. You have plenty of time to figure out how not to have Benny have to arrest you. I am not kidding, Du Pré. That happens I am going to get real mad with you."

Du Pré nodded.

"OK," he said. He put the papers in his pocket.

"Go and talk to Tapley now," said Susan. "He's there today. I checked. He's actually expecting you. I made an appointment."

"OK," said Du Pré.

"You have an hour," said Susan. "Now would you like a nice

drink? Breakfast? A cheeseburger? Case you are missing the threat, they will be the last ones you ever have in here you don't go."

"OK," said Du Pré.

"Men," said Susan Klein, "sometimes annoy me."

She shoved a ditch across the bar and Du Pré drank it quickly. Susan bared her teeth.

Du Pré went out and he got in his cruiser and he drove to Cooper. Tapley was in his office, boots on his desk, tossing balls of paper at a wastebasket stuck high on a wall.

He made a bank shot just as Du Pré stuck his head in the door.

"Good," said Tapley. "Susan called and said if you didn't show up she was going to make your life utter hell."

"Yah," said Du Pré.

He pulled out the summons and he put the pieces on the desk. Tapley glanced at them.

"They have a hotshot law firm in Dallas, where else, representing the abused and misunderstood Christians Texas sends up here to throw dead girls in our highway barrows," said Tapley. "They have a lot of money, they have hired some young and hungry lawyers and given them the scent of blood, and so here we are, thanks to Pidgeon, I guess."

"That is not fair," said Du Pré. "We know it is them, just not how and where they did this thing."

"If they did it," said Tapley. "I looked at the report from the medical examiner. It could have been a lot of things, none of them necessarily criminal. Disposing of a body like that is, but it sure would have been nice if there had been enough evidence to justify a warrant. There was not."

"So what do I do?" said Du Pré.

"Well," said Tapley, "I wuz you I'd find out a whole lot of things real fast, like before this deposition. You know what they do in depositions? They can ask you about anything at all and you have to answer. It is a favorite trick. They get you mad and you blow up and then they get you for perjury or for contempt."

"I am not answering their questions," said Du Pré. "I don't like these people."

"Not a defense," said Tapley.

"OK," said Du Pré.

"Gabriel," said Tapley, "I know you. If you have to do this, you take me with you. I can probably save you years in prison."

159

"OK," said Du Pré. "There is not a conflict of interest?"

"No," said Tapley. "Not yet anyway."

"Maybe I am in the mountains," said Du Pré.

"Just what they want," said Tapley, "is for you to do something dumb like that."

"Who are these bastards?" said Du Pré.

"Americans," said Tapley, "who don't like having the doors kicked down by thugs and people harassed for no good reason. They did not screw up, Du Pré. The state did, and first off the state is going to claim it got lied to by Cooper County lawmen. Lawyers live off messes."

"OK," said Du Pré.

"And don't kill anybody and make it worse," said Tapley.

Du Pré looked at him.

Tapley's eyes were twinkling.

Du Pré went back out to his cruiser.

He sat a moment, sipping from his flask, and then he drove down the back road to Benetsee's.

He walked round back and down the little incline to the flat where the sweat lodge was.

He sat on a stump in the shade.

The kingfisher flew past.

"Old man!" Du Pré yelled. "I am sitting here till you come. I sit here until I am bones on this stump."

Du Pré went half asleep, like he did when he was hunting deer.

A horsefly buzzed around his face, lit. Du Pré slapped and killed it. He looked at the big dead fly in his hand.

He went back to sleep.

He heard hooves far away, he woke, he looked over east at the benchlands.

Pallas and Moondog were coming, and fast.

The horse sailed over fences as he ran, clearing them by feet.

Pallas and Moondog pounded down the trail that led up to the mountains, jumped the creek not far from Du Pré.

"Gran'père!" said Pallas. "You got to go. Benetsee is coming, we got things we got to do!"

"I need, talk to him," he said.

Pallas had half her face painted black and half white. She wore an otter-skin wrap around the thick single braid that fell down her back.

"He got to talk, me," said Du Pré.

Pallas got down from Moondog and she walked him in a circle.

"You know why him not talk to me?" said Du Pré.

"He did already," said Pallas. "You got to go now, Gran'père."

"What he say?" said Du Pré.

Pallas looked at him. Her black eyes flashed.

"Him say it to you," she said. "How am I to know what he said? Now please go, Gran'père. I got to see him, six more times before I go."

Du Pré got up.

"I am sorry," he said. "I don't know what to do so it makes me mad."

"You are a guy," she said. "Guys get mad they don't know what to do. Women don't. We just wait."

Du Pré laughed. He went to Pallas and they hugged. He walked up the little steep patch and to his cruiser.

He got in and he started the engine.

A huge raven, a whitethroat, flew down and perched on the hood in front of Du Pré.

"You go to hell, old bastard," said Du Pré, and he backed up and the bird flew up and circled round the cabin.

I never see Benetsee change into anything, thought Du Pré.

But he does.

The Chinese sage who wondered if the butterly was his dream, or if he was the butterfly's dream.

Du Pré looked at his watch. It was near time to go and get Father Van Den Heuvel.

Du Pré got to the school a few minutes before four.

The same young man who had served the papers on him yesterday came out. He saw Du Pré and gave him a friendly wave.

Du Pré shook his head.

The young man put his attaché case in his sedan and he drove off.

The school buses had gone. Du Pré had passed one on his way into Cooper.

Father Van Den Heuvel and Lennart came out together. They each had summonses in their hands.

Du Pré got out and he sat on the hood of the cruiser.

"You get one of these?" said Lennart. "Christ, I can't just up and go for this nonsense."

The big priest looked at Du Pré.

161

"They are serious, aren't they?" he said.

Du Pré nodded.

The van with the Texas plates pulled in, and the Flowerses got out and the girl Du Pré had found hysterical, hiding behind Chappie's trailer.

She was pretty, and composed now.

The Flowerses marched up to Lennart and Father Van Den Heuvel, the girl behind them.

"Raylee will be in school tomorrow," said Flowers, "but I demand she not be sent to science class. Evolution is a lie."

Lennart looked at him.

"She cannot graduate unless she has science credits," said Lennart.

Flowers blinked at him.

"There's better science," he said. "Creation science."

Lennart colored but he didn't say anything.

"Creation science is religious nonsense," said Father Van Den Heuvel. "Now if you want your daughter to get an education, this is the place. If you don't, school her at home. So she can be poor and ignorant all her life. But do not ask the public schools to teach religious nonsense."

Flowers looked at him.

"You're a Catholic priest," he said.

"Worse," said Father Van Den Heuvel. "I'm a Jesuit."

Flowers smiled smugly.

"So what are you teaching?" he said. "*Religion?*"

"See you in the morning," said Father Van Den Heuvel.

He walked past the fat little man to Du Pré.

"Let's go," he said.

Flowers went on talking to Lennart.

"He won't stay," said Father Van Den Heuvel. "He's a good man and he loves teaching. But there are places he can go where he doesn't have to put up with this."

CHAPTER
31

"I don't got children in the school anymore," said Du Pré. "Why do I got to go to this thing?"

Madelaine looked at him.

"You have grandchildren," she said.

"I got a lot," said Du Pré, "of grandchildren. Jacqueline, she can go."

Madelaine was brushing her long silver-shot black hair.

"You are going," she said.

"I am going," said Du Pré.

"Good," said Madelaine. "I was about, getting the cattle prod."

"Do I got to wear a tie?" said Du Pré.

"You don't own a tie," said Madelaine. "Suit, either."

"I could go and get one," said Du Pré. "They got good suits, sale, Billings."

He went to the bedroom and he put on clean Levi's and polished boots and a heavy linen shirt Madelaine had made for him.

"New hat," said Madelaine.

"It is not broke in yet," said Du Pré.

Madelaine picked up his good old hat with thumb and forefinger.

"Take this in for sandblasting," she said.

"Little spot here and there," said Du Pré.

"Looks like you stuck it under your car, drained the old oil into it, you are changing oil," said Madelaine. "New hat."

Du Pré sighed. He found the hatbox way up high in the closet. There was a heavy beaver hat there, silverbelly, with a new horsehair band on it that had a beaded medallion of a fiddle and bow.

Du Pré looked at the medallion.

"This is pretty," he said.

"Yes," said Madelaine. "Now we got to go, Cooper, now."

They went out and got into Du Pré's cruiser and he backed and turned and headed toward the county seat.

The parking lot of the school was filled with trucks and cars.

Some had Cooper County plates but a lot of them did not.

The Flowerses' van was there.

The school board meeting was in the gymnasium. The bleachers had been pulled out and they were largely filled with people.

Du Pré looked at the crowd.

I don't know half these people, he thought.

The Flowerses and a lot of their congregants all sat together on the far side of the bleachers.

Bart and Pidgeon were sitting as close to the door as they could, on a couple of folding chairs. Most of the men in the place were stealing glances at Pidgeon.

"All right," said a big-boned, weathered woman in the center chair of five. "We have a new school board member. You know Bob had to move away, so the commissioners appointed the person who got the most votes the last election but didn't quite make it."

People fell silent.

Wilbur sat at the far end. He looked very uncomfortable.

"So Wilbur here is the new member," said the big-boned woman. "This is a special meeting of the school board. We have before us a decision. Some people in the community want a new textbook used in the science class."

Du Pré looked at Flowers, who was looking smug.

"This new textbook," said the big-boned woman, "teaches intelligent design, and enough of them have been donated by the Galilee Education Foundation so the school won't have to buy any. If we decide to use them."

Lennart and Father Van Den Heuvel were sitting together off on one side of the long tables the school board members sat at.

"The principal has a few comments to make," said the big-boned woman.

Lennart stood up. He looked pale.

"Thank you, Velma," he said, bowing toward the woman. He fiddled some change in his pockets.

"I haven't much to say but this: to adopt these books will be to break the law. The courts have decided over and over again that religion, which is what this new text promotes, may not be promoted in the public schools. If the board should adopt this textbook, then there will be a lawsuit, and the board will lose, and it will cost the school district a lot of money," said Lennart.

There was a ripple of whispers in the crowd in the bleachers.

"What if these new books is true?" said a rancher Du Pré knew, barely.

"I am not qualified to argue about that," said Lennart. "I have a master's degree in education. But Father Van Den Heuvel has a doctorate in geology, a very good background in science, and I would like him to address this," said Lennart.

The big priest was dressed in his cassock. He stood, big and dark, and he waited until the murmurs died away.

"This is a religious, not a scientific text," said the big priest, "though it may be called creationism or intelligent design, what it always is is dishonest as science. It has no merit at all."

"Evolution is just a theory!" yelled Flowers.

Father Van Den Heuvel rocked back and forth on his heels a moment.

The school board looked at him.

"I have a question for Mister Flowers," said Father Van Den Heuvel, "and I am going to give this"—and he walked to the woman chair and handed her a sheet of paper—"over to the board's chair. Now, Mister Flowers, would you define the word *theory?*"

Flowers opened his mouth, shut it, opened it again.

"A guess," said Flowers.

Velma looked at the paper.

"Nope," she said. She handed the paper to the next person, a gray-haired man. He took out spectacles and he stared at the paper.

"I haven't anything more to say," said Father Van Den Heuvel, "so I do hope you vote against adopting this book. It is a lie."

He walked out.

Lennart fidgeted in his chair.

He stood up.

"If the board votes to adopt this book," he said, "consider my resignation offered. I will not be a party to this."

He walked out, too.

Madelaine got up.

"Well," she said, "not much else we can do." She and Du Pré left then, and found Father Van Den Heuvel in the parking lot, talking with Lennart.

"I can't stand this," said Lennart.

Du Pré looked off at the ranks of cars.

There was one, a late model sedan with dark windows, that had Colorado plates on it and a radio antenna.

"Let's go over, sit on that car," said Du Pré.

Madelaine looked at him.

She nodded and she and Du Pré and the other two men walked over to it and they sat on the hood. The car sank down.

"Hey," said a man who had been sitting in it. He had put down the window and then he opened the door.

Du Pré looked at him.

"You're sitting on my car!" said the man.

The other door opened, too.

Another man stood up.

"Get off," he said.

"You are sitting on my land," said Du Pré. "Who are you?"

"Get off," said the man. He was about forty, dressed in a cheap, flashy suit and a black tie.

"I smell that marijuana," said Du Pré. He took out his wallet and he flipped it open and showed his badge and shut it and put it away.

"Out of the car," he said.

"What?" said the man.

"You, him, out of the car," said Du Pré. "Anybody else, too. You got drugs, you get out, you put your hands on the roof."

Madelaine and the priest and Lennart were looking on, eyes wide, and Madelaine turned away, so the men would not see her laughing.

"This is—" said the man.

Du Pré pulled out his 9mm and he waved it in the air.

166

Both men got out, looking stunned.

Du Pré pulled the doors open in the back. He riffled through some papers. He looked through some books.

The two men looked like they were in shock.

"OK," said Du Pré. "You are arrested. You got ID?"

The men nodded. They pulled out their wallets.

"Lennart," said Du Pré. "Find Tapley. He is in there I think."

Lennart raised his eyebrows and he went off.

"Madelaine," said Du Pré. "I got handcuffs the car."

Madelaine went off skipping and humming.

She came back quickly with two pairs of cuffs and Du Pré snapped them on the men's wrists.

"Sit down," he said, pointing to the ground.

They sat.

Du Pré started putting papers and books on the roof of the car. He found a satellite phone and he set it up there, too. He found two briefcases.

Lennart and Tapley came out of the school building.

Tapley had his hands in his pockets.

He came up to Du Pré.

Du Pré pointed at the papers and books.

Tapley looked at them for a moment.

His face broke into a big smile.

"My, my," he said. He read some of one book and he laughed. He picked up a letter Du Pré had found on the dash. He read that, nodding.

Benny Klein drove into the lot.

He pulled up.

Benny got out and he looked at the two men on the ground.

"What'd they do?" said Benny.

"Ah," said Tapley. "Wish I had a mustache to twirl."

"What?" said Benny.

"Conspiracy," hissed Tapley.

CHAPTER
32

Du Pré turned around to find the entire crowd from the school board meeting ranked behind him. The Flowerses stood in front of their folk, mouths open.

Lennart was standing with Father Van Den Heuvel.

Benny shoved the second man into the back of his patrol car.

The two men were silent, unbelieving.

"So what do I do now?" said Benny. "With the car I mean."

"Haul it to the county shop," said Du Pré. "Needs to be searched."

"I got to put these fellers in the jail," said Benny. "They will no doubt want to call a lawyer. Can you search the car?"

"Sure," said Du Pré. He slid into the driver's seat, poked around a little, and he came up with a small plastic bag full of green leafy stuff. It looked a lot like oregano.

Du Pré opened the bag and he sniffed.

"Pot," he said.

"All right," said Benny. "I hope you know what you are doing."

"Drug bust," said Du Pré. "Up against the wall, you know."

Benny shrugged and he drove off toward the low brick building that housed the three jail cells and the sheriff's office. Cooper was not large and it was not far away.

Du Pré shut the door of the sedan.

Madelaine was standing there, looking innocent.

"What is going on here?" said Wilbur. He looked genuinely puzzled.

"Those guys," said Du Pré, "they had drugs, their car. Selling to schoolkids probably."

Wilbur looked at Flowers who was merely looking stupid.

"We still have to take a vote," said Velma.

"I'd have to say no," said Wilbur. "I guess maybe we oughta stick with the old books fer a while anyway."

Velma looked at the three other board members.

Two nodded and one shook his head.

"Voted down three to two," she said, "and I declare the meeting adjourned."

Flowers was turning red.

His wife moved away from him, her eyes toward the ground.

Du Pré got in the sedan, turned the key, and he drove the sedan to the county shop. It was open. He drove inside and he got out and he pulled down the steel door and then he locked up the sedan and he went out the side door.

Tapley drove up in his pickup. He looked back at the school. The crowd was thinning, cars and trucks leaving close behind each other.

"I heard the stories," said Tapley, "but never saw you in action."

"What action?" said Du Pré. "I am sitting, their car, door opens, I smell grass. I am a deputy, you know."

"Auxiliary," said Tapley. "Christ, I hope you never get mad at me."

"Small place," said Du Pré. "They pick this one out, you know. They say, there are no people there, so we will do this thing. How much it cost the school, they get their dumb books, the science class?"

"Could be as much as a couple hundred thousand," said Tapley.

"Poor place," said Du Pré.

"Bart would cover it," said Tapley. "But there ain't one good reason why he should have to."

"Yeah I would," said Bart. He came in with Pidgeon close behind.

Du Pré found a white clasp envelope in the car, he wrote on it and signed his name. He put the little plastic bag in it and he sealed it.

"I want to talk to those guys," said Pidgeon.

169

Du Pré nodded.

"Soon," said Pidgeon. "Before they get a lawyer here."

Du Pré shrugged.

"Let's go," he said.

He took the evidence envelope and he walked back to his cruiser. Madelaine was in it smoking one of the cigarettes she kept in the beaded case. They had gold tips and were very long.

Bart and Pidgeon drove off toward the sheriff's office and jail.

"Some mess, eh?" said Du Pré.

"Maybe those guys know about that girl, the dead girl?" said Madelaine.

Du Pré shook his head.

"*Non,*" he said. "They are not that."

Madelaine nodded.

"You are close," she said.

"Yah," said Du Pré. "Maybe."

"I keep thinking about that poor kid I drove to Billings," said Madelaine. "She just cried, moped the whole way there. Wouldn't talk, so they admitted her. Wouldn't talk after she was in, so they let her go. Now she is back home, acting like nothing happened."

Du Pré looked at her.

"Don't make a lot of sense," said Madelaine.

"She is afraid of something and then she is not," said Du Pré.

"OK," said Madelaine. "So somebody talk to her."

Du Pré nodded.

"So you are going now," said Madelaine, "going to look."

Du Pré drove back to Toussaint and he dropped Madelaine off at her place and then he drove to Wilbur and Marge's place, a house set back from the road. It had a huge lawn and a Siberian elm shading a small pool of water that was thick with polliwogs.

Flowers's van was there, parked behind the house.

Du Pré knocked on the door and Marge came.

He could hear people praying in the back of the house.

Marge looked at him for a long moment.

"Come in," she said.

Du Pré stepped inside.

Marge just pointed back toward the praying.

Flowers and his wife and Raylee and the other children were on their knees on the floor, praying loudly for Wilbur to join the Children of God.

Wilbur was flushed and he looked very unhappy.

Flowers and his wife had their eyes closed.

Du Pré ran some water in a glass. He threw it in Flowers's face.

The little fat man blinked and choked.

"Get out," said Du Pré.

Flowers started to say something and then he thought the better of it.

They left through the side door.

Du Pré sighed.

"Good thing you said no," he said. "You said yes, there would have been bad trouble."

"It's my religion," said Wilbur. "We do got freedom of speech, you know."

Du Pré nodded.

"Where is Sonny?" he said.

"Hauling," said Wilbur. "Had to go to Great Falls, had a load of stuff they take there and nowhere else."

"Sonny doesn't live here now," said Du Pré.

"No," said Wilbur. "He's out at the old Self place. We got that for the junk."

"Where you keep your old cars," said Du Pré.

"Yeah," said Wilbur. "It's down in that little flat, you know, can't see it from anywhere around. The danged environmentalists put up such a stink about the old cars."

"You should have voted yes like you said you would," said Marge. "Whole church is going to be mad at us now."

"How long you been at the Self place?" said Du Pré.

"Four, five years," said Wilbur. "Picked it up for back taxes."

"We go there," said Du Pré, "see old cars. What else is there?"

"Hell," said Wilbur, "I don't know. Sonny highgrades the stuff folks leave at the dump. Lots of good stuff gets thrown out."

Du Pré nodded.

"Sonny, he was gone here awhile," he said.

"Ten years," said Wilbur. "In the service. Got divorced and in time he come back home here."

"You start going to the church he goes to?" said Du Pré. "Used to go, the Methodists?"

"For God's sake, Du Pré," said Marge, "it wasn't no good. They don't teach no Bible like it oughta be taught there, all this terrible stuff going on in the country. Abortion. Any girl can just up and go and get an abortion just like that. Got homos everywhere. All this stuff is of the Devil."

Wilbur nodded. He looked beaten.

"I got an old stove part I need," said Du Pré. "Off an old Monarch."

Wilbur looked at him.

"Sonny got one of them," said Wilbur. "He was crowin' about it. You remember about when that was, Marge?"

She shook her head.

Her lips moved. She was praying.

"Where is it?" said Du Pré.

"I imagine it is out the Self place," said Wilbur. "He got a couple mean dogs out there. Chows. Mean bastards, them black mouths and all."

"So Sonny takes you to the church he joins," said Du Pré.

"We were lost," said Marge. "Now we ain't."

Wilbur looked at Du Pré.

"We best go there, I guess," he said.

Du Pré nodded.

"The dogs won't mind nobody but Sonny," said Wilbur.

Du Pré shrugged.

They went out to Du Pré's cruiser.

"I can come!" said Marge. Her eyes looked desperate.

Wilbur shook his head.

She went back inside.

Du Pré started the cruiser and they drove off.

He looked in the rearview mirror.

Wilbur and Marge's pickup truck pulled out.

It stopped in the center of the road.

It was still there when Du Pré crested the first hill.

He kept looking for it, but after a moment he didn't anymore.

Wilbur sniffed.

He looked in the back seat.

He picked up one of the chair pieces, still thick with paint on the turnings.

"Sonny's got a stripping tank take care of this," he said. "Works good."

CHAPTER
33

Du Pré stopped the cruiser in front of the chain that stretched across the drive. A huge old brass padlock was set in the end links.

"That's new," said Wilbur.

Du Pré looked at him.

Wilbur got out and he fished a ring of keys out of his pocket. He opened the old lock and let the chain fall.

"Bring the padlock," said Du Pré.

Wilbur nodded, picked it up. He came back to the open passenger door and he got in.

"I don't want to do this," said Wilbur. "It was your boy, would you?"

Du Pré said nothing.

"Don't kill him," said Wilbur. "Please don't kill him, Du Pré. I know you done that before. I know you have."

"I am not killing anybody," said Du Pré.

"We was happy oncet, then Marge got the vision," said Wilbur. "Said she done saw Jesus, saw him walking down the road."

Du Pré drove slowly. They went through a narrow cut in the rocks and then there was a small circular valley, a hole in the ground, a few small and rolling hills now all covered with old cars and trucks, ranked in rows.

There were three old garbage bins, huge things the size of a semitrailer. They had panels missing from them and showed rust in the paint.

"Who got religion first," said Du Pré, "Marge or Sonny?"

"Sonny," said Wilbur. "Marge went down to Texas where he was stationed to see him after his wife walked out on him and she come back *saved.*"

Du Pré stopped the cruiser. He got out and he put his 9mm in his belt and he put two extra clips in his pockets. He picked up the heavy five-cell flashlight that sat on the back window ledge.

"What are you lookin' for?" said Wilbur.

"A cell," said Du Pré. "A jail. A metal box maybe."

"Just them things," said Wilbur, "wouldn't hold nobody."

"There are six panels missing," said Du Pré.

Wilbur made a show of counting.

"There was a mine here," said Du Pré.

"I heard so," said Wilbur. "Don't know where it was."

Du Pré looked at him.

Wilbur was crying softly.

"You think he killed that girl?" said Wilbur. "My boy he couldn't do that."

"Where is that mine, Wilbur?" said Du Pré.

Wilbur pointed toward a wall of rock.

"Vanadium," said Wilbur. "Second World War, they found some vanadium there."

The mine entrance was screened by three old school buses, one piled atop the other two.

A dark hole into the rock sat just at ground level. It was about eight feet high and about that wide.

Du Pré turned on the flashlight.

He shone the light inside.

A metal sheet lay on the ground. There was water dripping someplace.

Du Pré picked up a chain lying on a bus bumper.

He chained Wilbur to the bumper and locked the chain with the padlock and he took the keys.

"I wouldn't have done nothing, Du Pré," said Wilbur. He looked utterly defeated.

"He is your son," said Du Pré.

"Yes," said Wilbur.

Du Pré went into the old mine and into the metal box that lay beyond the sheet on the floor. It had a door cut in it, one that had many holes.

There was a padlock but it was open.

Du Pré took the lock out of the hasp and he pulled the door open. It swung easily. Someone had recently oiled the hinges.

A cell.

There was a wooden bed, a chemical toilet, a water cooler with water in a big jug on top of it.

Candles.

A Bible.

Du Pré looked at the bed.

It was covered in soogans, now mildewed.

He shone the light on the floor.

Drag marks.

Du Pré backed out of the cell.

Wilbur was sitting on the old school bus's bumper, his head in his hands.

"It's bad, isn't it?" said Wilbur.

"Yes," said Du Pré.

Du Pré unlocked the chain and they walked back to the cruiser.

They drove out of the little blind canyon and Wilbur locked the chain across the road. He came back to the cruiser, stood outside.

"I did it," he said. "I killed the girl."

"No," said Du Pré. "No, you did not. You have been here before?"

"Long time ago," said Wilbur. "I was running the station, Sonny would bring me a part from here I needed one."

Du Pré looked round, lifted his cell phone up, and he punched in some numbers.

"I found where she died," he said. "You go out the ranch road past Five Forks. Bring Booger Tom. I am at the old Self place . . . Call Benny . . ."

"You call Benny," said Pidgeon.

Du Pré chuckled.

He punched in some more numbers.

"Old Self place," he said. "Sonny kill the girl."

"Oh, God," said Benny.

Du Pré shut the telephone back up.

Wilbur was crying.

"I didn't know about it," he said.

175

Du Pré looked at him.

"You didn't want to," said Du Pré. "You would not come out here because you were afraid of what you would find."

Wilbur nodded. He pulled out a kerchief and he blew his nose.

"What's going to happen to him?" he said.

"Trial," said Du Pré.

"Oh, Lord," said Wilbur.

"Let's find that stove part," said Du Pré.

They walked back through the cleft and Wilbur pointed to a big white stove, one with some dings in the baked porcelain finish.

Du Pré pointed to the firebox.

"That casting on the right," he said.

Wilbur nodded. He went to an old truck and he got some tools out of the box and he came back and he started to take the stove apart.

His hands flew.

Something he can do. Watch those hands, Du Pré thought.

Wilbur tugged and the cast-iron panel came free. He held it up.

"That looks like it," said Du Pré.

"You got one of these?" said Wilbur.

"Benetsee," said Du Pré.

"He talks to the Devil," said Wilbur. "Flowers said he did."

"Benetsee don't kill little girls," said Du Pré.

"Oh, God," said Wilbur.

Du Pré carried the panel back to the cruiser and he put it in the trunk.

He went back to where Wilbur was sitting, on an old hay rake.

"It was that woman he was married to," said Wilbur.

Du Pré stood, silent.

"God damn it, Du Pré," said Wilbur. "Whole country's gone to hell."

Du Pré said nothing.

"There's about nothin' left here," said Wilbur.

Du Pré rolled a smoke.

"My boy didn't do this," said Wilbur. "He loves the Lord."

Tires made crackling sounds as they went over gravel.

Du Pré turned.

Bart's big green SUV pulled in and he and Pidgeon got out, and after a moment so did Booger Tom.

176

The old cowboy had his Colt on his hip, a huge thing with ivory handles.

"Keep him here," said Du Pré.

Booger Tom nodded.

Du Pré led Pidgeon back to the old mine and the steel cage. She stood outside it, playing the beam from the flashlight over the walls.

The walls were covered in quotations from the Bible.

THOU SHALT NOT SUFFER A WITCH TO LIVE.

Pidgeon looked at the floor.

"Yeah," she said. "That's where he dragged her."

"Shut her up here why?" said Du Pré. "He don't fuck her, don't beat her up."

Pidgeon backed out of the dark into the sun.

"They are terrified of sex," she said, "of women and the sexual power of women. The girl was sent here because whoever was responsible for her felt she had to be broken of her thoughts. And you cannot break thoughts without a lot of effort."

"He mean to kill her?" said Du Pré.

"Probably not," said Pidgeon. "She died of a potassium deficiency perhaps. She might have had a lot of problems. But she would not have died if she hadn't been here and hadn't been terrified."

Du Pré nodded.

"All of the quotations are about women," said Pidgeon. "That fits."

"What we do with Sonny?" said Du Pré.

"Arrest him," said Pidgeon. "He didn't do this alone. He did it for somebody else."

"What we do with this?" said Du Pré, waving at the mine.

"I wait until we get a team here," said Pidgeon. "I already called them. Might be a couple hours."

"What about Wilbur?" said Du Pré. "Him don't have anything to do with this."

"Take him home," said Pidgeon. "He probably had something to do with it but not much. We can always pick him up later."

Du Pré and Wilbur walked back to his cruiser.

"We could leave them chair parts," he said, pointing at a tank on a steel frame. "That's the one tank. There's a bigger one someplace, I think still in a truck trailer."

Du Pré nodded.

He looked at the ground under the tank.

It was dark with fluid.

"Dang," said Wilbur. "Sprung a leak. Leave 'em anyway. Sonny kin strip 'em in the big one."

There was a big stainless steel table near the broken tank. It was six by eight, and had a rim three inches high. There were drains in the corners, and a long hose dribbled water on the ground.

"Stuff he uses," said Wilbur, "water works on, so you kin just hose it away."

CHAPTER
34

The two men arrested at the school sat in adjoining cells. They both had small New Testaments and they both were reading them.

"In a couple of hours," said Pidgeon, "federal agents are going to be here. You have pissant state drug charges against you. They are going to bring warrants for other matters. Either of you has anything to say you had best say it now."

The two men ignored her.

"Fine," said Pidgeon. "I'd as soon not talk to you anyway. Up here in Montana, they don't like putting murderers to death. Down in your native Texas, they love it."

The two men ignored her.

Pidgeon shrugged and she nodded to Du Pré and they walked out.

"Thanks," said Pidgeon.

Du Pré nodded.

"Now I guess finding Sonny is the next best thing. He went to the hazardous waste dump in Great Falls?" said Pidgeon.

"That is what Wilbur said," said Du Pré.

"So he should be back soon," said Pidgeon.

Du Pré shrugged.

"State patrol is looking for him," said Pidgeon.

"Semitrailer on that highway should not be hard to find," said Du Pré.

"They should have found him by now," said Pidgeon.

Du Pré nodded.

"I have known you long enough to know when you are thinking and not talking, Du Pré," said Pidgeon. "What is it?"

Du Pré shook his head.

"Sonny maybe just ran," he said. "What I think happened is, that girl, she was sick and died, terrible surprise for him. He takes her to the table he washes the wood he has stripped paint from, washes her so there is no evidence."

"Pretty good thinking," said Pidgeon.

"On the TV all the time," said Du Pré. "All those crime shows."

"Yeah," said Pidgeon.

"He puts her by the road so she will be found," said Du Pré.

"But who is she?" said Pidgeon.

"Maybe those two in there know," said Du Pré.

"But they won't talk," said Pidgeon.

"She is not from here," said Du Pré, "and neither are they. You find out where they come from, I bet you find out where the girl comes from."

"I thought of that," said Pidgeon. "And we have photographs of the girl and we are showing them round Texas, which is a very big state with a lot of people in it."

Du Pré nodded.

The little television on the front desk was tuned to an evangelist. The sound was off. The man was waving the Bible and pounding on the lectern.

"So," said Pidgeon, "where is Sonny?"

"I think maybe he call home, let them know he is on his way back," said Du Pré.

"Of course," said Pidgeon.

The dispatcher came out of the side room where she worked at the bank of phones and radios.

"They found Sonny's truck," she said. "About halfway between here and Great Falls. Just idling by the road. No Sonny."

Du Pré nodded.

"How far from here?" said Pidgeon.

The dispatcher thought a moment.

"Hour and a half, two hours," she said.

Du Pré sighed.

"I got to stay here until the agents come," said Pidgeon. "I hope these bastards don't have other women in boxes in the ground."

Du Pré went out and he got in his cruiser and he drove back to Toussaint to Wilbur's garage.

There was no one there. The doors were locked and Wilbur's truck was gone.

He went to their house.

Wilbur's truck was there, but Marge's old sedan wasn't.

Du Pré sighed.

The road west wound through the High Plains. Sometimes you could see for fifty miles, even more.

The hills were green still, the summer heat had not yet cured the grass to yellow-brown.

It was summer in the Wolf Mountains, the deer were fat, it was warm, there were lots of places to hide.

Du Pré pulled off on a bench road that went up to the mountains and then around their western flank, where the high reach of the peaks fell away into the earth.

Come up from there fifty million years ago.

Bunch of them in Montana, come up in the soup.

Du Pré drove along, looking at each spur road that went toward the mountains.

This was cattle country, pasture, and the cattle could drift up in the mountains for grass and nights that were cold enough the flies would not follow.

At the far end of the mountains there was a single road that wound up to the base and then rose up and went straight across to a creek that came out of a narrow cut in stone. There was a game trail there, big enough for horses but not for any vehicle.

Du Pré stopped on a hill, he could see the creek cleft easily. There was a packer's station at the end of the road, a big circular area with a couple of corrals and a loading chute.

Du Pré looked at his watch, fished his binoculars out of the glove box of the cruiser.

He put the lenses of the binoculars on the place where the packer's station was.

A couple of magpies flew up to a treetop and after a moment they glided back down the way that they had come.

Du Pré sighed.

He went to the driver's door and he got in and flicked on his radio, lifted the microphone. The thing was very old but it worked.

"Du Pré," said Du Pré.

"Yeah," said the dispatcher.

"You maybe call Bart's, get Booger Tom bring me a good horse and saddle?" said Du Pré. "I think I know where Sonny is, Wilbur and Marge, too."

"Call out the troops?" said the dispatcher.

"No," said Du Pré. "I just want Booger Tom, bring me a horse."

"OK," she said, "but I will have to tell Benny."

"Fine," said Du Pré. "You tell him I am going in and there is no reason, anyone else to do that."

"OK," said the dispatcher.

Du Pré flicked off the radio.

He got back out, looked up the road. There was no way back down other than this road.

"Christ," said Du Pré.

Be an hour or two before Booger Tom gets here.

Du Pré got his flask and he drank a little and he smoked a cigarette. A big beetle walked across the dusty road, a black tanklike creature.

It went into the grass.

The sun was hot. Du Pré went back and sat in his car with all the windows open.

Marge's sedan came into view. It stopped.

"Shit," said Du Pré.

Du Pré looked at the sedan. It sat there for half an hour and then it came on.

Two people were in it.

Marge was driving.

She stopped the old brown sedan a few feet from Du Pré. She got out. Wilbur sat in the passenger seat, staring straight ahead.

Marge had been crying.

Du Pré got out, opened the door for her.

"Sonny went up the mountains," she said. "You ain't gonna kill him, are you?"

"*Non,*" said Du Pré.

Marge began to cry.

Du Pré got some paper towels from the back seat and she took one.

182

"Sonny didn't know," she said. "He was told the girl was possessed by Satan. She was just supposed to be locked up a while. Then he found her dead."

Du Pré nodded.

"Who say she is possessed?" said Du Pré.

"Sonny didn't know," said Marge. "A couple men brought the girl one night, after telling him to make up a safe place for her."

"Steel cage in an old mine," said Du Pré.

"The Devil walks among us, Du Pré," said Marge.

Du Pré nodded.

"Sonny didn't mean no harm," she said.

"What he thinking of?" said Du Pré. "Sticking girls in prisons, so they die?"

"He was trying to save her," said Marge.

Du Pré sighed.

"You got no religion, do you?" said Marge.

Du Pré looked at her.

"I don't got one kills women," he said. "Thing about religions is lots of them kill women."

Marge looked at him.

"They were trying to save her," said Marge. "From the Devil."

She nodded, looked satisfied.

"It was the right thing to do," she said. "You wouldn't understand."

"No," said Du Pré. "I would not."

"Are the police coming?" said Marge.

"They will," said Du Pré.

"This is a godless country," said Marge.

Wilbur got out of the car.

He walked back to Du Pré's cruiser.

"Wilbur!" said Marge, "tell Du Pré! Tell him Sonny was just trying to save her!"

Wilbur looked at his wife.

"Oh, Christ," he said. "Shut the hell up, Marge."

CHAPTER
35

"You sure?" said Booger Tom.

Du Pré nodded.

"Sonny's kind of a hothead," said Booger Tom, "an' he's scared now. He got a gun?"

Du Pré nodded.

"Let the cops do it," said Booger Tom.

"Then they just kill him and maybe he kills some of them," said Du Pré.

"He might kill you," said Booger Tom.

Du Pré shook his head.

"He is scared," said Du Pré. "Me, I were him, I would be scared too."

"That goddamned Pidgeon," said Booger Tom. "She's gonna have half a brigade here. They are gonna wanta go and hunt Sonny."

"You tell her from me," said Du Pré, "they come and they got to kill me, too, and Madelaine, she will not take that well."

Booger Tom snorted.

"Wal," he said, "I brought you old Punkin and Jonesy for Sonny. You talk him down he probably oughta have something to ride."

"Good," said Du Pré.

They offloaded the horses and saddled them. Booger Tom had brought two bedrolls and a pack of food and some utensils.

"He's on foot?" said Booger Tom. "Won't have gone far."

"Eight, ten miles maybe," said Du Pré. "There is that cabin, Big Flat Meadows. Me, I would go there."

"Some shit, huh, Du Pré?" said Booger Tom.

"Tell Madelaine I be back maybe tomorrow," said Du Pré.

"Sure," said Booger Tom. "She sent this for you." He handed Du Pré a plastic half gallon of whiskey.

"A carin' woman," said Booger Tom, "is beyond rubies. I think that is in the Bible."

Du Pré swung up on Punkin, an orange-yellow horse with a cream mane and tail. He was middle-aged and gentle.

Jonesy was the same, a buckskin with a black mane and tail.

"You hear helicopters," said Booger Tom, "hide."

Du Pré nodded.

"Whyn't I go, too," said Booger Tom.

"No horse," said Du Pré. "You only brought two."

"The hell with me then," said Booger Tom.

Du Pré reached down and they shook hands.

Booger Tom stuffed the whiskey into a pack and Du Pré clucked and Punkin walked up the trail. Jonesy followed, without a lead. Good old horses.

Du Pré rode along, getting down every once in a while to see if Sonny had passed this way.

He was headed straight for the Big Flat Meadows.

At five miles in, Du Pré stopped and he got down and he put the horses in the shade. He climbed up a hillside to a rock promontory and he looked at the land ahead with the binoculars.

A raven circled a stand of lodgepole pines a mile or so ahead. The trail wound through trees there, and huge slabs of rock shed from the mountain.

Du Pré found some shade and he kept his eye on a little saddle that ran from one mountain flank to another. The trail wound up and over it, and Big Flat Meadows were about a mile past that.

Du Pré went to sleep. He was watching the saddle but time flowed past.

Movement.

Du Pré lifted the glasses.

Elk.

A cow with a dozen other cows and their calves went over the saddle.

Du Pré glassed the mountainside to his left.

More elk.

Then they stopped walking, staring downhill, and then they all turned and raced away from the trail.

Du Pré kept the glasses on the saddle.

Sonny walked swiftly up and over, moving as fast as he could across bare ground.

He had a big pack on, a sleeping bag slung underneath the back.

Dumb shit, you are waiting there to shoot me.

"Christ," said Du Pré. He looked up at the sky.

Three hours of light, then dark for an hour, and then the moon would rise.

"Shit," said Du Pré.

He walked back down to the horses and he mounted and he went on. When he came to the saddle he left them in the trees and he went from rock to rock to the top and he peered through an old Indian peekaboo, piled flat stones that screened movement.

Nothing.

He sat for a half hour, watching.

No squirrels chirred, angry at an intruder.

The light began to fail and Du Pré went on, letting Punkin pick his way along the narrow trail.

He got to the Big Flat Meadows when it was darkest. He hobbled the horses and set them to graze, left the gear on a flat rock.

Du Pré moved toward the cabin set in a grove of aspens near a spring about halfway up the Meadows, on the right where a mountain flank sank into the thick grass. He would move ten feet and listen, move ten feet and listen.

Nothing.

An owl flew past his face so close he could smell it, and it was gone, silent, hunting.

The cabin was in shadow.

Du Pré sat on a log, waiting for the moon. It took awhile to rise above the mountains.

Pale light washed across the meadow, the cabin sat dark.

Du Pré waited.

He will come out, take a piss, turn on a light.

The owl hooted.

Great Horned.

Du Pré went to sleep, a hunter's dazing sleep.

Nothing stirred.

He edged toward the cabin, a few feet at a time. He carried the flashlight ready to blind Sonny if Sonny was waiting.

Du Pré got near the door, standing open, a waft of wet air came out of the black hole.

He shone the light inside.

A bear had broken in and wrecked the place and then torn a hole in the roof getting out.

Sonny was not there.

Scared and running.

Du Pré flicked off the light.

He walked back to the horses, found a bedroll and the whiskey, drank some while he chewed deer jerky made the old way, un-cooked sheets of meat left to dry in the sun. The jerky was crumbly, and melted on his tongue.

He slept hard, woke early, chewed instant coffee and sugar for breakfast.

He saddled the horses and he went on.

Sonny had gone right by the cabin, his stride shorter. He was very tired.

Du Pré found the place where he had turned off the trail and made a dry camp in a small grove of firs, young and thickly grown, good cover.

He is thinking some.

Maybe he calm down some.

Du Pré found some wrappers from food bars, pressed nuts and dried fruit and chocolate.

Du Pré went on.

Sonny had left before dawn, and his tracks in the dew-wet soil were fresh and stark.

Du Pré came to the place where the trail forked. One, the right, went between two peaks and on into the back country, the left went over a low pass and down to the dry plains to the north of the mountains.

Sonny had gone to the right.

What you do, Sonny? Eat mountain sheep and wait for the snow?

I get someplace where he can see it is just me, maybe he come in then.

Du Pré rode on, not stopping, until he was no more than an hour behind Sonny by the age of the tracks.

The sun rose up hot.

Du Pré went up the mountainside that reared steep to the south. The trail wound back and forth, up to a saddle, and then on to a high basin with several glacial cirques ringing it. There was snow up there ten months of the year and sometimes twelve.

A few tiny lakes sat at the foot of cliffs or scree slopes, lakes sapphire blue and without much life in them. They were shallow and froze solid every winter.

Du Pré stopped, took out the binoculars, looked around.

Nothing.

He probably see me and he is waiting.

Du Pré went on, following Sonny's tracks.

They left the trail abruptly, and went almost straight up a scree slope at the side of a high rock knee, bone of the mountain.

Du Pré looked up.

Sonny was on top of the knee, just sitting on a slab of rock.

"Sonny," said Du Pré. "It is just me!"

"Hi, Du Pré," said Sonny. "Sorry things are the way they are."

"Come on," said Du Pré. "You spend some time, prison, you did not mean her to die."

"Prison," said Sonny.

Du Pré waited.

"A cage like the one I put her in," said Sonny. "Years and years of a cage."

Du Pré waited.

"If there was a God," said Sonny, "he wouldn't let things like this happen."

Du Pré waited.

"God," said Sonny, "would you tell the girl's family how sorry I am?"

Du Pré waited.

"You help maybe find those people," said Du Pré, "they give you time off."

Sonny didn't say anything.

"I'm those people," he said. "Besides, you'll figure it out."

Du Pré saw Sonny come over the edge of the rock, saw him turn once in the air as he gained speed.

A wet thud, heavy, final.

Du Pré sat down.

"Shit," he said.

CHAPTER
36

"These bastards won't be happy until there is an iron stake in every town square to burn witches at," said Pidgeon, "and I don't see one fucking reason why I should be tolerant of such ambitions."

"Pidge," said Harvey Wallace, "calm down."

Du Pré nodded.

"So this Sonny feller just took a dive," said Harvey. He was standing on the boardwalk in front of the saloon, dressed in jeans and running shoes and a windbreaker that had FBI in big yellow letters on the back.

"Yah," said Du Pré.

"You knew him," said Harvey.

Du Pré nodded.

"And his parents," said Harvey, "the ones that are in jail for aiding and abetting."

Du Pré nodded.

"The two doofuses you planted the grass on are in federal stir," said Harvey, "and they are so afraid of the fair Pidgeon they are babbling away. Were you there when our dear and beautiful Pidge interviewed them?"

"No," said Du Pré.

"Did you twist off their testicles?" said Harvey to Pidgeon.

"Oh, come off it, Harvey," said Pidgeon. "I know what the agency parameters are."

"*Parameters*," said Harvey, "that word again. Someday someone will explain what it means to me."

"Those assholes transported that poor girl from Texas to here to stick her in a steel box in an old mine shaft," said Pidgeon, "and God knows how many others how many other places."

"We are finding out much," said Harvey.

"I gotta retire," said Pidgeon. "Serial killers were one thing. These nutcases are worse. Come to think of it, the worst serial killers claimed they did it for the sweet love of Jesus or because the Devil told them to."

"We need you, fair Pidgeon," said Harvey. "Come with me to Beautiful Texas."

Bart came out of the saloon, looking miserable.

"I will only be a couple weeks, honey," said Pidgeon.

Bart nodded.

"You don't have to do this," he said.

"Yes, I do," said Pidgeon. "Believe me, I have to do this."

Bart sighed.

"OK," he said. "Just be careful."

"Always," said Pidgeon.

Pidgeon and Harvey got into a tan government sedan and they waved as they drove off.

"She said she was going to stop," said Bart. "I am afraid every time she goes off on one of these."

Du Pré nodded.

"See you this evening," said Bart. "Madelaine is feeding me."

Du Pré nodded. Bart went to his big green SUV and he got in and he drove away.

Du Pré went inside.

Chappie was sitting at the bar, and Madelaine was on her stool, beading.

Du Pré slid up on a seat. He sipped from the half-gone ditch that he had left there.

The parcel service man came in, looked round the bar, saw Du Pré.

"Got a package for you," he said. "Thought I would find you here."

Madelaine snorted.

Du Pré signed the weird electronic clipboard and the parcel man left.

"It is the rosewood," he said. "For Pidgeon's rocking chair."

"You do better when you work in wood," said Madelaine. "Go do that now. You are not much good anybody, sitting there, all dark."

"I come along," said Chappie. He got off his stool and carefully set his phony leg.

Du Pré and Chappie went out to the cruiser and they got in and drove out to Du Pré's old place, where Jacqueline and Raymond lived now, and their passel of kids.

"Jacqueline's kids are getting older," said Chappie.

"Yah," said Du Pré. "Me, too."

All in school, couple already gone.

Du Pré slid back the big sliding door and the woodshop smell billowed out, a blend of machine oil and thinners and sawdust from many species of trees.

Du Pré opened the box and he slid out a short plank of rosewood.

"How much that cost?" Chappie said.

"Seven hundred dollars," said Du Pré.

"For a piece of wood," said Chappie.

"Yah," said Du Pré.

"Jesus," said Chappie, "that is a lot of money."

"Ebony costs more," said Du Pré, "a lot more."

Du Pré put on a shop apron and he brushed sawdust away from the platform the bandsaw blade plunged through. He found the ripping jig and he fixed the plank of rosewood in it and he went to the side and eyed it to check aspects.

Du Pré switched on the bandsaw and he began to make slices of wood from the plank. When he had eight of them he shut the saw off. He picked up the slices, long pieces five-sixteenths of an inch thick, and he took them to the small planer and he ran them through.

Shorn of the rough saw marks the wood came to life, glowing rich red-brown.

"What I can do?" said Chappie.

"Maybe look the pieces," said Du Pré, "sand off any glue on those tenons."

Chappie looked at him.

Du Pré laughed.

"These," he said, "where they fit into the legs or rockers or crossbars, these round ends."

Chappie took a sheet of sandpaper and he began to sand the old wood.

Du Pré ran the flat back pieces through the bandsaw again to taper them top and bottom. Then he took a palm sander and he cleaned them and they glowed even more.

"How you get this stuff off?" said Chappie.

"Sonny had a tank of stripper," said Du Pré.

"Tank," said Chappie.

"Big tank of chemicals," said Du Pré. "You put the stuff in there, it dissolves the paint. Has a filter on it, pumps the chemicals through, filters out the paint. Fish out the wood it is pret' clean. Just a little stuff down in the grain."

Chappie nodded.

"You like this?" he said. "I liked wood shop, school."

Du Pré nodded.

"You know that teacher, blond girl, Sarah?" said Chappie. "I like her a lot. I hope maybe we get something going, but she says no."

"They got a choice," said Du Pré.

"Yah," said Chappie. "I think maybe she don't like me I don't got one leg, one eye, and I am sad about that. But she is very nice, she tell me she don't like *men*."

Du Pré nodded.

"So I don't feel so singled out," said Chappie, and he laughed.

"What you going to do now?" said Du Pré.

"I been sitting round, feeling very sorry for myself," said Chappie, "but you know after a while it gets boring, sitting around, drink a lot, feel sorry for yourself. So I am thinking, I go back to school."

"OK," said Du Pré.

"I got the money to do that," said Chappie.

"What you want to do," said Du Pré.

"Teach maybe," said Chappie. "Little schools like Cooper, they have a hard time getting good teachers. I taught in the marines. I liked it, showing people how to do things."

Du Pré nodded.

He picked up a rocker and he looked it over. There were a few blooms of old paint faint as shadows on the wood. He took the rocker outside and he looked at it in the sunlight.

Du Pré put the piece on a table outside and he sat with a piece of fine emery paper, carefully rubbing the old stains away.

Chappie came out and joined him.

Sarah's little station wagon pulled in and she and the old dog got out. His coat was brushed and shiny and he had bright and curious eyes now.

"Hi," she said. "I'm back. Poor Father Van Den Heuvel, I guess he got a lot of crap while I was gone."

She sat on the other side of the table. The old dog curled up at her feet. "Him doing well," said Du Pré.

"Yeah," said Sarah. "They don't ask for much."

"You teach again Monday?" said Chappie.

"Yeah," said Sarah. "I have only four more weeks anyway, then I have fulfilled my contract. I'm movin' on."

"Can't blame you," said Chappie.

"Too much has happened here," said Sarah. "I'm going to make a fresh start. Someplace where there haven't been all these fights."

"You take the dog?" said Du Pré.

"You bet," said Sarah. "He's a good buddy. Smart as hell. I don't know how those people can treat other creatures that way."

Du Pré nodded.

"Nice wood," said Sarah. "What is it?"

"Rosewood," said Du Pré.

She picked up the rocker that Du Pré had set down.

She put it to her nose and she sniffed.

"Wow," she said. "That stinks."

Du Pré looked at her.

"I have a real good sense of smell," said Sarah.

Du Pré looked at the wood.

"Smell like what?" he said.

"Rotten," she said. "Smell the hole there." She pointed to the hole the leg went into.

"Well," said Sarah. "Got stuff to do." And she walked away.

Du Pré rolled a smoke and then he went back to sanding the wood.

CHAPTER 37

The men got out of the big van and they went to the back of it and they pulled out flat white packages.

White moon suits, to wear around hazardous materials.

"We wear 'em when we clean up meth labs," said the gray-haired man.

Du Pré nodded.

"Now where is this tank?" said the gray-haired man.

Du Pré pointed to the huge semitrailer. The back pins were thrown and there was a padlock in the hasp.

"How big a tank is it?" said the gray-haired man.

Du Pré shrugged.

"Well, we'll cut her open and see what's what," said the gray-haired man. He went to the back of the van and started putting his suit on.

Benny Klein stood there, frantically chewing tobacco.

"Go," said Du Pré to Benny. "Just go. I take care of this, anything is needed."

Benny looked at him.

"I'm the sheriff," he said.

"You get sick at the sight of blood," said Du Pré. "This will be a lot worse than that."

Benny swallowed.

"Go," said Du Pré.

Benny went to his cruiser and he got in and he drove off.

One of the men in the moon suits picked up a pair of bolt cutters and he went to the rear of the trailer and he snapped the shackle of the padlock. He brushed the piece of steel out of the hole, flipped the pins, and pulled. The door swung open.

Du Pré stood back.

The moon-suited men brought a platform with a set of steps set in it and they put it below the box and one man got up on it and he shone a light inside.

"Big sucker," he yelled. "Three thousand gallons at least."

Du Pré squinted against the sun. He couldn't see into the interior very well.

"I don't see anything," said the man on the platform.

"Hell, I hope you see the tank," said another man.

Du Pré couldn't tell who was who. They all wore the odd plastic suits and helmets and face masks.

"Check for booby traps," someone yelled.

"There's nothing here," said the man on the platform. "There's a hand winch lifts the top of the thing. Hell, it has to be big enough to put a bedstead in."

One of the men on the ground handed the man on the platform some black box with wires and probes hooked to it.

The man on the platform put the probes into the tank.

He looked at the box.

"I think it is just paint remover," he said. "Just petrochemicals. I don't see any nitrates."

"OK," said someone.

"Well," said the man on the platform, "everybody back off. I got the short straw. I'll lift this up. Holler when you are far enough away."

The other men walked back toward Du Pré.

"Move back please," said a moon-suit.

They backed away for about two hundred feet.

"OK!" someone yelled.

The winch scrawked, there was a sound of thin metal flexing. Racheting.

"Fucker's heavy," said the man on the platform, "but give me another five minutes."

Racheting.

The metal boomed, like a tiny thunderstorm.

Racheting.

"OK," said the man on the platform, "I see a hand."

"You were right," said a moon-suit to Du Pré.

"This stuff is awful murky," said the man on the platform. "There's something else at the other end."

"What do we do?" said a moon-suit.

"Drain it, I guess," said the man on the platform. "We got a truck here?"

"Not yet," said the moon-suit.

There was the sound of gears thrashing, and a septic tank pumper pulled up. The driver got down from the cab.

"What the hell is this?" he said.

"Pumping a tank," said a moon-suit.

"Put him with the other guy," said the man on the platform. "Tell him thank you and his truck has been commandeered by the Great State of Montana."

"I gotta call my boss," said the driver.

"We'll call your boss," said the man on the platform. "You got a place to take old chemicals?"

"Sure," said the man. "Funny thing to call shit."

One of the moon-suits went to the man, took him by the arm, and led him to where Du Pré was standing.

"Stand here," he said, "and you are likely to see things you don't want to see. I was the two of you, I would just up and go. We get paid for this. Not near enough, but we do get paid. We get nightmares, too, but we get paid."

The septic-cleaning company driver looked at Du Pré.

"I don't want to watch," he said.

Du Pré nodded.

He pointed toward the old Self house, still sound though lacking paint.

"Wait over there the porch," he said.

The driver trudged off.

One of the moon-suited men took off his protective clothing, went to the cab of the tank truck, started it, turned, and backed up to the semitrailer. Other moon-suits took the wired hose down and coupled it to the valve.

"You know how to run one of these?" said a moon-suit.

"Yeah," said the man. "I drove one one summer when I was in college."

He fiddled some valves and he nodded.

The man inside the trailer stuck the end of the hose in the big vat.

The truck engine speeded up when the man at the pump controls flipped the brass levers.

"It's taking it," said the man in the trailer.

"It could be evidence," said the man in the truck.

Two ambulances pulled in. Their crews got out, pulled out gurneys and black body bags. Then they put on moon suits, too.

"Pump faster," said the man in the trailer.

"It don't suck shit any faster," said the man at the pump controls. "It would bust its gusset, it would."

The truck engine whined and the pump whined.

"We got at least two," said the man in the trailer. "Jesus, this is awful."

Du Pré walked away then.

He found the man from the septic tank cleaning company sitting on the porch.

"Where you come from?" he said.

"Great Falls," said the man. "I thought it was kinda strange, so far out here."

"I get you back there," said Du Pré. "You don't want to stay."

"There are bodies in that thing?" said the man. "Mother of God."

Du Pré nodded.

"Yeah," he said. "I guess they won't need me."

"If they keep the tanker, evidence in it, no, not for a while," said Du Pré.

"Fuckers could have told us," said the driver.

Du Pré got his cruiser and brought it round and the man got in.

He had no hat or jacket.

"What is this about?" said the driver.

Du Pré shook his head.

He drove the man down to the highway and on to the gas station at the crossroad where the north-south road and the east-west one came together.

"Here," said Du Pré. "There is a bus in an hour. Get you to Great Falls tonight, goes roundabout."

The man nodded.

"You need money, the ticket?" said Du Pré.

The man looked in his wallet.

"I got forty bucks," said the man.

Du Pré gave him two more twenties.

"They are going to be pissed at the company," the man said. He got out and went into the gas station.

Du Pré turned around and he drove back to Toussaint.

Madelaine and Susan Klein were in the kitchen, cooking for the Friday night diners. The kitchen smelled of baking bread and spices.

There was no one else in the bar.

Du Pré made himself a ditch and he drank it.

Benny came in, looking worn.

"How'd it go?" he said.

"They said they found two bodies, had the rest of the tank to pump out," said Du Pré.

Benny nodded.

"I can't believe Wilbur and Marge knew about this," he said.

Du Pré shook his head.

"Sonny, either, come to think on it," said Benny.

Du Pré shrugged.

"You hear from Pidgeon and that Harvey character?" said Benny.

Du Pré shook his head.

"What would make people do this?" he said.

"Fear," said Du Pré.

Benny nodded.

"Fear," he said.

Du Pré made himself another ditch.

"Thanks for tellin' me to go," he said.

"Sure," said Du Pré.

They sat there for a while, and then Madelaine and Susan came out of the kitchen. They were laughing.

Du Pré and Benny walked round the bar and Du Pré hugged Madelaine and Benny hugged Susan.

Very hard.

CHAPTER
38

"You've got some friends with weight," said the young woman. She was dressed in a dark blue suit and she carried a Glock 9mm in a shoulder holster.

Du Pré nodded.

"But you smoke," said the agent. "Hardly anyone does anymore, at least not in the FBI. I don't plan to live forever myself." She drew deep on a filtered cigarette.

Du Pré drew in the last of his cigarette's smoke. He put the butt in the sand in the urn. All the other butts had little white filters on them.

"You roll your own," said the young agent, "out here in Montana, where I thought there were plenty of cowboys. I see people in hats and boots, but I don't know if they are cowboys or not."

"Miles City," said Du Pré. "Most of them are there."

The young agent stubbed out her butt.

They went into the federal lockup, and the agent checked her gun with a uniformed guard.

"You don't have a gun?" said the guard.

Du Pré shook his head.

The young agent handed the guard a form. The guard looked at it and then there was a clicking sound and the door opened.

They went through another door, guarded by a woman in uniform in a booth. The glass in the booth was thick and had a greenish cast.

The young woman opened a door and they went into a room painted pale green which had cheap stacking chairs and a green-topped table. There was no clock, no ornament of any kind.

"This isn't privileged," said the young agent, "so we will be listening. You knew that."

Du Pré nodded.

"He asked to see you," she said. "If he hadn't wanted to, you wouldn't be here. If you didn't know Harvey Wallace you wouldn't be here."

"I am here," said Du Pré.

He sat and in a moment the young woman left, and not long after she did, the door opened and Wilbur shuffled in. He was dressed in an orange jumpsuit and he had a belt round his waist his hands were cuffed to and shackled on his ankles joined by a chain just long enough so he could shuffle.

The young agent closed the door.

Wilbur turned and sat in the chair that Du Pré pulled out for him.

"Is that priest you are with so much a communist?" said Wilbur.

"I don't know," said Du Pré.

"My boy's dead," said Wilbur. "Marge took to praying so much and so loud they hauled her off to some nut hospital. I sleep when I can in a white room that they leave the light on in all the time. Any old time they come and haul me out and ask me about killing women and I don't know nothing."

Du Pré didn't say anything.

"You knowed me a long time," said Wilbur. "I didn't know Sonny was doing any such thing. I don't think he was. I think these bastards framed him."

Du Pré nodded.

Wilbur sat looking off into some far place beyond the cinder blocks.

"You know how it was," said Wilbur. "You remember, when you was a kid there was ranchers makin' good livin's. They wasn't gettin' rich, but they was all right. We had loggers, too, had that mill in Cooper, just a stud mill but it was jobs. Young feller could work there a while till he found something better."

Du Pré nodded.

"All changed, didn't it?" said Wilbur. "Them liberals raised the interest rates. Folks couldn't keep going, started to leave. Then them damned liberals shut down all the logging, said it was bad fer the *environment*. Sonny, he tried to hang on but the bank got our old place, Marge and me moved to town then, I had the garage, but most folks do their own mechanickin' cause they can't afford to pay nobody do it."

Du Pré nodded.

"Sonny's wife left, took their two little girls, moved to Billings and married a cop. The kids was real young and she talked him into lettin' the cop adopt them and then he couldn't see them no more," said Wilbur.

Du Pré nodded.

Wilbur cleared his throat.

He looked at the floor.

"Now they are sayin' there was a bunch of bodies out to Sonny's, and they are sayin' I did it or I know who did and I don't, and I bet Sonny don't, either. It was that one girl in the . . . the mine died. Sonny found her. She wasn't supposed to be there but till next afternoon."

"Who put her there?" said Du Pré.

"Sonny didn't know," said Wilbur. "God, he didn't know, Du Pré."

Du Pré nodded.

"You used to go, Methodist church?" said Du Pré.

Wilbur nodded.

"When there was one. But the people, well, there was less and less and we all had to pony up more and more while we was all goin' under and all the damn parson would say was that times was changin' and we had to change with it. He left it there. So it closed up."

Du Pré nodded.

"Marge started readin' the Bible hard and watchin' them preachers on the TV," said Wilbur. "Then she somehow got hold of one of 'em and this feller came, talked about the End of Days and how there was saved folks and all the others would burn and how the Bible was unmistaken . . . they got a word for it . . ."

"Inerrant," said Du Pré.

Wilbur nodded.

"So we made that old schoolhouse over to a new church and we took turns preachin' in it and time to time somebody would come up," said Wilbur.

"Sonny had a big tank, used to strip paint off wood, old furniture," said Du Pré. "Where he get that? There was not a furniture refinishing business in Cooper or Toussaint when I was small."

"Big tank and a small one," said Wilbur. "Small one held maybe three hundred gallons, the big one was huge, I don't know how much."

"Sonny got them someplace," said Du Pré.

"He never said," said Wilbur.

Du Pré leaned forward. He put his clasped hands on the table.

"There were four bodies in that big tank," said Du Pré. "Chemicals embalmed them. Been there a long time maybe. Four young women. Like the young woman Sonny washed off on the table, left by the road."

"Four," said Wilbur.

"Where did he get the tanks?" said Du Pré.

Wilbur started to cry.

"He went down to Texas twice I know," said Wilbur. "Second time he took that big old Peterbilt tractor he had, came back with a trailer, parked it out in the yard, and that was that. Hell, I figured it was scrap, had a cracked frame or something. We had about two hundred cars and trucks out there and an old trailer wasn't that odd."

Du Pré nodded.

"So he has the small tank out front," he said.

"Yeah," said Wilbur. "Where I done sent them pieces you couldn't get cleaned."

"Wilbur," said Du Pré, "Sonny, you were close. The girl died and he washed her up and he left her by the road. You were there, too, you helped him carry her."

Wilbur's head shot up.

Color drained from his face.

"You was always a good tracker," said Wilbur.

"Sonny did not expect the girl to die," said Du Pré.

"God, no," said Wilbur. "She was . . . possessed, that was the word he used . . . possessed, and he was to keep her locked up with her Bible to git rid of—"

"The Devil," said Du Pré.

"Devil's around," said Wilbur. "Been around a lot lately. Corruptin' men's hearts and leadin' them off the true path."

"Who sent the woman to Sonny?" said Du Pré.

"Some feller Sonny knew, I don't know his name, out of Great Falls," said Wilbur.

"How you know that?" said Du Pré.

"I was out there to the yard one night gettin' a water pump from an Oldsmobile," said Wilbur, "an' this van had Great Falls plates comes in and Sonny goes to meet them and they go on into the yard. I thought they was looking for a part."

Du Pré tapped the table.

"The van was from Great Falls," said Du Pré. "The people weren't and you met them."

"We prayed together," said Wilbur.

"How many?" said Du Pré.

"Three men in the van and me and Sonny," said Wilbur. "We prayed fer strength and the hand of the Lord to be with us."

"What was the girl doing?" said Du Pré.

Wilbur looked at the floor, his eyes filled with tears.

"She was screaming," said Du Pré.

Wilbur nodded.

"And then they dragged her to the old mine," said Du Pré, "and they shut her in that metal box and you couldn't hear her any more."

Wilbur closed his eyes.

"I could hear her," he said.

"You went back," said Du Pré.

Wilbur nodded.

"She was a-screaming in the box. I'd go for a part and she'd scream. She never stopped."

"How long?" said Du Pré.

"Week maybe," said Wilbur.

"Then she stopped," said Du Pré.

"I thought maybe they had come and took her away," said Wilbur.

"Wilbur," said Du Pré, "When they come with the pictures of men for you to look at . . ."

Wilbur looked at him.

"If you don't tell them who brought that girl, I will put you in hell, and you know I can," said Du Pré.

204

"That's it," said the young woman, coming swiftly through the door. "You may not threaten prisoners."

Wilbur looked up at Du Pré.

"Devil was walking there, our home, Wilbur," said Du Pré, "and you dance along with him pret' good."

CHAPTER
39

Du Pré watched Wilbur shuffle away.

He sighed, got up, went out to the hall.

"Be back in a minute," said the young agent. She was guiding Wilbur toward a gray metal door with a viewport in it.

Du Pré took a pinch of tobacco and he put it behind his lower lip.

He waited for half an hour, then he walked to the door they had come in.

"I need to go," he said to the speakerbox.

"Agent Simms needs to speak with you first," said the woman.

Du Pré nodded.

He walked back and forth for another hour.

He went to the box again.

"Quit playing stupid games," he said, "or Harvey Wallace comes in."

There was no answer.

The door at the far end of the hall opened and the young woman came through it and she walked down toward Du Pré, her heels tapping briskly.

"Sorry," she said. "Something came up. I have some questions for you. Why don't we go back to the interview room?"

Du Pré shook his head.

"It won't take long," she said.

Du Pré just looked at her.

"We can hold you," she snapped.

Du Pré looked far off and he began to whistle.

Baptiste's Lament.

. . . the forest is so dark and my love is so very far away . . .

"How did you know about the tank?" she said.

Du Pré looked at her.

"Have Harvey call me," he said. "I tell him, I don't tell you."

Simms stood for a moment.

She went to the speaker.

"Simms," she said. "We are coming out."

The door clicked and they went on through.

They went through the second door and Simms got her sidearm back and she took off her suit jacket and she put it on.

They went out into the sun.

"I'm sorry," she said.

Du Pré shrugged.

"I tell you now," said Du Pré, "you should not do that, people. They will help more you don't."

Simms nodded.

"I am fixing this old rocking chair, got paint on it, I try to take it off and can't. So I mention it to Wilbur. He says Sonny has a tank. I think it is the small one. I see that, but when I am there, there is a break in it. It don't have the chemicals in it, a seam opened, there is a big stain on the ground. I got to go then. Few days later, Wilbur brings me the pieces, I set them by, because I am busy. When I get to them, this young woman comes by, says one piece stinks. So I think, why is this? And there is another tank, not the little one."

Simms looked at him.

"No one told you about it?" she said.

Du Pré shook his head.

"The dead girl, I think she was washed off, the big drain table came with the tanks. Stainless steel, got drains on it, use it to hose off pieces of wood after stripping. Sonny does that to her, then Sonny, Wilbur, take her body out by the back road. They are carrying her, and maybe there is a light coming, something, they drop her and they go."

"So Wilbur was in on it," said Simms.

Du Pré nodded.

"Sick," said Simms. "Those poor girls."

"Pidgeon, she say this is about sex," said Du Pré. "I think it is more about some men being sure that their daughters are not having sex, not wanting to maybe."

Simms nodded.

"I apologize for keeping you," she said.

"It is OK," said Du Pré. "Tells me I don't want, end up in one of those places."

They both laughed.

Du Pré went to his old cruiser and he opened the door. He looked in.

Agent Simms was walking back to the building.

"Hey!" said Du Pré. "You go through my car!"

Simms turned and gave him a huge smile.

"Patriot Act," she said. "It's still under the front seat and the backstock is still in the trunk."

"Ver' funny," said Du Pré.

"Harvey said you had a machine gun," said Simms. "He said that."

"I don't got one," said Du Pré.

Here I don't got one.

"He was pissy about it," said Simms. "He has a thing about machine guns."

"That Harvey," said Du Pré. "I fix his ass."

Simms waved and she went inside.

Du Pré reached under the seat and he got his flask and he had a drink. He rolled a smoke and he lit it and then he started the engine and he backed and turned and drove to the west side of Billings. He took a back road, found the address he had written on the paper scrap in his shirt pocket.

The low ranch house was set well back from the road, and had three black pickups parked near it.

Du Pré drove in and he stopped and got out.

A gray-haired man with a carefully trimmed pointed beard came out.

"I am Du Pré," said Du Pré.

"Ah, yes," said the man. "I'll get it and the ammo."

He came back out with a big flat black case and a tall plastic box with a handle in the lid.

He carried them to the cruiser. He set the black case on the hood and he put the green plastic box on the ground.

The man flicked the latches open and he lifted the lid.

A big rifle sat there. It was finished in a dull black, and a bipod sat folded in a slot under the barrel. The stock was in another slot.

"Fifty-caliber sniper," said the man, "and two hundred rounds of ammo. You want more, it is on special today."

"How much?" said Du Pre.

"Another four hundred rounds for two hundred dollars," said the man. "Overstock."

Du Pré counted out the hundred dollar bills.

The man went back in the house and he came back out with two more of the heavy plastic boxes.

Du Pré stowed everything in the back seat of the cruiser.

He went back to the expressway.

He got gas at the turnoff where he headed north, and when he was over the first hill he opened it up.

He pulled into Toussaint in the early evening.

Madelaine was at home.

"You got the funny camera," he said.

"Yes," she said.

The door opened and Pallas came in.

"I want, some pictures," said Du Pré, "sent to that Harvey."

Pallas looked at him.

"Sure," she said.

Du Pré got the black case and he took it out in the back and put it on the picnic table.

He opened it and he took out the receiver and barrel and he put the stock on and the telescopic sight and the bipod.

He went back and got a box of the ammunition.

It was on belts, thin canvas strips.

He draped two of the belts over his shoulders.

He picked up the very heavy rifle.

"OK," he said.

Pallas clicked the camera a few times.

"You want me to send these, Harvey?" said Pallas. "You want to say anything, too?"

"Tell him keep his nose out, my car," said Du Pré.

"What kind of rifle is that?" said Madelaine.

"Fifty-caliber sniper," said Du Pré.

"Fifty caliber," said Madelaine. "Twice as wide as your deer rifle."

Du Pré nodded.

She fingered one of the shells, which were almost eight inches long.

"Artillery," she said.

"Go through two inches of steel plate," said Du Pré.

"Good for gophers," said Madelaine. "Their armor won't help them now."

Du Pré put the rifle back in the case.

He carried the case and ammunition back to his car and he put it in.

Pallas came out of the house.

"You send them already?" said Du Pré.

"Computers are very fast," said Pallas. "I could show you how."

Du Pré shook his head.

"Don't want to know," he said.

"OK," said Pallas, "I am taking Raylee for rides, you know."

Du Pré looked at her.

"They let her do that?" he said.

Pallas nodded.

"She got on of those laughs that is close to screaming," said Pallas.

"She was in, the hospital," said Du Pré.

Pallas nodded.

"You want to know why?" she said.

"Yes," said Du Pré.

"I tell you tomorrow," said Pallas. "Maybe tonight, maybe."

"I come late," said Du Pré.

Pallas nodded and she went back in the house.

CHAPTER

40

Du Pré sat at the bar. Madelaine was sitting behind it, beading. It was late and there was no one else in the place.

The fat little Texan came in, red-faced and with his mouth working silently.

"Where is Raylee?" he said. "She was supposed to be home an hour ago."

"She went riding with Pallas," said Madelaine. "Maybe they got distracted. You know how kids are."

"I want my daughter home when she is supposed to be home," he said.

"I go and look for them," said Madelaine. "I maybe find them."

The man would not look at Du Pré.

Madelaine made a telephone call.

Susan Klein came in the back door two minutes later.

The fat little man was still standing where he had been.

"I go and see," said Madelaine.

"I worry about her," he said. "It is dangerous out there."

Madelaine looked at him.

"Not so bad," she said. "She can always get an abortion things get out of hand."

His eyebrows shot up but she was already out the door.

He blinked, turned, ran after her.

The door closed and after a moment it opened.

"Where is she?" he screamed.

"Get out," said Susan Klein.

He shut the door.

"Lord," said Susan.

Du Pré laughed.

"You know where those kids are?" she said.

Du Pré nodded.

"I think," said Susan, "Madelaine may have ruptured his mind. When you go out, see if his brains are all over my boardwalk."

Du Pré finished his drink, held up the glass, and Susan made him another.

"Who were those crackers came up with him?" she said.

"Ardreys," said Du Pré. "They are still here, don't come in here, though."

"Why weren't they arrested?" said Susan.

Du Pré shrugged.

"Maybe they don't have nothing to do with anything," he said. "It was Sonny and Wilbur, you know."

"And poor Marge," said Susan.

"She start it," said Du Pré.

"What a mess," said Susan. "I had not a clue that tribal magic was alive and sick among my neighbors."

"Some of it is," said Du Pré. "Some is still pret' good."

"Yeah," said Susan. "After I got my Achilles' tendons slashed old Benetsee showed up when I had given up on the damned physical therapy. Christ, I hurt all the time. He stuck me in the sweat lodge and burned some sweetgrass and things got better. Got better each time he did that."

Benny came in the back door, looking tired.

"That little fool wants me to call search and rescue for his kid," he said. "Isn't she with Pallas?"

"Yah," said Du Pré.

"They'll come on home," he said. "Two teenagers stay out past curfew. That has never happened before."

Du Pré nodded, sipped his drink.

"If I did that I'd die," said Benny. "You run on that stuff."

"I don't do it I die," said Du Pré.

He got up.

"See you tomorrow," he said.

Du Pré got in his cruiser and he drove off toward Benetsee's. The van that Flowers drove pulled out behind him and followed.

"Not smart," said Du Pré.

He parked a mile away from the rutted track that led to Benetsee's cabin and he walked quickly up and over a hill, on the back path that came in to the creek behind the sweat lodge.

Du Pré looked back.

A flashlight shone on the ground.

It danced along the path.

Du Pré went on. The path was clear in the starlight, at least if one knew what to look for.

And for a time it was fairly wide, since several game trails converged down low and did not branch until rising up nearly to the benchlands above.

Du Pré stood in a small grove of aspens, watching the flashlight beam bob up and down.

Suddenly it pointed skyward.

Fall on his ass, that one.

Du Pré stopped again about a half mile from the sweat lodge.

The flashlight beam was on the wrong trail, heading up toward the butte that sat next to the mountains, where Benetsee sat to think on this earth.

Du Pré went on, and he came to the creek. He smelled smoke and steam.

The sky was clouding over, a sudden thunderstorm had come in from the west.

Du Pré sat on a stump. There was faint singing and then he heard it get a bit louder.

Then it stopped and there were splashes.

Laughter.

He waited, out of sight of the pool.

The splashing stopped.

"It's so cooooollld!" said Raylee.

She sounded happy.

Du Pré waited for two minutes, then he whistled, like a meadowlark. They were all asleep now.

"Yah," yelled Madelaine. "You come in now, Du Pré."

He dodged his way through the thick alders and willows, came to the log that spanned a narrow place in the creek below the pool, and Du Pré stepped swiftly across it. The water danced, black on black below.

Madelaine and Pallas and Raylee were dressed, their hair wet, and they all looked at Du Pré when he came to the fire in the stone ring by the logs.

"Ah, Du Pré," said Madelaine, "a good sweat and sing, you should have come."

Raylee flushed.

Madelaine put her arm around her.

"We don't make you scared," she said. "It is all right."

"I want to stay with you tonight," said Raylee.

"Sure," said Madelaine, "but we got to tell your parents."

Raylee sighed and she nodded.

"I could just stay here," she said.

"We will tell them in the morning," said Madelaine.

Raylee brightened.

She was a pretty girl whose eyes were too old and tired for her age.

"OK," said Madelaine. "I am driving back."

"Moondog will take Trapper home," said Pallas. "We talked about it."

The black horse whuffled in the pasture near the cabin.

"You go on home, Moondog!" yelled Pallas.

Hoofbeats, a neigh, and the two horses were silhouetted for a moment against the sky. There was a patch of moonlight.

Moondog was nipping Trapper's butt to move him the way Moondog wanted to go.

"It is late," said Madelaine. "I am going home."

The three women walked up the little incline and Du Pré heard Madelaine's small station wagon start and move.

Du Pré pulled the flask from his hip pocket and he had a drink. He rolled a smoke and he sat by the fire.

Little gusts of wind kicked up, sparks danced above the red coals.

Benetsee appeared just beyond the fire, grinning.

"Old man," said Du Pré, "you hurt my feelings."

"You got things to do," said Benetsee. "So do I."

"I wanted help," said Du Pré.

"The Good Lord helps those who help themselves," said Benetsee. "I read that, the *Wall Street Journal*."

Du Pré laughed.

214

"So," he said, "it is not over, but mostly."

"*Non,*" said Benetsee. "Not over much at all."

Du Pré looked at him.

"Never over," said Benetsee. "Always the people, they get lost."

The wind came down the flanks of the mountains then, roaring through the pines far away, sounding like a distant sea.

Du Pré and Benetsee made for the cabin. They went inside and Benetsee started a fire in the stove.

"You fix this?" he said.

Du Pré nodded.

"Where you find that part?" said Benetsee.

Du Pré shook his head.

"In my other pants," he said.

Then rain began to pound down, and lightning flashed so close the thunderclap was simultaneous.

The rain had some ice in it and the sleet plopped as it hit the ground.

"Bad night be out," said Benetsee.

Du Pré nodded.

"Only a fool would be walking around out there, this," said Benetsee.

Du Pré nodded.

Benetsee found a jug of wine in the woodbox and he opened it and he filled an old jam jar and he drank the thing down in one long swallow.

Du Pré sipped whiskey.

"I suppose," he said, "I should go and get that fool."

Benetsee shook his head.

"*Non,*" said Benetsee. "*Non,* he will be all right."

"He could die out there," said Du Pré.

"Him too busy to come home," said Benetsee.

Du Pré looked at Benetsee.

"Him busy seeing things," said Benetsee.

CHAPTER
41

Du Pré was out at Bart's oiling the old saddle that had carried both his father and grandfather, a much-worn Coggeshall stock saddle now more than a hundred years old.

Du Pré looked at some of the rawhide ties. They were cracked. He found some strips of babiche on a shelf. They would do. He took out his knife and he measured and cut.

"Du Pré?" said Pidgeon from the open door.

"Yah," he said.

She came in and she stood, her eyes wide open, but she could not see well yet.

"That sun is very bright," she said.

"Yah," said Du Pré.

"We found out who the girls were," said Pidgeon.

Du Pré nodded.

Pidgeon came to the workbench. She slid onto a tall stool. She had a few papers in her hands.

She waited. Du Pré cut. He sawed a little. The rawhide parted.

Du Pré put the knife back in his pocket.

. Pidgeon handed him a sheet of paper.

There were drawings of four women, some artist's rendering of dead faces.

"Sisters," said Pidgeon, "four girls fourteen through seventeen. Autopsy showed how they all died. Drowned. Drowned by their father with help from his brother, uncle to the girls. Aren't families great? Papa was a self-made man of God. Traveled all over, preaching. But the girls were girls and they acted like that, so he killed them all. One an evening for four days. Drowned them in the swimming pool. The girls fought back. We found skin from that son of a bitch under their nails."

Du Pré sighed.

"Their uncle had a furniture business. Papa and kindly Uncle Joe were a bit worried that the heathens might not understand that they had killed the girls so their souls were safe. Oh, yes, all of them had been raped. Papa and Uncle Joe are each accusing the other, of course."

Du Pré looked at the four faces.

He shook his head.

"They give Sonny the tank, and tell him to keep it safe. Poor Sonny. He was not the brightest feller ever hatched," said Pidgeon. "And the girls were very hard to trace. They had no tracks to speak of. They did have birth certificates, even though all of them were born at home."

"How you find this?" said Du Pré.

"Like we find out most things," said Pidgeon. "One of the idiots who had his soul saved by Papa—name was Ockford Nelles—case you wondered—got caught selling illegal weapons. But he had heard some rumors about the sisters. He was eager to make a deal. Once you get one of those rodents to rat, you go right on up the pole. Ockford and his brother Jobert got nervous. The girls hardly appeared on the screen. They were homeschooled, of course, and kept away from temptation, at least their own. Their male relatives were another matter, and the first rat squealed on another one, who was making bombs to use on abortion clinics. He hadn't yet, but when we find bombs we get mad anyway, and so forth and so on. And the four girls had been gone for a long time. Ockford and Jobert, it seems, had been seen drowning one of the girls, by some congregant who came by for counseling, who the brothers were able to convince silence would be the true path of righteousness, but when it got sticky he fessed up. An eyewitness is a good thing."

Du Pré shook his head.

"I have found several other instances," said Pidgeon. "Other

217

places where young women in these cracker cults have gone missing. Since the parents don't go to the police, we as yet have no idea of the size of the problem. It could be called an interesting sociological problem if I didn't want to fry these bastards in oil."

"And they come all the way up here," said Du Pré, "find people here to help them."

Pidgeon nodded.

"You want to look at this stuff?" she said.

Du Pré shrugged.

"I don't think that there are more here," he said.

"Not yet maybe," said Pidgeon. "Country is in very bad shape, case you didn't notice. You know what I worry about? That there will be a crematorium someplace and women will be reduced to ashes and scattered and there will never be any evidence at all."

Du Pré nodded.

"Flowerses are leaving," he said. "Some people left that church there is no money to pay them."

Pidgeon nodded.

"The others are, too. Nobody is moving here now, they are all leaving," she said, "and that is very sad."

"It was empty before," said Du Pré. "Will be again."

Pidgeon nodded.

"I want to smoke," she said.

They went outside. The sun was very bright so they walked to the copse of Siberian elms and lilacs that was set near the little creek that ran near the house.

There were some wooden Adirondack chairs in the shade of the lilacs. All the blooms were long gone, but the leaves gave off a clean, bitter scent.

"You have lived here all your life," said Pidgeon. "And it is beautiful."

Du Pré nodded.

"This happens, though," said Du Pré. "World falls out from under people and then they get ver' scared. New York, Erie Canal opens, New York farmers go broke, all these churches spring up, they have so many revivals they call New York the Burned-Over Land."

Pidgeon looked at him.

"Ghost Dancers," said Du Pré. "Like the loggers, Cooper, they blame the environmentalists, there is no logging. But there is no logging because they cut all the trees."

"Poor Wilbur, Marge, Sonny," said Pidgeon. "I don't think they had a clue where this would end."

"They did not want to know," said Du Pré.

"Ah," said Pidgeon. "That."

They smoked.

"Benetsee around?" said Pidgeon.

Du Pré shrugged.

"Who is he?" said Pidgeon. "Where did he come from?"

Du Pré shook his head.

"He was friend my grandfather," he said. "He was old I was young, he was old my father is young."

"Catfoot," said Pidgeon. "I would have liked to have known him."

Du Pré laughed.

"So you can arrest him, killing Bart's brother?" said Du Pré.

Pidgeon shook her head.

"He did not have to do that," she said.

Du Pré nodded.

"Maybe he did," said Du Pré. "You got to remember how rich Gianni Fascelli was. Aunty Pauline is a trouble woman, she made trouble her whole life. She make trouble when she sleeps, wakes, any time. Ver' beautiful, like you, she made Gianni crazy. I know Catfoot don't like having done it."

Pidgeon looked at him.

"I find old priest, ask if Catfoot confessed, repented. Priest can't say, but I have an old missal, I hold it out, I say, if Catfoot was sorry, take it. Priest, he looks at me, he takes it. So Catfoot is sorry," said Du Pré.

"So he knew it was wrong," said Pidgeon.

"Those girls," said Du Pré, "they never had their pictures taken."

"No," said Pidgeon, "not that we have found. We found any number of studio photographs of Ockford. He had a pompadour. He had a hairdresser. But the girls might become vain."

Du Pré snorted, he rolled some more smokes, lit them, handed one to Pidgeon.

"When they kill women, these men you hunt," said Du Pré,

"they always say God thinks it is a good idea. Maybe God is speaking to them, maybe they read their Bible and find it there, but it is always that?"

"Always," said Pidgeon.

"Not much of a God," said Du Pré.

"Not much human in any of it," said Pidgeon.

Bart came out of the house with a tray holding glasses and a pitcher of iced tea. It was hot.

He set the tray down on the table.

"Thank you, honey," said Pidgeon.

Bart poured glasses, passed them to Pidgeon and Du Pré.

"We were talking about bad gods," said Pidgeon, "and the people who worship themselves."

"Oh," said Bart. "Them."

"Those poor girls," said Pidgeon.

"But you say the father and uncle were arrested?" said Bart.

Pidgeon nodded.

"Too late for the young women," said Pidgeon.

"Yes," said Bart. "It is very sad."

"It reached all the way here," said Du Pré.

"A dying place," said Pidgeon.

"The place is fine," said Du Pré. "This place, it has never been easy for people. Indians come here, hunt buffalo, but winter they camped someplace else."

"I wish I could think of something," said Bart, "but I can't."

"How many people were in Cooper in say, 1946?" said Pidgeon.

"Maybe twelve hundred," said Du Pré.

"And now?"

"Three, maybe," said Du Pré.

"Toussaint?" said Pidgeon.

"Five hundred maybe," said Du Pré.

"Nothing left," said Pidgeon.

Du Pré looked off toward the Wolf Mountains through a hole in the lilac leaves. Something moved on the benchland set in the mountain.

Benetsee.

The old man trotted along, covering the ground pretty quickly.

Two coyotes trotted behind him, about a hundred feet.

They dipped down behind a fold in the earth and Du Pré did not see them again.

CHAPTER
42

Du Pré backed the horse trailer up close to the big cargo plane. There was a zigzag ramp going up to the loading door.

Pallas got out and she went to the rear of the trailer and she opened the door and she went in and Moondog backed out and he snorted and reared just a little. A jet took off with a heavy rumble.

Pallas petted his neck.

Moondog calmed down.

Pallas led him up into the cargo bay and she disappeared in the dark interior.

Du Pré stood a moment, then he went to close the trailer doors.

He carried Pallas's luggage up the ramp. She was standing at a stall, Moondog rubbing his head on her shoulder.

"Your things," he said.

"I better stay with him," said Pallas. "I would be scared, too. I am scared every time I ride in one of these things. Are you scared when you fly, gran'père?"

"I don't fly," said Du Pré, "then I am not scared."

"Now I know why I am so brave," said Pallas.

Moondog nosed Du Pré's arm. He fished an apple out of his pocket and he gave it to the big black horse.

"Loading check," said a voice on a speaker. "If you don't want to go to gorgeous New Jersey, get off now."

Du Pré and Pallas hugged.

"Madelaine would have come," said Du Pré, "but she is a mother and she is with Chappie."

"Screwing his pants down to a chair," said Pallas. "He will be all right now, I think."

"Be a good teacher," said Du Pré. "Then he get a kid like you and he quit."

"Oh," said Pallas, "I almost forgot. Harvey send these for you." She gave Du Pré a brown envelope about the size of a sheet of typing paper.

"Beautiful New Jersey," said the voice on the loudspeaker, "will be the fate of all on board in one minute. One goddamned minute."

"I like this," said Pallas. "Not so mealymouthed as regular airlines."

Du Pré nodded, turned, walked back down the ramp. The door began to lift up into the fuselage.

A man with a little tractor came and hauled the zigzag ramp away.

Du Pré walked back to the big green SUV. He got in and he rolled a smoke and he pulled away the strip of tape that sealed the envelope.

He slid a photograph out of the cardboard bracings.

A man holding a huge fifty-caliber sniper rifle stood in front of a green banner which had Arabic inscriptions on it.

The man had a headdress, the gingham tablecloth kind.

It was Du Pré, the photograph he had had Pallas send Harvey.

A little yellow stick-on note was on the back of the photograph.

"You wanna play, we'll play," Harvey and Ripper.

Du Pré heard a tap on the window.

Simms, the young FBI agent.

Du Pré flipped the switch that unlocked the door.

Simms got in and she sat. She took out a filtered cigarette and she lit it.

"We are dumping poor old Wilbur back on Cooper County," she said. "He didn't know anything and it seems that all he did was help his son dispose of the girl's body. He just happened to go out there when Sonny was washing her down and so he and his son ended up dumping her in the ditch. He swears Sonny didn't know about the girls in the big tank. I think I believe that, too."

Du Pré rolled a cigarette.

He lit it and he blew smoke out his open window.

"We may never know who the girl on the roadside was," said Simms. "You know why? She may have been born at home. They don't even get birth certificates for their kids, these crazies hate the government so much. The kids are homeschooled. They aren't visible. In a way, that girl never existed. A whole *otherworld* right here in the good old USA."

Du Pré drew on his cigarette.

"Harvey told me to have a chat with you," said Simms. "He said it was better to have you inside the tent pissing out than outside the tent pissing in."

Du Pré handed her the photograph.

"You got one of them?" said Simms. "They are gonna be outlawed soon enough."

Du Pré shrugged.

"Very funny," said Simms. "Your mustache and all. You look good there, Du Pré."

"So we don't know anything," said Du Pré.

"Not much," said Simms. "It seems there are a lot of people who would like it to still be about 1200 A.D."

"So," said Du Pré.

"So," said Simms, "you hear anything let us know."

Du Pré nodded.

Simms got out.

"Do you have a machine gun?" said Simms. She grinned and shut the door.

Du Pré drove off then, out the automatic gate the guard opened for him.

He cruised along the Interstate to the turn north.

The country opened up, far and wide.

Pastels shaded from brown to yellow to purple on the distant horizons.

A prairie falcon shot past, dove behind a hill and did not rise up.

Du Pré had to drive slowly because the empty horse trailer could overturn if he went fast.

On a long stretch of road he saw a person walking, one with a big backpack made of bright blue cloth.

The person had his left arm out and thumb pointed north.

Du Pré slowed and stopped.

A blond young man with a short beard carrying his home on his back.

Du Pré waited until the man had stowed his huge pack in the rear seat and climbed in.

"Thank you," the young man said. "My name is Chip Hannon and I am headed for the Wolf Mountains."

"So am I," said Du Pré, "Du Pré."

They rode along in silence. Hannon was not one of those people who pay for rides with mindless chatter.

An eagle sat on a dead deer in the barrow pit. The huge bird was tearing at the deer's flesh with his curved yellow beak.

Hannon stared at the eagle.

"I have never seen one up close," he said.

"You are from the east," said Du Pré.

"Yup," said Hannon. "Boston."

"First time out here?" said Du Pré.

"One summer my parents took us to Yellowstone Park," said Hannon, "but I was six and I don't remember it well."

"You are backpacking and camping?" said Du Pré.

"Yes," said Hannon. "I am actually doing research for a paper. I'm in the Divinity School at Harvard."

"What you going to write about, the Wolf Mountains, Harvard?" said Du Pré.

"The Idea of God," said Hannon. "It seems to have been found in the wilderness and specifically the desert, and I thought I might go and see about that."

Du Pré rolled a cigarette. He lit it and he rolled down his window.

"There's no one out here, is there?" said Hannon.

"There are people," said Du Pré.

"It must be lonely," said Hannon, "and what I am looking for I think one must find alone."

Du Pré nodded.

"I don't mean to be a bore," said Hannon. "Just because I'm enthusiastic it doesn't mean others are."

"It is all right," said Du Pré. "I don't mind God being an idea. I always thought that anyway."

They laughed.

Du Pré turned off east and the Wolf Mountains rose up, blue and high, with white peaks.

"Wow," said Hannon.

"I am going, Toussaint," said Du Pré. "It is easy to get to them from there."

"Fine," said Hannon.

Du Pré pulled in to the field across the road from the saloon.

"Do they have food?" said Hannon.

"Yah," said Du Pré.

"I'm starving," said Hannon. "I had been walking for hours before you picked me up. I have food but I was saving it, you know, the freeze-dried stuff."

Hannon got his huge pack out of the back seat and he carried it to the boardwalk in front of the saloon. He started to take it off.

"Bring it in," said Du Pré. "They don't care."

They went in.

Booger Tom and Father Van Den Heuvel were there. The big priest was sitting on the stool. Not half off it.

"You get the stitches out?" said Du Pré.

"Yup," said Father Van Den Heuvel.

"Now he wants me t'go back up there," said Booger Tom. "I got things I got to do and I ain't got time, so he's whinin'."

"I can go alone," said Father Van Den Heuvel.

"Hooper and Noodles will take good care of ya," said Booger Tom. "They like this idiot. Can't ever tell about mules."

Hannon sat on a stool.

So did Du Pré.

The ordered cheeseburgers and Susan Klein went to cook them.

"You find that roadkill on the way here?" said Booger Tom, glaring at Hannon.

"Yah," said Du Pré. "Him going up into the Wolfs to look for God."

"Oh," said Booger Tom, "I see."

Father Van Den Heuvel looked at the young man.

"I'm doing a paper on the Idea of God," said Hannon.

"That just give me one," said Booger Tom. "How is you at first aid?"

"OK," said Hannon. "I took a course before I set out."

Father Van Den Heuvel looked at Hannon.

Father Van Den Heuvel moved to the stool on the other side of Hannon.

"Praise Jesus," said Booger Tom.